MS. PERFECT

LADY BILLIONAIRES

DARCI BALOGH

KNOWHERE MEDIA

For all of my film friends, old and new. I treasure my experiences making movies with you and enjoy using those stories in my books. Never give up on your dreams! And remember, you can always fix it in post.

CHAPTER 1

Grace flipped her oversized square sunglasses from where they rested on top of her head down onto the bridge of her nose. They made a great headband, but the midday sun made her squint, and squinting, of course, led to wrinkles. Best to be cautious. Besides, this was Hollywood, anyone who was anyone wore sunglasses practically all of the time.

"I still can't believe we got Zac," Phoenix Sutherland said as she pushed the air fried sweet potatoes on her plate around with a fork before popping one into her mouth. One of Grace's hand picked producers, Phoenix was in her early 30's, thin with bland blonde hair that was always pulled back into a limp ponytail, and earnest hazel eyes that were magnified by black framed prescription glasses.

Roger Rigby, Grace's other producer, known to his friends and colleagues as plain old 'Rigby', nodded emphatically, his mouth full of Portobello burger. A once handsome, maybe not so much anymore, movie producer in his late 40's, Rigby had been a driving force in Grace's career since almost the beginning. Still chewing, he grunted his enthusiasm and raised one finger in the air, waving it around like it was a flag and they were in a parade.

The Zac they were referring to was Zac Foster, a hot young actor who had reached stardom in his late teens and was, many believed, on his way to super-stardom now that he had reached maturity, which was just under 30 in Hollywood years.

Zac was tall-*ish*, with natural thick blonde hair, disgracefully attractive blue eyes, and that special mix of masculine and feminine bone structure in his face that made him both handsome and beautiful. Known for his excellent physique, Zac Foster had the body to carry off all of the beach scenes in their script and steal the audience's heart along the way.

Grace's team had landed Zac in the lead role of her newest pet project, tentatively titled, Heart of Mine. Everyone was pleased. Really, really pleased. Grace was just as pleased as her producers, though perhaps not quite as obsessed.

"Yes, Zac will be perfect," Grace declared, hoping this would end the praise fest of Zac Foster that had been going on at their table for the past five minutes. They needed to move on to other important details. They were in the middle of lunch at a popular Los Angeles eatery, one of the top locations to have a production meeting. "Now, what do we have locked down in Australia?"

Phoenix and Rigby both froze mid-chew and stared at her, Phoenix's eyes grew even bigger than normal behind her glasses. At the exact same moment, they stole a sideways glance at each other then looked back at Grace, still silent and boggle-eyed.

Rigby finally cleared his throat and said, "We thought Australia was on the back burner…now that we have Zac."

"Why would that make any difference?" Grace asked. Again the two producers shared an infuriating sideways glance and Grace gave them a sharp look, which was lost behind her sunglasses. "Would someone please explain to me why we would hit pause on the locations in Australia? And explain it to me quickly?"

"Well, Grace, it's just that with Zac as the male lead…well, we thought the obvious choice for the female lead was Indigo," Phoenix said, looking quickly to Rigby for support.

Rigby nodded his head enthusiastically. "Right. That's what we discussed, wasn't it?" He looked at Grace as if expecting her to agree.

"Indigo?" Grace's throat tightened as she said the girl's name, twice, "Indigo Lee?"

Indigo Lee was a gorgeous starlet with raven black hair and emerald eyes not dissimilar to her own. She had excellent acting skills and that certain something that charmed an audience through the lens of a camera. The same certain something Grace had always possessed. The same certain something she had felt slipping away of late.

Still, Indigo was barely out of her teens. Grace wasn't even sure the girl was 21-years old yet. How could Indigo Lee play Scarlet Kensington, the intense and broken female lead in this romantic drama?

Anger rose in Grace's chest as she cocked her head to the side, indicating that she hoped she had misheard what her producers had just suggested.

Before she had a chance to argue, Rigby spoke quickly, "You know the script, Grace. The beach scenes, the nude scenes, the sex scenes, these are all going to be better…" he searched for the right word and found it, "*Received* if the female lead is younger than the male lead. You know that." He gave her a 'what are you gonna do' shrug and a wan smile.

Grace glared at him from behind her sunglasses and wondered briefly what it would feel like to pop him right in the mouth and wipe that smug little smile off of his face. Not the first time she had wondered something similar in their decades long working relationship.

Instead of punching Rigby, she took a deep breath and in the coolest tone she could muster, which was quite cool, she was a brilliant actress, after all, asked, "Are you saying I'm too old for the part?"

Denial rose in unison from the two producers, reaching such a crescendo that Grace had to shush them both before they drew too much attention to their table. Rigby, at a loss to explain, took another huge bite of his Portobello burger, leaving Phoenix to do the dirty work.

"It's not that you're too old, Grace. Of course not," the girl gushed before glancing dismally down into her plate and building up the nerve to continue. "It's just that you're not… you're not young."

Still cool on the surface, though this conversation sent palpitations through her chest, Grace asked, "I'm not young?"

Phoenix's big eyes panicked. "Not that you're not young… not exactly. You're not…smooth." Phoenix's face froze in shock, as if she was just as surprised as anyone else at the word that had escaped her lips.

Grace's facade slipped and she set her jaw so she spoke through nearly clenched teeth. "Not *smooth*?"

All of the insults to her looks she had ever received as an actress, which were broad and varied, raced through her mind, temporarily obstructing any chance at a witty comeback. Grace had built up a fairly thick skin after years of putting herself on view to the public and receiving both adoration and negative comments. She knew that both came with the territory.

Recently, the sting of being automatically set aside for major romantic roles and instead offered what she had always thought of as 'old lady characters' had been hard to ignore. That's why she and her production company had taken on this project, after all, to show that she still had what it took to play a romantic lead and play it well.

The silence at their little table was heavy. Neither Phoenix nor Rigby were bold enough to continue eating as they waited uncomfortably for Grace to speak.

Grace lifted her sparkling lemon water, took a dainty sip, placed it back on the table, and let her fingers slide down the glass to rest on the tablecloth. She tapped the base of the glass with one French manicured fingernail thoughtfully.

"What, exactly, do we have a DP for if it's not to provide flattering lighting?" she began, her fingernail continuing its slow clicking on the glass as she spoke. "What, exactly, do we have makeup people for if it's not to…smooth me out?" She emphasized the word 'smooth'. Phoenix cringed. "I am not hiring Indigo Lee or anybody else to play Scarlet Kensington. I am playing Scarlet Kensington. End of discussion."

"Gracy," Rigby always called her that when he thought she was being unreasonable. "It's not that we don't think you'd be a great match with Zac. It's just…do we…" he opened his arms as if encompassing the other people in the dining room, in Hollywood, in all of Los Angeles and the rest of the world in the royal 'we', "…do we think it's believable?"

"Believable?" Grace shot back at him. She bent her head lower and gave them both pointed looks over the top of her sunglasses. "I'm an actress. Believable is what I do."

He let his arms drop to his sides. "There's a ten year difference between you and Zac," he offered, though his tone was more pleading this time.

"There's a ten year difference between Zac and Indigo, at least. Is she even 18 yet?" Grace asked sharply. Rigby and Phoenix shared a look and Grace was happy to note it was one of resignation. This conversation could be put to an end and they could go back to her original question. "So tell me why we haven't locked things down in Australia?"

Phoenix cleared her throat and responded, "Indigo had a lot of reservations about Australia. Too many poisonous spiders I guess."

"I see," Grace said curtly. Then, in a show of her willingness to put the Indigo Lee conversation behind them forever, Grace let loose with her world famous smile. "So we can move ahead with Australia now, right?" Both Phoenix and Rigby nodded. "Excellent," Grace said with finality. "I love Australia!"

"Me too," a man's voice came from behind her, and before she could turn around to see who it was, his hands were on her shoulders and he leaned in from behind and gave her a quick peck on the cheek.

Nobody in the restaurant would guess that Zac's anxiety levels were peaking as he casually kissed the amazing, the legendary, the timelessly beautiful, Grace Woods on the cheek. He had mastered the art of covering up his emotions as a child, long before his first acting class. It was one of the reasons he enjoyed acting as a career. If he was constantly pretending to feel one way or another he never had to show his true emotions.

"Zac," Grace cooed as she turned in her chair and looked up at him. "So glad you could make it."

"I wouldn't miss it," Zac took the empty chair next to Grace and smiled casually at Phoenix and Rigby. Though his stomach twisted with nerves, his hands were steady and his smile, he knew, exuded confidence.

"We were just finalizing Australia as the location," Grace explained.

"That's great!" he answered. There was no reason to hide his enthusiasm for being the romantic lead in this film. It was a big deal to be chosen by Grace Woods to do anything. He would have said 'yes' to being an extra or even a grip on one of her films. Well, maybe not a grip. "So, Fiji was a no?"

Phoenix and Rigby tensed at his question. Zac held his smile and pretended not to notice, instead focusing his blue eyes on Grace who seemed unmoved.

"Fiji was never the best option," Grace informed him. "Australia is gorgeous…with more of a…oh, I don't know, a rugged vibe. Don't you agree?"

Zac's smile ticked up at the corner of his mouth in a mischievous way. His rakish look. He'd worked on it in the mirror for a solid month before getting it perfect. Grace's hand had brushed against his when she said 'rugged' and an electric charge jolted up his arm. She may be older than him, but dang if Grace Woods wasn't one of the sexiest women he had ever encountered. On or off the screen.

"I do," he answered. He wondered how Indi was going to take this news. She was not about working in Australia. A distant relative of hers had been bitten by a poisonous spider there once upon a time and almost died. She had all but made a solemn vow never to go to the place. Indi was all about holding grudges, even against entire countries. "I'm sure Indi will warm up to the idea," he added.

Phoenix and Rigby tensed up so hard and so fast they looked like they were frozen in place. Only their eyes moved, flicking to Grace then back to each other, waiting for a secret bomb to explode.

"Do you mean Indigo?" Grace asked coolly.

Zac nodded, uncertain what was going on, but sure he sensed a problem in the air. He decided not to say anything else unless absolutely necessary. The movie business was run on relationships and personalities. One misstep, one insult, and his career could plummet. He did not want to jeopardize anything by sticking his foot in his mouth, however innocently. He took a sip of water and waited for someone else to continue the conversation.

Rigby finally picked up the ball, clearing his throat comically before saying, "There's been a change…" he glanced at Grace whose lips pursed almost imperceptibly. A slight pause while Rigby reorganized his thoughts, then he started again, "We've decided to stick with the original casting." He glanced at Grace, no pursed lips. He grinned like he was about to tell them a secret and continued, "I mean, why bring in just anyone when you have the best there is right at your fingertips?" He gestured both hands palms up towards Grace who dipped her head in the tiniest of bows to his compliment.

"That's exactly right!" Phoenix chimed in, her thin ponytail bobbing as she nodded in agreement. "I mean, who else in this world could play Scarlet Kensington any better than our one and only Grace." Phoenix lifted her water glass to Grace in salute. Rigby followed quickly with his scotch and soda.

Zac looked back and forth between the two producers. What was happening? Indigo was supposed to play Scarlet Kensington. That's what all the buzz around town had been for weeks and weeks. That's why he had befriended her, charmed her, romanced her. That's why he had declared his feelings for her and given her the key to his apartment just the other day.

He always worked better if his romantic interest on screen was his romantic partner in real life. That was his process and it worked like a dream. His process had won him MTV's Award for Best Shirtless Performance, the Teen Choice Award for Male Hottie of the Year, and the People's Choice Award for Best Sex Scene…two years in a row!

Zac's heart raced in his chest. The beginnings of a stress headache pressed against his forehead. Still, he controlled his expression, choosing to don his placid, non-committed look, the one he'd perfected playing the sociopathic bank robber in Dirt Dogs. The look had come in surprisingly handy in a variety of awkward social situations since he made that film.

Everyone was looking at him, waiting for a response of some kind, but Zac's mind wasn't working fast enough. He was still grappling with the fact that his relationship with Indi was all for nothing.

"Do you have reservations about me playing Scarlet?" Grace asked.

Her tone was as cool as a cucumber and Zac couldn't read her eyes because of those damned sunglasses. Not that that would have mattered much. An accomplished actress like Grace Woods wouldn't give away much in her eyes.

He cleared his throat and switched to charming mode. "Absolutely not. I'm just a little overwhelmed by this amazing opportunity. I mean," Zac turned up the humble response and tried to exude earnestness, "I just hope I'm up to the challenge of working opposite someone of your talent."

"Hmm," Grace responded with a quiet smile.

"Great," Rigby took over the conversation, wrapping it up for all of them. "Everything's settled. All you two need to do is study the script and pack for down under."

Zac nodded with enthusiasm. He would study the script, learn his lines, and work with Grace. He would also extricate himself from his romance with Indi…and get his key back. He had to remember to get his key back.

CHAPTER 3

Grace stared out the window of the private jet as the rays from the rising sun created one single reflected line on the ocean below. No clouds obscured her view and the plane was banking slightly, which allowed her to take in the glimmering beauty of the great wide ocean waking up.

She was thankful she had been able to hitch a ride on Faye's jet, leaving hers available to fly her producers and key cast and crew. As much as Grace loved making movies, sometimes the togetherness of it all got to her. Especially this movie.

The initial insult she had felt about being thought too old for the part by her producers was over and had been replaced by a sadness she couldn't quite push away. Then there was the awkward moment she had found out Zac and Indigo Lee were romantically involved. Even though he insisted it had been casual and they were no longer an item, Grace had basically fired his girlfriend. Very uncomfortable.

Then there was Syd. In hindsight she had to admit hiring her ex-boyfriend to direct Heart of Mine may have been a little optimistic. She shifted in her seat, the uncertainty of how that decision would pan out during this shoot made her fidgety.

"I don't know how you're going to survive this experience," Faye had said to her over dinner on the plane the night before. "I can't imagine working with one of my exes."

Grace had wanted to point out that Faye had never had anything even resembling a real job, so it would be difficult for her to imagine working with anyone, let alone an ex-boyfriend, but she held her tongue. It was no good to start a tiff with Faye while stuck on a jet flying somewhere over the Pacific Ocean.

Still, Faye's comments had given rise to a nugget of doubt in Grace's mind. She had made the decision to have Syd direct because of his talent and their previous success working together. She was counting on both of them to act like professionals. After all, in their world it wasn't unheard of to end up on set or on location with former lovers or spouses. It was a common occurrence.

But…what if it went badly? That sudden thought made her stomach sink. What if Syd took revenge on her by purposely making her look bad? Grace had a lot riding on Heart of Mine. A lot of money, as always, but it was also her chance to prove that a woman didn't have to be in her early twenties to carry a romantic movie.

She shook her head as if warding off the possibility of Syd sabotaging the film, silently scolding her overactive imagination.

Don't be ridiculous. Maybe Syd and the DP, the extremely talented Kendra Piotto, would have to work a little harder to 'smooth' her out, but they were more than equipped to make her look good next to her younger leading man. Besides, it had been Syd who had broken up their romance. He had no reason to take revenge. Or at least none that she could imagine.

To take her mind off of Syd and their failed relationship, Grace allowed it to wander to Zac. A few butterflies flitted around her stomach. What a handsome young man.

"Handsome man, Grace. You don't have to call him young," she said softly to herself. The sound of her voice met the nearly silent hum of the jet engines and she glanced around the seating area.

She was alone. Faye was still zonked out in the jet's master bedroom, softly snoring her little heart out. And the crew had disappeared after bringing Grace a fresh cup of coffee when she woke before dawn. Though they were most likely hovering nearby, perhaps close enough to hear her talking to herself.

She set her lips together to keep from speaking out loud again and allowed her inner voice to continue the chastising commentary. She had to stop calling Zac a young man, it took away from her ability to see him as a love interest. She had to focus on how attractive he was, how sexy and appealing.

Grace smiled to herself. What an assignment. If she could get over the needling thought that she was too old for him, it wouldn't be at all difficult to fall a little bit in love with Zac Foster. For the good of the movie of course.

Grace leaned back and snuggled into the plush leather of her seat, allowing Zac to fill her mind. Again, she smiled. This acting life wasn't half bad once you got past your insecurities. Maybe her and Zac's on screen love affair was too much for stuffy old suits at big studios, but Grace thought the dynamic between them would be extremely believable. It might even be Oscar material by the time they were done.

"You're gonna have to sell this, Gracy," Rigby had warned her. The press release about her starring with Zac had created a flurry of media attention, most of it focusing on their age difference, and Rigby had been all wound up about it. "You've got their attention, you need to make sure you keep it."

Grace had shooed his concerns away with the wave of her hand. "You're not telling me anything I don't already know," she answered, trying to appease his worrying spirit. Still, the wrinkle of concern remained on his forehead. Sometimes Rigby appeared to be in a continual state of wincing, especially when they were embarking on a new project. Grace had to laugh. "Try not to worry so much. It's all in place. We have Zac, we have a beautiful location, Syd will do a great job, and the script is brilliant. Really brilliant. Everything will be wonderful."

The jet straightened, forcing her view away from the reflections of the sunrise on the water below to the sunrise itself. Pink and orange and utterly gorgeous, Grace took it as a good omen. Everything would be wonderful indeed.

"Did I miss it?" Faye asked, her voice still thick with sleep. She came out of the master bedroom wearing a sweeping silk dressing gown that reminded Grace of a black and white 1940's movie. Though sleekly dressed, Faye was unsteady on her feet.

"What are you doing up so early?" Grace asked, trying to think of the last time she had seen her friend rise before 10:00am.

Faye plopped down in the leather seat opposite Grace so she, too, could look out the window. "I want to see the swirly water," she answered with a yawn. A brisk crew member brought hot coffee, cream, and croissants to them without Faye uttering a request. "I didn't miss it, did I?"

"No, I don't think we can see anything yet," Grace said.

Faye harrumphed and let her head fall back against the seat. Her blonde hair was pulled up into a loose knot and she didn't have a speck of makeup on. "I told them to be sure to fly over it before we land. It's so pretty."

Grace had seen pictures of the famous hill inlet at Whitehaven Beach that swept turquoise water in wide undulating swirls over pure white sand, creating an incredible sight, especially from the air. She had never seen it in person, however.

"Have you been to Whitehaven Beach often?" she asked Faye as she tore one of the croissants in half. Days before she was scheduled to be in front of the camera Grace didn't want to overeat, but the croissants were warm and smelled delicious.

"Oh, a gazillion times," Faye answered, taking a sip of her coffee.

Grace grinned. Sleepy morning Faye reminded her of teenage Faye, making this trip feel like something between a girl's night out and a sleepover.

"I hope it's as magical as they say it is," Grace said.

Faye nodded. "You'll love it. And your movie will be gorgeous because of it...and because of you, darling." Faye took another sip of coffee and, obviously waking up, added, "And because of that Zac person. I understand he is unbelievably attractive in person?" Faye's eyes twinkled mischievously over her coffee cup.

"That he is," Grace said, trying to appear nonchalant.

"Tell me, since you and Syd are old news do you think you might end up involved with Mr. Tall Blonde and Handsome?"

Grace deflected the question by shrugging noncommittally and looking out the window again. Her tendency to become involved with the men she made films with was a well known fact, but she didn't want to give Faye too much fodder for her imagination. Relationships on set could be delicate, she didn't need Faye, or anyone else, spreading rumors and causing problems.

Daylight grew stronger by the minute, revealing bright blue waters beneath them. So blue they didn't seem real.

A crewman appeared suddenly beside them and announced, "The Captain wants you to know we'll be flying over the inlet in just a few minutes."

Faye nodded and waved at their empty coffee cups indicating they needed refills. "Good, good, I didn't miss it." Faye was almost fully awake and delighted.

Within a few minutes, both of them sipped fresh hot coffee and peered out of the window as their pilot skillfully maneuvered the plane so they were at the best angle to see the inlet below. The view was truly magical. It looked to Grace like an angel had spilled paint of the deepest turquoise and purest white then swirled them slowly, lazily together from one side of the inlet to the other.

Except it wasn't paint, it was water and sand, a completely natural phenomenon that seemed like something created in heaven instead of on earth.

A flicker of excitement moved through Grace. Then another.

No matter how many times she started working on a film the thrill of the creative process gave her a tingling sensation. The magnificent view below them added that special intangible element she always found especially inspiring. Definitely a good omen of what was to come.

"My goodness," was all she could think to say while Faye, for once, remained silent.

CHAPTER 4

incoln Reeves stood knee-deep in a gaping hole right in the middle of his kitchen floor.

He was annoyed.

Not so much at the fact that his six-foot three-inch frame had caused the rotting spot in the original Mackay cedar flooring of his Granddad's house to give way right under his feet, although that was a problem. No, Lincoln was annoyed at a bigger problem, his younger brother, Luke, whose phone call had caused him to reach for his cell and take the one misstep that caused the cedar to crack and crumble.

Plus, Luke was whining on the other end of the phone. Lincoln hated it when Luke whined.

"Come on, Link, just this one time," Luke asked for what seemed to Lincoln like the millionth time.

"No, I don't have time to cover for your mistakes."

Luke groaned and coughed. The sound was wet and phlegmy. He sounded as hungover as he claimed to be, but that wasn't Lincoln's problem.

"What are you doing today that's so important?" Luke wanted to know.

Lincoln looked down into the hole in the floor where his feet had disappeared. "I'm busy at Grandad's."

"Jeez, Link, you're always gonna be busy up there at that dump."

Hackles on the back of Lincoln's neck stood up at the insult. The hill house on Hamilton Island was old and in disrepair, but it was not a dump.

His eyes roved up from the rotten flooring to the hand-made cabinets and the solid wood beams in the cathedral ceiling that encompassed both the kitchen and the great room. He glanced at one of the long windows lining the living room seating area. They opened out onto a wide deck that stretched the length of the house and provided a view of the thick groves of palm and gumtrees just outside and the beautiful Whitsunday waters stretching out from the island far below.

Their Grandad had built this house with his own hands and though it had suffered from neglect for quite a few years, Lincoln considered the hill house a diamond in the rough. Not to mention that it was the only connection he still had with his Grandad. Besides Luke, of course, and the boat they had inherited, which Luke had taken charge of…for the most part.

"It's not a dump. It needs a lot of work, though," Lincoln answered. "Which is why I don't have time to cover for you every time you hit the bottle a little too hard."

Luke groaned again, a mixture of his hangover and the frustration of not getting his way.

Lincoln carefully lifted one leg out of the hole, found more solid footing, and climbed out of the mess, balancing his cell between his shoulder and chin as he did. "Why don't you just cancel the charter if you can't do it?"

Luke scoffed. "Give up the money? That's no way to run a business."

Lincoln was too busy dusting off his legs and inspecting the brand new hole in the floor to point out that getting hammered and being too hungover to take a bunch of rich tourists around on a boat was no way to run a business either. Besides, it would have fallen on deaf ears. Luke never listened to anybody, least of all him.

"And it's not just any old group of tourists," Luke continued. "It's a Hollywood movie studio. For the movie they're making on Whitehaven Beach."

"Yeah, yeah, yeah, I know about that." Everybody on Hamilton and all of the surrounding islands knew about the movie. The locals talked about it incessantly. It didn't surprise Lincoln that Luke had gotten in on some of that action. Though Lincoln was a little surprised a big movie studio would bother hiring a one-off charter boat when there were whole fleets available.

"It's a big deal, Link. Grace Woods and Zac Foster are starring in it. Syd Masters is directing."

Lincoln knew who Grace Woods was, but the other names didn't ring a bell. "If it's such a big deal you should throw back some coffee and do it yourself," he suggested.

"I can't," Luke whined. "I'll get sick on the water."

Lincoln didn't respond.

"That's no kind of first impression," Luke continued. He sensed an opening in his brother's silence. "It could be a big break for me and the boat."

Lincoln sighed. He ran his hand through his hair, looking around the kitchen and living room of the hill house. There was so much work to be done. Weeks, even months' worth, and it would cost a lot of money. He had talked to the bank about helping him out with some of the raw materials costs. He could do the labor. He'd trained under his Grandad as a carpenter until drink had taken over his Grandad's personality and eventually sent him to his grave, much like it had he and Luke's father decades ago. But the bank hadn't given him a solid answer yet.

"Link?" Luke's voice nudged him hopefully.

Lincoln sighed again. A sigh of resignation. Any money Luke could bring in on the boat would be that much less he would ask Lincoln to loan him, which would help keep him on track with the repairs until the bank came through. He supposed delaying construction work on the house by one day wouldn't make that big of a difference in the end.

"Is that a yes?" Luke pressed.

"All right, but just this once."

"Beauty! I'll text you the details," Luke said quickly, then hung up before Lincoln could change his mind.

Lincoln scowled, grumbling to himself, "A fine thank you, little brother."

He took one last look at the hole in the floor, his eyes flicking to the pile of unused supplies in the corner of the room. Some he had picked up from the hardware store and some had been ferried to the island. It had taken weeks to get everything in place in order to get started on the floor, the plumbing, and the electrical that needed fixing. He did have loads of work to do on this place, but once it was done it would be his to enjoy. A little piece of paradise on earth, gifted to him by his Grandad.

His phone buzzed with Luke's text.

8:15am. 6 people. Full tour. Sell them on another booking before they get off the boat!

Lincoln mumbled a few choice words about his brother as he grabbed his keys to leave. It seemed like he had been cleaning up after Luke's irresponsible messes his whole life. Today was no different. The last thing he wanted to do was stop everything, trek down to the dock, and ferry a boatload of spoiled Hollywood types around the island like they owned the place and he was their chauffeur.

He stepped out into the morning that was just beginning to break and climbed into the old golf cart he used to get around the island. It was a little dinged up, but it got the job done on a car free island. The cart buzzed heartily as he drove it down the long driveway onto the winding road that led down the hill.

Lincoln took in a deep breath of the fresh morning air and steered the cart deftly around the sharp curves in the road. He would bite the bullet and get this tour done, then be back at the house by mid-afternoon. How bad could it be?

CHAPTER 5

Zac couldn't sleep. He never could sleep on an airplane, no matter how exhausting the trip.

The private jet made things nice at least. Definitely nicer than coach on a commercial flight. And flying on Grace Woods' private jet was even better. Minus Grace Woods, though. That was a bummer.

He wondered about that fact as he stretched out in one of the reclining seats in the main cabin. Worried about it was more like it. Had he done something already to offend her? Or…maybe she was pissed at someone else on the flight.

Zac dropped his head to the side and craned his neck to get a better view of some of his fellow passengers. Kendra, the DP, and the assistant director, Max, were sitting side-by-side. Rigby's assistant was sitting next to Rigby, though Zac's view of the producer was obstructed by the high backs of the reclining chairs. Syd and his girlfriend, Shandra, a sappy younger actress Zac knew from a previous project, were in the main bedroom. The other producer, Phoenix, had the smaller bedroom. It was still early in the morning, barely daylight, and all of them were asleep.

He let his mind wander with the possibilities of what any of them might have done to make Grace so upset she didn't want to fly with them. He quickly concluded it was probably Syd bringing his girlfriend. He sighed. Women made things difficult.

"You up?"

A voice came from behind Zac, startling him.

Rigby's face appeared, looming over the back of Zac's chair, "Sorry, I didn't mean to scare you." Rigby said in a hoarse whisper.

"No problem," Zac said. "I didn't know anyone else was awake."

"Want some coffee?"

Zac nodded and Rigby's looming face disappeared. Moments later he was at Zac's side, settling into the empty seat next to him. Moments after that a member of the staff brought them a coffee service with two cups and placed it gently on the table between them.

"Can't sleep?" Rigby asked.

Zac nodded, shrugging it off as no big deal.

Rigby chuckled as he poured his coffee. "At your age, I don't imagine it makes that big a difference. Me? If I don't sleep I gotta take all kinds of stuff to get me through jet lag." He offered to pour Zac a cup and Zac nodded. Rigby paused mid-pour and gave him a pointed look. "If you need anything…you know…to help you through jet lag…let me know."

"I will," Zac said. He understood what Rigby was offering, assistance in getting medication, legal or illegal, but Zac didn't partake in pharmaceuticals. They tended to age the user, add unwanted bags under the eyes, plus wrinkles. Zac valued his looks too highly to do anything that might damage them. His looks made him a lot of money and offered him the possibility of a star on the Hollywood Walk of Fame. Not worth the risk. "I should be fine. I brought some vitamins and herbal tea," he said.

Rigby paused and blinked a few times. Zac noticed that the older man had those dreaded bags and wrinkles. Producers didn't have to worry so much about their appearance.

Suddenly, Rigby burst out laughing. He tried to hold it in, keep it quiet so as not to wake everyone else up, but it was definitely a belly laugh. Constraining it made the laughter come out in short, whining bursts.

Zac smiled his best camaraderie smile, as if he and Rigby were old friends and agreed on the humor in all situations. He held the smile as Rigby's laughter continued long after Zac considered the appropriate amount of time. He kept thinking that if they were in a scene the director would have already yelled cut.

Finally, wiping his eyes, Rigby stopped laughing and sighed happily, saying, "You're funny, kid." Rigby eyed Zac with some newfound respect and gave his knee a meaty smack. "You get it. I can tell." Rigby nodded with satisfaction.

Zac wasn't sure how to respond. So he didn't. He toned down his camaraderie smile to a contented listening expression and waited to see if Rigby would keep talking. Not surprisingly, he did.

"You know, that's the thing that's gonna make your career. Not everyone gets it. But you do," Rigby pointed a thick finger at Zac and stabbed the air between them. He leaned back contentedly in his chair, still turned in Zac's direction. Watching him. Waiting for a response.

"That means a lot coming from you," Zac said.

Rigby's eyes glittered with amusement and he gave his head a shake, as if conceding to Zac's superior intellect. "You see? That's the perfect thing to say. You always know exactly what to say."

Zac touched his forehead as if tipping an invisible hat.

Rigby kept gazing at him. He seemed to be weighing something heavy in his mind. For one instant Zac wondered if the older man was going to hit on him, but when Rigby leaned in closer to speak again it felt more like he was about to share a secret than make a pass.

"I've been thinking about you and Grace," Rigby said.

Zac raised his eyebrows. "Me and Grace?"

Rigby nodded, glancing past Zac, making sure everyone else was still asleep. "You and Grace are gonna make a great couple on screen. I really think your styles are gonna mesh, you know?"

Zac nodded. Not sure where this was going.

"The thing is, Zac, I don't think the world," he moved his hands around in tight circles through the air in front of them, "is ready to accept the *age difference*."

Zac raised his eyebrows again. He had decided not to bring the younger man older woman thing up since he heard that Indigo was out. He wasn't in a position to insult anyone, especially not Grace Woods.

Rigby leaned in closer, intent on getting his point across. "I was thinking that if you and she were…you know…" Rigby wiggled his eyebrows up and down, "…an *item* in the real world, then maybe the whole thing will play out better with the audience." Rigby leaned back in his chair and studied Zac's reaction.

Zac, for his part, thought he was taking the suggestion very well. He didn't let his calm, contented expression falter. Instead, he allowed the corners of his mouth to lift ever so slightly, indicating he was secretly enthralled with the idea.

He was, in a way.

Zac had pondered that very thought himself, though he had pushed it aside as too risky. What if his attempts at engaging Grace in a real life romance failed? That might affect the filming and, worse, crumble his reputation as one of the most desirable bachelors in Hollywood. But if he had a powerful man like Rigby helping him along the way, maybe it would work.

"You think Grace and I should get together? Date?"

Rigby nodded, eyes still glittering with the possibility of it all.

Zac shifted in his chair and cleared his throat, letting the producer believe that his idea was a brand new concept.

"You like her well enough, don't you?" Rigby asked.

Zac nodded. "Yeah, yeah, of course. She's…well, she's Grace Woods."

Rigby laughed. It was almost a giggle and Zac wished he hadn't heard it, it kind of gave him the creeps. He shook it off. Even if the delivery was less than perfect, Rigby's idea was palatable. If he and Grace were a couple it would also solve his dilemma of giving his best performance in the film.

Zac had one more question. "Do you think she'll go for it? I mean, do you think I really have a chance with someone like her?"

Rigby chuckled and patted Zac's knee again reassuringly. "You've got nothing to worry about, kid. If you're up to it, I will make it happen."

CHAPTER 6

Grace parted ways with Faye after they landed. The former wanted to check into their luxury hotel and freshen up, which probably meant taking a nap until late morning. Grace, however, wanted to get out onto the island. Being cramped up on the plane all night had given her cabin fever and seeing the beautiful water from the sky had been a literal inspiration.

Lucky for her she had a boat ride around the island scheduled just after 8 o'clock on a small charter boat named the Lady Jane.

With all of the last minute arrangements being made for their trip to Australia, someone had booked the boat ride much too early in the morning.

"I can reschedule," Phoenix had told her over the phone, calling from Grace's jet to Faye's.

"No, don't do that," Grace had told her. "Book something that everyone can attend after you land. I'll go on this one alone."

She didn't tell Phoenix, but she was glad for the mistake. She wanted to go alone, sans producers, sans Syd and his girlfriend, sans Zac. She wanted to decompress from her trip. A solo boat trip would do just the trick.

As she stepped onto the pier a few minutes before 8:00 she had the sense of a thrilling new adventure. A balmy tropical breeze lifted her hair off of her face and she breathed it in, letting the beauty of this place fill her lungs and feed her creative soul.

Grace needed to immerse herself in this world. To play Scarlet Kensington who, according to the script, ran a beachfront gourmet restaurant, Grace needed to become an islander. The sights, smells, and sounds of this place needed to permeate her body just as Scarlet's character permeated her mind.

She took slow, careful steps down the long pier, taking in the shining white boats tied to their docks with thick ropes while French blue waves lapped at their sides. She smiled quietly at the sound of sea birds on the water and closed her eyes for a moment, inhaling another deep breath of this amazing place. Grace could almost feel the spirit of Scarlet Kensington in the soft peaceful breeze.

"Excuse me," a man's voice sounded sharp and loud from behind her, accompanied by the hollow thumping of someone running on the pier.

Grace's eyes flew open. In the instant it took to turn around and see the man her mind raced through all of the security protocols she had broken to get to the pier. She had left her security team behind to travel in Faye's private jet. Then, dismissing Faye's offer to have one of her people escort her, Grace had opted not to take the shuttle. Instead, she had hired a seemingly nice man with a golf cart, or buggy as they called them on this car free island, to take her to the marina.

As the thumping runner fast approached, fear rose in her chest. Years of living with fame and the money that came

with it had made Grace cautious of the outside world…
normally. Had she let her guard down on this enchanting
little island only to be robbed, kidnapped, or worse, within
an hour of landing? On the other hand, would a kidnapper
say 'excuse me'?

She wasn't sure, so she grit her teeth, gripped her Chanel
tote firmly with both hands, and silently cursed her mistake
as the man rushed towards her.

He was tall and well built despite being a little shaggy and
unkempt. His olive green cargo shorts were spattered with
paint splotches and his shoes were actually worn work boots.
He carried a raggedy knapsack that clunked as he ran. He
was fumbling with a white polo shirt, trying to pull it down
over his bare chest. The action made his forward progress
awkward, but he didn't slow down, even when the shirt was
wrapped almost completely around his neck and face,
obstructing his view.

Grace gasped. The wild man was barreling blindly
towards her on a pier with no room for her to escape, but
that wasn't why she gasped. The gasp came from somewhere
deep in her chest near her heart, a purely visceral reaction to
the sight of him.

His bare chest was tan and extremely well formed. A lean,
muscled, stomach practically stared her in the face as he
moved closer, wrestling with his shirt. Not the rock hard six-
pack that would lead her to believe he spent too much time
worrying about his appearance, but the sexy hard stomach of
a man who built his muscle from real manual labor. His
abdomen and torso flexed and writhed as he tried to twist
the white polo into place.

He was almost on top of her and Grace couldn't move.
Frozen in shock, she tried and tried, but could not get her
breath. She couldn't even call out a warning to tell him he
was about to run smack into her.

Just as she thought they were doomed to collide and go careening off the pier into the blue water, he freed the shirt and yanked it down so it was out of his face. Grace had half a heartbeat to take in the shock of blonde hair, the 5 o'clock shadow on a strong jaw, and the perfect white teeth in a surprised smile.

"Whoops," he exclaimed as he saw her right in front of him. Without slowing down, he turned sideways, sucked his stomach in to keep their bodies from bumping, raised his awkward knapsack high in the air so it just skimmed over the top of her head, and carried on past her, still running. He called out over his shoulder in an unmistakable Australian accent, "Excuse me, sorry!"

Grace was dizzy as she watched him run away. Even though she hadn't moved as he passed by, somehow she felt as if she had spun around in a full circle and been left flapping in the breeze caused by his departure. His backside grew smaller and smaller as he quickly moved down the pier, and she noted that it was just as attractive as his front side.

It took her a few moments to regain her composure. Finally, she pulled in a shallow breath, then another, and realized that her whole body was trembling.

"It's okay," she whispered. One more breath, deeper, more calming, and she would be fine.

She relaxed her grip on her tote bag and glanced up and down the pier to see if anyone had noticed the running man or her reaction. There were just a few people on a handful of boats preparing to go out for the day. Mostly she could only see the tops of their heads from her much lower position on the pier. None of them seemed to be paying any attention to her or the stranger who had been in such a hurry.

Grace smoothed her black hair and tugged the front of her blue-green chambray shirt back in place. The trembling was gone, except for a small ball in the center of her stomach, and she felt a little foolish.

What in the world had come over her? She had worked with some of the world's most glamorous and attractive men and had never lost her ability to speak. Probably the mixture of jet lag, fear, and a little bit of island mojo was affecting her senses. She needed to get to her boat and settle in for a relaxing ride.

Glad nobody had been watching to see her go into palpitations over a random good looking Australian sailor, she reoriented to her task and continued down the pier to look for the Lady Jane.

CHAPTER 7

incoln boarded the Lady Jane in three long steps. A little out of breath, still agitated because of all the problems he'd had getting there, it was a relief to finally arrive. Only a couple of minutes before 8:00am, so he wasn't late. Even after everything that had happened.

Halfway down the hill Lincoln had realized he wasn't dressed properly to Captain the boat for tourists. He had to turn his buggy around, go back to the house and find a clean white polo and his grey Reefs, which were old and a little gnarly around the edges, but the only deck shoes he had. No time to put them on, he shoved them in a knapsack and took off again.

When he was already past the small town full of closed shops, almost to the marina, Luke texted him.

Don't forget champagne.

"Champagne?!" Lincoln shouted at his cell phone.

Pulling his second U-turn of the morning, he muttered a few choice words about his little brother. Even choicer words came to him when he pulled up to Lyra's Bottle Barn and saw a 'CLOSED' sign. Too early for any of the shops to be open, Lincoln thought about running to the resort and buying a bottle of their champagne, then came up with another possibility.

A quick trip to Lyra's house to ask a favor of the elderly island woman with a missing front tooth got him one bottle of champagne. This was her personal stock that she happened to have in her fridge.

"Thanks again, Lyra," he called to her as she watched him climb back into his buggy with the bottle.

"No worries, Link," she smiled happily, the gap in her teeth enhancing her good humored expression instead of diminishing it. "Tell your brother he needs to place an order like normal folks."

"I will," Lincoln gave her a wave and zipped off, still with plenty of time to get to the boat before the luxury guests arrived.

And he would have made the trip with ease, if his buggy hadn't run out of power halfway there.

"You've got to be kidding," he exclaimed in disbelief, slamming his fist on the center of the steering wheel. Too many trips carrying construction supplies for the house up and down the hill had run the battery down, and he had forgotten to recharge it before his current adventure. Not forgotten, exactly. He'd been interrupted by Luke's hangover phone call. "Unbelievable," Lincoln muttered, shaking his head.

Lincoln stepped out of the buggy. It had died unceremoniously, lurching to a spot in the middle of the lane. He fought the urge to pick up one side of it and roll it off the road into the ocean. Instead, he picked up the front end and moved it as far as he could, then did the same on the back end, eventually getting it enough out of the way that other buggies could pass.

"I'll deal with you later," he told the cart as he took off his work shirt and tossed it in the back. He pulled the white polo out of the knapsack, shoved the bottle of champagne in, and took off running towards the marina.

Lincoln took a deep breath. All of that was over. He had made it on time and just needed to put a few things in place before the Hollywood types arrived.

He kicked off his work boots and rummaged through the knapsack, pulling out his deck shoes. He had this under control. Despite Luke's careless attention to business, he was safely on board the Lady Jane with plenty of time to–

"Hello?"

Lincoln whirled around at the sound of a woman's voice.

"This is the Lady Jane, correct?" The woman was already up the ladder and standing on the deck, confident that she had the right boat without his answer.

Lincoln stood barefoot and frozen, his deck shoes still dangling from his hand, stunned not so much by her presence or her question, but by something more primal.

She was dressed simply, nothing overtly sexy, but the shape of her body, lithe with curves in all the right places, was hard to ignore. Black hair, high cheekbones, full lips, eyes hidden behind sunglasses, she was the picture of beauty and elegance. Stunning–literally.

Lincoln opened his mouth, but his brain was numb with some kind of testosterone rush and he couldn't form words. He was more attracted to this stranger standing in front of him than he'd ever been to any woman in his past, and he had dated some real beauties. None of them, however, could compare to Grace Woods.

Because this was Grace Woods, standing right in front of him, Lincoln had no doubt. Even with her famous green eyes hidden behind sunglasses he recognized the movie star and understood like he never had before how she had made her fortune on the big screen.

Grace dipped her chin and peered at him over the top of her sunglasses.

Lincoln felt his heart skip a beat when her eyes caught his. They really were an electric emerald green.

A tiny pucker appeared between her eyebrows. "It's you," she said.

The accusation surprised him out of his silence and he realized his mouth was still open. He closed it, cleared his throat to make sure his voice didn't come out as a croak, and asked, "It's me?"

She waved her hand in the general direction of the marina and said, "You almost knocked me into the water back there."

"I did?" His brain still in a daze from the sight of her, Lincoln thought through his race to get to the Lady Jane. Yes, right, there had been a woman on the pier that he had run past. He remembered. But that hadn't been Grace Woods. Or had it?

"I didn't see you," he said.

"I know you saw me. You spoke to me. You said 'Excuse me.'" She was complaining, but it wasn't coming off as angry. More like she was trying to get the story straight, make sure all of the facts were lined up.

She pushed her sunglasses to rest on top of her head as she spoke and a stab of yearning pierced him right in the gut. What was his problem? He had to get it together. He wasn't some kind of star struck school kid. He was a grown man.

"I saw you, but I didn't know you were *you*," he explained as he motioned towards her, deck shoes flopping in his hand.

"Oh, you didn't recognize me." She winced, a barely imperceptible movement at the corners of her eyes, but Lincoln caught it. A shade of melancholy passed across her beautiful face and another stab of yearning pierced him, this time in his heart.

He needed to explain himself, un-insult her if that was possible, and break out of this strange mesmerization.

"I saw you, of course I saw you," he motioned towards her again with the deck shoes, looked at them as if they had just appeared in his hand, and decided to put them on. It didn't make any sense to stand there holding his shoes like an idiot. As he hopped on one foot and then another to slip the shoes on, he started talking, and the words just kept coming out, "I just didn't realize you were *the* Grace Woods. Not that there's another Grace Woods. I mean, I knew the real Grace Woods would be here, I just didn't know that was you." He paused, shoes on, watching her watch him, still not sure how to fix the situation. "I thought you would be…bigger."

Grace's green eyes filled with confusion, then amusement. The corners of her mouth lifted into a small smile and that smile turned into a laugh.

At that moment, to Lincoln Reeves, it was as if the Whitsunday sun, unmatched for its brilliance, had dropped out of the sky and landed right on the deck of the Lady Jane.

CHAPTER 8

Grace had walked down the pier with trepidation. Not a feeling she was used to having. Yet there it was, she was nervous.

As she passed each boat one by one and read the name painted on the side she could plainly see none of them were the Lady Jane. Knowing that the man who had almost sent her reeling into the ocean while simultaneously driving her senses wild with some kind of animal magnetism had disappeared onto one of the boats at the end of the pier, she also knew that the odds of him being aboard the Lady Jane increased every time she walked by another boat. Thus her sweaty palms and fluttering stomach.

For the first time since she left LAX she wished Phoenix or Rigby were with her. The comfort of a producer would be nice if she ended up face-to-face with that...that...*man*. She tried to convince herself that she was offended by his behavior, but deep down she knew that wasn't the problem.

When she did climb onto the Lady Jane and found him standing with his back to her, his feet bare, holding a pair of old shoes, she was flustered. She had let her gaze linger on his incredibly appealing backside, and travel down to his unusually attractive feet, before regaining control of her senses.

Really? Distracted by his attractive feet? She was being ridiculous.

Then she had said hello and he had turned around and Grace's butterflies burst free from her stomach, filling her whole body with wild flutterings before escaping and covering every inch of her skin with tiny feathery kisses. Shivers ricocheted up and down her back and arms and Grace sucked in her breath, holding it in tightly. It took everything in her power to remain calm on the surface and keep him from seeing her reaction.

He was magnificent. An Adonis.

His features were sculpted, heavy, masculine, but not perfect, which only made them more appealing. Thick sandy blonde hair kissed by the sun so that the ends of it gleamed. Blue eyes, but that was an understatement. Blue like the waters that surrounded the island. Shining turquoise. Unbelievably blue.

Maybe it was the gentle movement of the boat, but Grace's knees felt wobbly and she had thought she might actually faint. She had to do something to gather herself, so she resorted to scolding him for his earlier behavior. A defense mechanism. Deflect emotion onto the other person and make them figure out what to say next.

It had worked, sort of. He had tried to explain himself, talking too long and too fast, but then he had made her laugh as he struggled to put on his shoes and admitted he thought she would be bigger in real life. Nobody had ever said that to her and it struck her funny bone.

Grace regained control of herself and stopped laughing, deciding to forgive this beautiful example of a man for running past her without realizing who she was if he would only stop making her feel like a schoolgirl.

Suddenly he stepped forward and stuck out his hand.

"Lincoln Reeves," he said. "Welcome aboard the Lady Jane."

Grace took his hand gingerly, afraid touching him would send an electric shock through her body. His hand was strong, but gentle. There was no electric shock, not exactly. More like a deep warmth that permeated her skin and soaked up her arm.

"Lincoln?" she asked, her arm limp and heavy with the heat of his touch.

Maybe it was strange to question his name, but she couldn't think of anything else to say. Holding his hand was turning her brain to mush. Thoughts of Abraham Lincoln popped into her mind, though it seemed odd for an Australian to be named after an American president. And Grace could tell by his accent he was definitely Australian.

He was still holding her hand, gazing down into her eyes with those brilliant blues of his own. He opened his mouth to speak and her eyes dropped to his full, thick, warm—she imagined—lips.

Quietly, because they were so close together and perhaps, she hoped, because he felt the same intimacy she did, he said, "My Dad liked cars."

Grace blinked. Once. Then twice. She lifted her eyes to his and found a mischievous gleam in them, which enhanced their amazing blue to something almost ethereal. A sigh almost escaped her lips, but she clamped them shut. He grinned. She decided to allow the smallest of coy smiles of her own when a giggle unexpectedly bubbled out of her throat, taking them both by surprise.

"Oh," she started to apologize for laughing when another giggle, this one louder and longer, came over her.

Lincoln watched with curious amusement as she stepped back from him, pulled her hand out of his, and covered her mouth, trying to suppress the laughter.

She failed. Miserably.

The ridiculousness of her situation, hand clamped over her mouth, standing on a boat with a total stranger, unsuccessfully controlling gales of laughter, came over her again and again, which kept the laughter flowing, erupting in little spurts through her fingers.

Concern furrowed Lincoln's Adonis brow. "Are you all right? Can I get you some water or something?"

Grace shook her head 'no' with such force her sunglasses flopped off the top of her head and became entangled in her hair. The need to save them from falling to the deck brought her out of her laughing fit. She continued to shake her head with less vehemence while she carefully extracted them from her hair.

"It's okay, I'm sorry. It must be jet lag or someth–" a loud hiccup stopped her from finishing her sentence, surprising them both again. She looked at Lincoln with wide eyes.

He chuckled with relief, "Right, that makes sense. I'm not usually *that* funny."

"Maybe I should have taken a nap at the hotel before I came out here."

"You just flew in?"

She nodded, still working her sunglasses out of her hair.

Lincoln smiled and motioned towards one of the seats on the side of the boat. "If what you need is to relax, we can take care of that, no worries. You sit here and as soon as the rest of your party gets here we'll be on our way."

"There is nobody else."

He paused, his hand touching the waterproof cushion on the seat. "I thought there were six in your group?"

She shook her head 'no' again, re-tangling a section of

hair she had just freed. "No. Change of plans. They're not going to arrive until much later."

"Oh," he looked a little confused, awkward even.

"Is that a problem?" she asked as she sat down in the seat he had offered.

"No, no problem." Lincoln glanced around like he was looking for something then realized he didn't need it. He clapped his hands together once and announced, "I guess we're ready to go then. Party of one." He made like he was heading to the helm then stopped suddenly and turned back. "Are you all right there? Do you want something to drink while I cast off?"

Grace started to shake her head again, then stopped, her sunglasses were still tangled in her hair. "No, thank you. Let's just get going."

She was glad to have him busy somewhere else, where she wasn't staring at him making a fool of herself. She needed a minute to get her act together, plus this particular chair he had settled her in was pretty comfortable.

"Great," he said, starting towards the helm again. With a sudden movement, he turned back once more. "Where do you want to go exactly? Since you're the only passenger there's no sense going anywhere you don't want to be."

Grace looked up at Lincoln, sunglasses dangling, flustered at his presence, her mind in a jet lag fog, and said, "Why don't you decide. I want to go somewhere relaxing and beautiful."

Lincoln gave her a long look as a wide smile took over his face. His smile reawakened the butterflies she thought had left her stomach and she tried to smile back without swooning.

"Relaxing and beautiful?" Blue eyes twinkling, he told her, "I know just the place."

CHAPTER 9

aye ran her finger down the list of lunch options on the menu. With the waiter on standby, she was trying to decide between the soft shell crab salad and the cold seafood platter, which had prawns, salmon, and her favorite, oysters.

She was positively starving. After collapsing on the bed in the private beach house, the only space in the hotel that was sufficiently secluded enough for Faye's taste, she had slept for almost two hours. When she woke she checked in with her staff, took a quick dip in the infinity pool, showered, and dressed for lunch. She had been alone all morning and decided to dine amongst the people.

One of the people, the waiter, stood patiently alert at her side.

"Oh, just bring me both of them," Faye conceded, handing him the menu and releasing him to his duties. The long trip had made her hungry and it was seafood after all, not terribly fattening.

She took a sip of sparkling mango infused water and let

her eyes wander across the tables full of diners and the view beyond. All of the restaurant seating stretched along the edge of a long covered deck that hung just above a pristine beach, which offered a wonderful view of gentle blue waves rolling peacefully up and back, up and back. The green hills of this and neighboring islands rose up out of the waters beyond. A lovely vista to be sure, but not quite interesting enough for Faye.

She rather despised dining alone and wondered when Grace would return to the hotel to get some rest and join her. Faye pressed her lips together in a discreet grimace. Grace would probably be busy with her film and not take any time to relax. The woman was a certifiable workaholic when she was filming.

Faye sighed. She might have to find some other distraction while she was here. Luckily, her table was situated at the far end of the deck and gave her an excellent vantage point to watch the other patrons.

There were several couples, mostly young, mostly beautiful, none of whom she recognized. She did recognize a politician she had met at a party in Sydney the year before, though she wasn't sure he recognized her. He was not a young man, but was seated with an extremely young woman that Faye decided was not the wife she had met at the party. Perhaps he didn't want to be recognized. That was a possible intriguing bit of information.

Before he noticed her noticing him Faye turned towards the ocean as if captivated by the view. Not that it wasn't gorgeous, but it wasn't quite as interesting as a heavy hitting politician attempting to have a secret affair just a few tables away.

As she gazed nonchalantly at the water a sensation filled the air around her, an electrical excitement that moved through the entire dining room. A buzz of sorts.

Faye carefully, slowly, keeping her expression cool and sophisticated, turned to see who had entered the restaurant. It had to be someone obscenely famous for her to feel the reaction of the room like that. Perhaps a rock star or one of those spotlight loving business moguls who were always pandering to get on the cover of Forbes.

She was wrong on both counts.

"Is that?!" A woman nearby whispered excitedly to her lunch companion, too thrilled to complete her question.

As the individual causing such a stir followed an attentive waiter to Faye's section of the restaurant, more and more distracted people stopped their conversations and watched. Faye could see why. The electrifying arrival was none other than Zac Foster, Grace's new co-star.

"My, my," Faye said under her breath

He certainly was a handsome thing. Astonishingly attractive features, well built, poised, and confident as he walked by obvious fans and pretended not to notice their reaction. Faye could honestly say she had never met the boy in person and his film work was not exactly her taste, but she understood why Grace had chosen him to star opposite in her movie.

For a brief moment she was overcome with jealousy, knowing that Grace was going to be working side-by-side with this gorgeous specimen, doing love scenes even, but then she remembered how depressed Grace had gotten after breaking up with Syd. Faye dismissed her juvenile feelings and chose to be happy for her good friend's distraction.

"Good for you, Grace," Faye spoke under her breath again.

A woman appeared behind Zac. Then a man. Both seemed to be following him to the table and both were quite familiar to Faye.

"Hello," she called to Phoenix and Rigby, waving at them then beckoning them over to her table.

"Well, hello, Faye," Rigby greeted her with a smile.

Phoenix noticed the single place setting at Faye's table. "Grace isn't with you?"

"No, she's out on her boat tour," Faye said in her disappointed tone. "But now that you're all here you can join me so I don't have to dine alone." She motioned to the waiter to seat the three Hollywood arrivals at her table.

Zac, who had followed Rigby and Phoenix to her table with only the slightest confusion, stood back from them, waiting politely for them to finish speaking.

Faye looked past the two movie producers and made eye contact with Mr. Blonde and Handsome, "You, too, darling."

"We don't want to intrude," Phoenix said.

"I insist," Faye said, keeping her eyes on Zac as she patted the seat next to her.

Zac looked to Rigby for clarification. The older man, well acquainted with Grace's close friendship with Faye, made an executive decision and gave him a nod.

"Thank you, we would love to join you," Rigby said. As if reading her mind he continued, "Zac, have you met Faye Clemonte? She's a dear friend of our Grace."

Zac's eyes flashed at the mention of Grace's name. Well, well, well, was that a little spark she saw? Interesting.

"Nice to meet any friend of Grace's," Zac said as he took the hand she offered him and lifted it gently to his mouth, almost brushing it with a kiss. Faye was smitten. What a doll.

As they ate lunch she made it her priority to find out all she could about Grace's gorgeous co-star. He seemed eager to give her details, which wasn't surprising. Faye had always possessed a strange ability to get people to tell her things. Intimate things. Things they were surprised they had shared the moment after they shared them.

"No, I'm single at the moment," Zac responded with a laugh after Faye teasingly asked if he was taken. "I think maybe it's a good thing, what with playing a romantic lead to someone like Grace."

"Oh," she raised her eyebrows and shared a look with Rigby before giving Zac a flirty smile. "Does that mean what I think it means?"

Zac, who Faye decided was either a hopeless romantic or a skilled actor, blushed. He leaned back in his chair and looked at his hands in his lap, trying to compose himself all the while glancing surreptitiously at Rigby.

Phoenix, bless her little soul, blinked at them all from behind her thick glasses, obviously missing the innuendo of a possible romantic attachment between Zac and Grace. Faye felt sorry for Phoenix sometimes. She was so…academic.

Rigby cleared his throat, attempting to interrupt the flow of the conversation and save the star of his current project any further discomfort. "I think it means that it's good to stay focused on the script and the work, you know? Give the best performance possible."

Faye only partially accepted this explanation. Zac seemed to relax. She had no need to press the matter so she allowed the topic of conversation to be steered to more mild subjects as she chewed over what she had just learned.

She definitely had learned something intriguing.

Faye prided herself on reading body language and picking up on the most subtle nuances in conversation and she understood exactly what was happening. Rigby was protecting Zac and Grace from outside gossip.

She forgave him for interrupting her friendly interrogation of Grace's leading man. He had a duty as a producer to keep the movie production flowing and make sure his stars were happy after all.

She would back off for now, but there was no denying

Faye was excited. The possibility of playing a role in getting the two lovebirds together piqued her interest. After a rather slow morning on the island, Faye was thrilled.

CHAPTER 10

The funny thing was that as Lincoln cast off and maneuvered the Lady Jane out of the marina and into the open waters off the island, he couldn't stop thinking about Luke. He kept thanking Luke over and over again in his mind for being such a partying flake, because it was the antics of his little brother that had landed him on this boat with Grace Woods.

Not that he was particularly excited that she was a movie star. Lincoln didn't care about that kind of thing. What he did care about was how his chest tightened and sent a million sparks across his shoulders and down his back whenever he looked at her. There had even been a few moments as they were talking that he realized he wasn't breathing.

Finally, he broke away from Grace's bewitching presence and got busy skippering the boat. Without another hand on board there was a lot to do. It wasn't impossible, but he needed to focus.

A fresh, damp ocean breeze blew in his face as he steered. The smell of the Whitsunday waters never failed to lift his spirits and Lincoln smiled as the motor pushed the Lady Jane and its precious cargo further and further away from the marina. Since Grace didn't have an agenda of her own he wanted to show her some of his favorite areas around Hamilton Island, which equated to some of the most private and pristine places.

Lincoln waved at a few old skippers as their boats passed nearby, people who had been living and working on this island for almost as long as his Grandad. Their decks were full of tourists, laughing and talking, drinking and getting out fishing equipment, generally enjoying their ride. Suddenly he felt the urge to check on Grace and make sure she was okay on her own. A safe enough distance out that he knew the Lady Jane wouldn't accidentally drift into another craft, he put the engine on idle and popped out of the helm.

"Are you sure you don't want a dri–" Lincoln stopped mid-question when he saw her. This time it was not because he was tongue-tied.

Grace Woods, gorgeous, elegant Hollywood legend, was slumped sideways in the seat where he'd left her, fast asleep. Her head had slid awkwardly off the low cushioned back and lolled to the side, which in turn had made her mouth drop open. For an instant, he had the horrible thought that she had dropped dead, but a rather un-elegant snore reassured him she was merely asleep.

Lincoln winced at the angle of her head, knowing when she woke she would probably have a sore neck. "And a sunburn," he said quietly as he glanced up into the cloudless blue sky. He hadn't thought to ask her if she had put on sunscreen.

He considered his dilemma. He could hardly put sunscreen on her without her permission and he wasn't keen on the idea of waking her up. His eyes wandered across the deck and landed on the bright orange umbrella with the weighted stand Luke had recently purchased. That might work.

Within a few minutes Lincoln had moved the umbrella, which was not only weighted, but also tied down to the deck, so it was positioned right next to Grace. Turning the crank slowly, to keep the clicking sound as low as possible, he got the umbrella fully opened without waking her up. Pleased, he saw that the shade it provided completely covered her.

Another snore brought his attention back to her head flopping to the side. He couldn't leave her like that.

Carefully, he sidled up as close as he could get without touching her. Leaning down, he spread the fingers of both hands apart and gently, ever so gently, slid his fingertips under both sides of her head. He didn't relish the idea of her waking up and finding him looming over her so he moved swiftly. Trying not to jar her, he lifted her head up and back onto the cushion.

Stepping back, he surveyed his work. Her head was no longer hanging sideways, which was good, but because the cushion on the chair topped off just below her shoulders her head now hung straight back, her mouth gaping open even wider.

Another snore, this one much louder than the first.

"Uh-oh," he said under his breath. He might have made things worse.

Lincoln pulled the cushion off of the unused seat next to Grace and, using his wide finger approach, lifted her head up slightly, pushing the cushion underneath. There, her mouth closed and she didn't look like she had been knocked unconscious anymore. She simply looked like she had leaned comfortably back, closed her eyes, and drifted peacefully off to sleep.

He watched her, allowing his gaze to wander over her beautiful features for a few moments. In rest, she was even more attractive, if that was possible. Lincoln shook his head, he needed to step away before she woke up and found him gawking at her like a creep. As if she had read his mind, Grace murmured and shifted her head on the pillow. Lincoln turned on his heel and hurried back to the helm.

When he got to the wheel and put his attention back to steering the Lady Jane, he realized they had drifted further out into open water than he had intended. Cursing under his breath he checked his instruments and the fuel levels. They were fine, but he couldn't believe he had gotten so distracted.

"Focus, Dipstick," he said.

"There you are!"

Grace's voice startled him and he bumped his elbow on the wheel as he turned to face her.

"Here I am," he responded.

"I must have fallen asleep and one of your people put an umbrella over me," she said, motioning behind her. He could just see the edge of the orange umbrella through the windows at the back of the cabin. "I tried to find them to thank them, but I guess they're all…downstairs?"

"My people?"

"You know, your crew. Are they downstairs? Is that what you call it on a boat?"

"In the cabin?" Lincoln shifted from one foot to the other before adding, "There's no crew. It's just me today."

"Oh," Grace stared at him for a beat, then said, "I thought you would have another crew…person." She waved her hand towards the door of the hatch.

"You thought we might keep a spare crew member in the cabin to bring out when needed?"

She blinked at him. "I just thought there would be more than you, by yourself."

"Nope, just me." Lincoln tried to sound confident, which he was, although with Grace watching him he was less confident than normal. "Don't worry, we have a radio if we need help. And we're not too far off." He nodded toward the islands in the distance, which were only low humps on the horizon since they had drifted further out than anticipated. Maybe he shouldn't have pointed that out.

Grace considered the barely perceptible islands for a long moment then turned back to him with her eyes full of concern. "What if something happens to you?"

"Nothing's going to happen to me."

"That's fine…but what if something does happen to you? I don't know how to drive this thing or use the radio for that matter."

It was Lincoln's turn to consider her comment. With her green eyes on him, intelligent and unwavering, waiting for an answer, his mind felt a little dull and he couldn't think of a good reason to brush off her concerns.

Lincoln took a small step back, his heart beating harder than it should, and motioned for her to stand at the controls.

"I'll show you."

A twinkle of delight washed away the concern in her eyes and she smiled. "Really?"

Lincoln shrugged like it was perfectly normal for him to include a skippering lesson with the island tour. "Why not?"

Grace moved into place right in front of him. So close he could have wrapped his arms around her if he wanted to, which he did, but he managed to control himself and show her the basics. They went over the buttons on the radio to send a message and to receive, how to control the speed of the Lady Jane and how to adjust for the current and wind when steering.

During this tutorial she was an attentive student, picking it up quickly, and looking back and up at him whenever she had a question. Lincoln did his best to keep everything respectful and professional, but he couldn't help but breathe in the citrusy scent of her ebony hair as it blew softly in the breeze.

Together they maneuvered the Lady Jane back in the direction of Hamilton Island. When they were pointed in the correct direction, Lincoln asked, "So where do you steer if you want to get there." He pointed straight ahead towards the island.

After just a moment of hesitation, Grace pointed about 10 degrees to the left and said, "There. Because the current will push us as we go."

"Spot on, Ms. Woods," he exclaimed. Grace looked back at him, laughing, obviously pleased with her new steering skills. Pleasure at her happiness once again stabbed his heart and he almost winced. Instead, he moved away from her. "Are you hungry?"

"Yes, a little," she answered.

"Great. You take care of the skippering and I'll go get us a snack."

He flung open the hatch and ducked as he climbed down the steep stairs to the sound of Grace's shocked complaints.

"You want me to drive this thing?!" Her voice was a mix of fear and excitement, which made Lincoln grin as he made his way to the galley. "Lincoln?" she called after him.

Lincoln ignored the electric thrill the sound of her voice saying his name gave him and squatted down next to the small refrigerator in the even smaller galley. He would grab the chilled champagne and whatever fancy grub Luke had stored in here for their guests and be back up top in a jiffy.

The door popped open and Lincoln's good mood deflated. There was no champagne. He had never put it into the refrigerator. The bottle he had picked up this morning was still stuffed into his knapsack on deck and had been baking in the sun all morning.

Hot champagne. Great, and from the looks of it very little

grub of any kind in the refrigerator. Luke must have cleaned out the food when he'd been drinking last night. All Lincoln could see was a block of cheddar cheese and a half empty jar of olives.

Before he had a chance to think too long about his flaky little brother, he heard Grace cry out his name followed by a terrifying shriek.

In three bounding leaps, Lincoln was back on the deck.

CHAPTER 11

Nobody was looking, at least not that Zac could see.

Rigby and Faye were wrapped up in a conversation Zac had lost track of, and Phoenix was typing madly into her phone. Their waiter was nowhere in sight and everyone seated near their table who had been keenly interested in their arrival seemed to have returned their attention to their meals.

Without any eyes on him, Zac was left with his own thoughts…and those thoughts were doozies.

What had started as a casual suggestion by Rigby, that he start up a romance with Grace for PR purposes, had taken an unexpected turn when her friend, Faye, had made similar, and much stronger, innuendos about that possibility. Was this going to happen? Was he really about to embark on a love affair with one of the biggest Hollywood stars on the planet?

Zac continued to nod and smile at Rigby and Faye as they carried on their conversation, but his mind was racing.

"Are you all right?" Phoenix leaned towards him, a curious pinch in her forehead.

Zac hesitated, but only for a microsecond. He smiled reassuringly, "Sure, I'm fine."

Phoenix pulled away from him, a frown in her eyes. She wasn't sure if she believed him, he could tell, which was unusual. Usually Zac could get anyone to believe anything.

"Really," he said again, lifting his water to his lips to take a sip and avert his eyes from hers. Her extra thick lenses made her eyes so much bigger than a normal person, like a cartoon bug. He felt like he was being scrutinized through a magnifying glass.

Phoenix went back to typing into her phone, only shooting him an occasional look now and again. It was a little disconcerting. He decided Phoenix might disapprove of his romancing Grace for PR reasons. She wasn't as imaginative as Rigby and she was a female. Probably a feminist.

"Don't you think, darling?" Faye asked Zac as she reached out and placed her cool hand on his bicep, a flicker of attraction gleaming in her lovely grey eyes.

"What don't I think?" he answered, leaning back into the conversation and allowing his gaze to respond to hers with a mischievous look of his own. It was natural for him to flirt. Especially with attractive friends of his co-star and producers. Part of the job description.

"I said you should join Grace, and me, for dinner. I'm sure she'll be back from her little boat trip soon enough, but she may be too tired to socialize. However, dinner would be wonderful. Surely you two have a lot to talk about." Faye squeezed his bicep gently and cooed, "Lines and such?"

Zac grinned, shooting a look at Rigby for guidance. The older man had a sly grin of his own as he gave Zac a quick wink and nod of approval.

Zac understood. Both Rigby and Faye were 100 percent

behind fixing him up with Grace. This was an opening, a chance for him to spend some intimate moments with her and kick on the charm.

"I'd love to," he said.

"Marvelous," Faye patted his arm and went back to eating her seafood.

The mood at the table shifted, as if a big decision had been made, an important detail locked into place. The shift was so powerful that Zac imagined he heard an audible click. The fate of the movie and his career were on the line and the stakes were high.

Goosebumps rose on Zac's forearms and he moved his hands into his lap to hide them from the others. The thrill of the chase. Nobody understood how exciting Zac found the decision to pursue a woman, especially a woman like Grace. Although, he realized, he had never pursued someone quite like Grace. She was everything he aspired to be, rich, famous, a Hollywood legend...and he was about to make her his girlfriend.

"Hmph," Phoenix grunted softly, interrupting his thoughts.

Zac looked at her, wondering if she had read his mind, but she was still tapping on her phone, unaware of what he, along with Rigby and Faye, were planning.

CHAPTER 12

"I saw a whale!" Grace shouted.

Hands clutching the steering wheel, eyes frozen on the waves, she heard Lincoln burst out of the hatch.

He was at her side in a split second, which was good because Grace thought she might faint. With both of her hands white-knuckling the steering wheel, she was managing to stand even though her body trembled, but she wasn't sure how long she could hold on.

"A whale? Where?" He scanned the waters in the distance.

Grace shook her head vehemently. "No! Not out there. Right here!"

She couldn't point since her hands were stuck to the steering wheel. Grace nodded her head repeatedly in the direction where she had seen some kind of giant mass lift up out of the ocean next to the Lady Jane.

"Right next to the boat?"

"Yes, right next to the boat," she said. He looked skeptical, which was infuriating. "What, aren't there whales out here?"

Lincoln surveyed the water around them. "It's not impossible to see a whale this time of year, but they usually keep further out. Are you sure it wasn't a dolphin?"

Grace's last nerve snapped. "I don't know what it was. Maybe it was a dolphin, but I don't think so. I only saw a piece of it and that piece looked way too big to be a dolphin."

"I'll check, stay here," he said.

Grace didn't want to tell him she couldn't have let go of the steering wheel even if she wanted to, let alone walk over to the edge of the boat and look down into the water, which was what he was doing.

Fear jumped into her throat as she watched Lincoln deftly lean out over the open water, only one hand holding onto the outside rail. He appeared to be taking her concerns seriously, shading his eyes with his free hand as he peered down into the blue beneath, even if he didn't quite believe that she had seen a whale.

Every shark attack movie Grace had ever seen, one of which she had starred in, came flooding into her mind and she wished he wouldn't lean out quite so far.

Suddenly, he stiffened.

"What is it? Is it a shark?" Grace tried to control the shrill tone in her voice.

Lincoln pulled back onto the deck and bounded to her side. He reached in front of her and killed the engine.

"What are you doing?" she asked.

"We don't want it to get hurt."

"We don't want *what* to get hurt?"

He looked down at her, his eyes glittering with excitement. "The whale. It's a humpback whale."

"A humpback…" Grace's voice trailed into a choked whisper. All of the fear that had been coursing through her veins plummeted to the floor under her feet, making the rise and pitch of the boat more extreme. All that remained in her body was a floating feeling as she disengaged from the reality of their situation. When she spoke her voice was high pitched and sounded far away. "Aren't those the biggest kind? We don't want the giant whale to get hurt? What about us?"

"It won't bother us."

The whale chose that moment to make its next appearance.

A great blue-grey hulking mass pushed up out of the water only yards away from where Lincoln had just been looking over the edge and sprayed a blast of ocean water into the air. Grace sucked in her breath, yanked her hands off of the steering wheel, and grabbed hold of Lincoln's arm.

"Oh, my goodness!" she whispered hoarsely. Her heart was pounding so hard in her chest she could barely speak.

"Come on," he said. Before she could protest, Lincoln slipped his arm around her waist and moved her to the edge of the boat where the humpback was lingering on the surface of the water. The animal was huge–absolutely huge–as it turned slowly onto its side.

"Heya, big fella," Lincoln said in a low, calm voice. He was speaking to the whale with confidence, but Grace could feel a tremor move through his arm on her waist. Instinctively she moved even closer to him, pressing her back into his chest.

They watched in silence as the whale floated quietly, its large, strange eye seeming to take them in. It pushed forward, lowering its head back under the water and revealing the white underside of a long slender fin on the side of its body. Before it completely disappeared back under the water, the humpback slapped the surface with the fin, sending saltwater droplets directly into their faces.

They both laughed out loud in surprise as they watched the massive shape move away from the Lady Jane. The whole event could only have taken 30 seconds or so, but to Grace it felt like forever.

"He's so beautiful," she whispered as the beast's shadow melted into the ocean.

"Yes, beautiful," Lincoln agreed.

She looked back at him to find he was already looking down at her. When their eyes connected she became intensely aware of their bodies pressing together, but couldn't quite get herself to move away. Legs shaky, a mix of euphoria and fear pulsing through her veins, Grace felt stronger up against Lincoln.

"Have you ever seen one that close before?" she asked, a little breathlessly. She should at least try to normalize the conversation. Lincoln didn't answer right away, so she kept talking. "I suppose you see them all the time," she said, making up her own reason why he wasn't answering her question.

"No, no…I don't see them all the time."

"I thought he was amazing," she continued, shifting her gaze out over the water. "Did you think he was amazing?"

"He was…"

Grace looked up at him again, he seemed to be lost in thought.

"I saw Migaloo once…with my Grandad," he said.

"What's a Migaloo?"

He grinned. "He's a pure white humpback whale. They think he's 30 or 35 years old now."

"Oh, wow," Grace was impressed. That must have been an amazing sight. "His name is Migaloo?"

"Yes, the aboriginal council named him. It means White Fella."

Grace giggled. "You all have a thing about calling whales 'Fella' in Australia?"

He chuckled, "I guess we do."

Every time he spoke or laughed Grace felt the sound resonate through his chest and into her back. It was a delightful feeling and not one that she wanted to end, but she knew it must.

Carefully, trying not to make him feel as if he had over-stepped by grabbing hold of her, Grace pulled away from him and turned to face him straight on. The ocean breeze was extra cool on her back where Lincoln's body had been keeping her warm just moments before. She tried to avoid the amused look on his face as she crossed her arms in front of her and looked nonchalantly around the deck.

Grace sensed he was waiting for her to speak, but she couldn't think of one thing to say after such a magnificent experience.

Luckily, Lincoln had the perfect question to get them back on an even keel. "Are you hungry?"

Her stomach grumbled and she nodded emphatically. "Yes, I am."

He clapped his hands together, rubbing them briskly like a cartoon chef. "Well, you're in for a treat, Ms. Woods. Not only do we provide up close and personal whale encounters on the Lady Jane, but we also serve only the best We-Forgot-to-Stock-the-Fridge hors devours. How does old cheese, stale crackers, and hot champagne sound?"

Grace threw her head back and laughed. When she stopped laughing she took in the gorgeous man with twinkling eyes waiting for her answer and nodded. "That sounds delicious…and you can call me Grace."

Lincoln grinned from ear to ear. "Grace it is."

CHAPTER 13

"I just don't understand what her problem was," Faye said, her voice pumping directly into Ronnie's inner ear at full whine through her earbuds.

"Maybe she was tired," Ronnie offered. She stood in front of the mirrored wall in the workout room of her New York penthouse doing bicep curls with fashionably cute purple hand weights.

Faye had called early, very early, to complain about Grace ruining her dinner party or something like that. Ronnie still wasn't clear on the details. She hadn't been completely awake when she answered the phone. When Faye, who only vaguely understood the time difference between New York and Australia, had continued to drone on and on about Grace's strange behavior, Ronnie had decided to get in a workout.

"She wasn't tired. I made her take a nap when she got back from that boat trip so she would be fresh for dinner. I had everything planned and she…she…"

"She what?"

"She ruined everything!"

Ronnie rolled her eyes. Faye's drama was a lot to take this

early in the morning. Normally she would have called Presley, not Ronnie, but Presley was pregnant and Faye thought she needed her rest. This was a nice sentiment, but Ronnie was growing a little weary of being Faye's sounding board for every little perceived insult in her life.

Ronnie set the 20-pound weights down, picked up two 15-pounders and lifted them up and down over her head. At least Faye's tendency to be long winded would give her time for a long workout.

"I don't understand what she ruined, Faye. What exactly did she do that was so terrible?"

"It was awful. She kept going on and on about seeing a whale on her boat trip and positively gushing about the captain, or skipper, or whatever they call them here."

"Grace saw a whale? In the wild? What kind was it?"

There was silence on the other end of the line and Ronnie sensed that her response was unappreciated.

Finally, Faye spoke, "Whales live in the ocean. I don't see what a big deal it was for her to see one while she was out there."

"Well, what did you want her to talk about at dinner?"

Faye let out a frustrated sigh before answering, "Zac, Ronnie. I wanted her to talk about Zac Foster. Or to Zac Foster, I should say."

"Oh…and Zac Foster was there?"

"Yes! Haven't you been listening?"

Barely. Ronnie pressed on, "And why did you want her to talk about, or to, Zac Foster?"

"He's her co-star, darling. And he's gorgeous. And I think he likes her…and I think it would be good for her to have a little fling while she's filming this movie. That horrible Syd is directing, you know."

"Oh, I see. You're matchmaking," Ronnie teased.

"Of course I'm matchmaking! I'm not going to sit around

and let that Syd person parade his new, much too young, girlfriend around in front of our Gracie. She deserves her own much too young love interest."

Ronnie winced and not because of the weights she was lifting. Faye interfering in someone's love life hardly ever worked out well. For Grace's sake, she set the weights down on the rack and focused on the conversation.

"Did Grace ask you to set her up with Zac Foster?"

Faye scoffed, "Of course not! She doesn't know what she wants right now. You know how she gets when she's making one of her movies."

Ronnie grabbed a white and lavender hand towel and wiped the sweat from her brow as she made a face at herself in the mirror. Grace did tend to get emotional and maybe a little flighty when she was working on a project, but Faye on some kind of self-imposed matchmaking project made her nervous.

"I think–" Ronnie started, but it was too late, Faye was moving on with the conversation without her input.

"It will be fine. I'm changing my plans and staying on here for a while. I can set something else up between them, right? Something romantic."

Ronnie tried to think of something to dissuade her. "Won't they be working?"

"That's right! They'll be working together every day and bonding."

"No, I mean, shouldn't you let them focus on the mov–"

"Oh! I know! I'll throw her a birthday party. That's perfect!"

Grace's birthday was over a month away and Ronnie distinctly remembered her requesting to postpone any big celebrations until after she was done shooting the movie.

Ronnie shook her head 'no' as if Faye could see her. "She

didn't want to do a party right now, remember? She didn't want the distract–"

"Nonsense, everybody wants a birthday party. She just didn't want to fuss with anything while she's working. But she has me! I'll plan everything."

It was too early in the morning for Ronnie to think of a good response, one that would keep Faye's determination under control.

"You'll come, won't you?" Faye asked.

"Of course…and if you need me to help plan any–"

"No need! I can do it all. I want it to be a surprise, though. Don't tell her. This all has to be hush-hush if I'm going to pull it off *and* get her and Zac together."

Ronnie winced again, but didn't try to argue. She would talk to Presley about Faye's matchmaking plans. Presley was better at persuading their very headstrong friend, maybe she could get her to back off playing interference in Grace's love life.

Faye was still talking, "…worked out so well for Presley and Hobie. I had a hand in their romance, you know, and now they're so happy. With a baby on the way and everything!"

Ronnie could hear the excitement in Faye's voice and knew her enthusiasm came from a place of kindness. Still, she decided, for Grace's sake, that she would carve out a chunk of time to get to Australia and help curb Faye's involvement–if that was possible.

CHAPTER 14

It was a beautiful morning on the white sandy beaches of Hamilton Island. The rising sun had turned the sky pink and orange against the vibrant blue ocean. The film crew had captured glorious images with Grace strolling along the water's edge. Then with Zac strolling along the water's edge. Then with both of them strolling along the water's edge. Then with them embracing at the water's edge, their silhouettes locked together gracefully, carefully orchestrated by Syd to look as beautiful as possible.

Every image was stored safely 'in the can' to be used as needed at different points in the film or cut out of the final version altogether. One never knew the fate of any given shot during filming.

When the brilliant colors of the sunrise disappeared, Syd directed the actors and crew to move on to shooting their first scene with lines. Grace's stomach was tight with nerves. Despite decades of experience acting, the first day of any shoot always gave her anxiety.

"Are you ready?" Zac asked.

He sat next to her on a giant beach blanket with fat fuchsia and white stripes. Zac's extremely bright yellow swim trunks stood out against the stripes and complimented her green swimsuit, which had been selected to bring out the emerald in her eyes. The costume designer had called her bikini 'leaf green'. Grace thought the green was more of a grasshopper green. Ever since that thought had crossed her mind she couldn't shake the feeling that she looked like a giant grasshopper sitting on the beach in a bikini.

There was no changing any of their clothing at this point, however. Everything they wore or touched had been painstakingly selected specifically to make them look their best and to coordinate with every other scene in the movie. She was stuck with her grasshopper swimming suit and Zac was stuck with his banana yellow swim trunks.

He watched her expectantly and she remembered that he had asked a question.

"What did you say?" she asked.

A flicker of embarrassment passed through his eyes before he repeated, "Are you ready?"

Grace glanced around at the half dozen crew members who were adjusting giant diffusion screens to filter the sunlight over them and make their skin as perfect as possible. There were also three sound guys fiddling with equipment, several more grips, and a couple of production assistants surrounding her and Zac in a large half-circle. The sand between their beach towel and the ocean remained empty and undisturbed to act as the background of their scene.

Just behind the worker bees, Syd, the DP, Kendra, and Max, the assistant director, stood behind the main camera while the cameraman made adjustments. The entire crew had to finish making all of the last minute technical adjustments for the shot before the camera rolled.

Grace smiled patiently and answered, "Yes, I think so. The question is, when are they going to be ready?"

Zac followed her gaze to the buzz surrounding them and laughed nervously. "Right. Hurry up and wait."

Grace considered him for a moment. Ridiculously bright swim trunks aside, his perfectly muscled body with its six-pack abs glistened in the sun. Hair and makeup had done an excellent job adding to his natural good looks and making him next level attractive.

However, he was acting strange. If she wasn't sitting right next to him she may not notice, but so close on the beach towel she easily picked up on his micro-fidgets. Maybe it was part of his process, releasing nerves before the scene, but come to think of it, Zac had been acting strange ever since they had dinner at Faye's.

She leaned into him, careful not to let their skin touch so their makeup wouldn't smear, and said reassuringly, "I'm sure Syd will be over here soon to get us started."

"You look beautiful," Zac replied.

The compliment took her by surprise. Again, the image of a grasshopper in a bikini flashed through her mind. This time it was joined by a giant bright yellow banana with six pack abs. In her imagination, the grasshopper and the banana strolled along the beach and embraced at the water's edge.

A small laugh escaped Grace's throat and she noticed the confusion in Zac's eyes at her response. Before she could backtrack and accept his oddly timed compliment graciously, Syd called out to them from behind the camera.

"Move back a few inches, Grace…please."

The 'please' was an afterthought.

Grace complied and averted her eyes from Zac's weird expression. She hoped she hadn't insulted him right before their scene. Then again, in this scene they weren't lovers yet.

The possibility of a relationship between their two characters was still very much up in the air. Maybe it would work.

"Grace, a little bit more," Syd called out. She moved her torso away from Zac a little. "No, your whole body," Syd called again. She carefully lifted her behind off of the beach towel and placed it gently a few inches further. Looking back at the camera she could see Syd hunched over the director's monitor shaking his head. "What happened here?" he shouted at nobody and everybody.

The entire crew paused in their work. Grace felt Zac's body tense. Kendra and Max stood on either side of Syd and looked blankly at the monitor, obviously not understanding the director's complaint. Somewhere in the crowd that had gathered on the perimeter of the movie crew a woman's voice called out, "I love you, Zac!"

Grace grinned and looked at her co-star. It was difficult to tell in the bright sunshine, but Zac seemed to be blushing. She nudged him good naturally only to draw a sharp reprimand from Syd.

"Don't touch each other! We don't have time for makeup before we lose this light."

The crew gasped at his tone. None of them would dare speak to Grace Woods in that tone. Grace knew that Syd wouldn't dare either except for the fact that they used to be intimate.

She turned her gaze coolly towards the waves rolling lazily onto the white sand. Ignoring him and his little tantrums was usually sufficient to calm him down, though it didn't do much for the anger boiling in her stomach.

The sound of Syd complaining drifted into the background as Grace looked out over the water. Small white shapes floated on the turquoise water in the far distance. Boats.

Suddenly she was transported back to the deck of the

Lady Jane, Lincoln pressed against her as they watched the magnificent humpback whale disappear into the ocean. A shiver moved down her neck and she raised her shoulders to contain it.

"Are you cold?" Zac, ever attentive, ever ready to impress, interrupted her thoughts, concern wrinkling his handsome forehead.

"No," she shook her head and came back to reality. "I'm fine."

She couldn't tell if Zac believed her, but it didn't really matter. Lincoln was her little secret, even if she had talked about him incessantly after the boat ride.

All of her stories about the whale sighting and the amazing tour he had given her had fallen on deaf ears. Faye wasn't one to care much for a man who served stale crackers and hot champagne to his guests, and Zac hadn't been too keen to hear about him either.

Grace was left alone with her memories of that boat ride and she rather liked it that way.

"Grace!" Syd was calling her, and when she turned her attention back to him she found the whole crew watching. Syd must have been trying to get her attention for a while.

"For real?" Syd snapped. He pushed his way out from behind the monitor, stomping over to Grace and Zac's beach towel. "Did you hear anything I said?"

"No," Grace answered, wondering what in the world was bugging him so much.

"I need you to mo–" Syd put his hands on her shoulders to guide her into position, but stopped suddenly. "Well, that's the problem."

"What's the problem?" Grace asked, not liking the way his eyes were boring into her bust line.

"That!" He let go of her shoulders and pointed directly at her breasts. "Those!"

"These?" Grace instinctively covered her chest with crossed arms.

Syd waved at Kendra and Max to join him, then at someone unexpected, Shandra, his girlfriend.

"Look at these then look at these," Syd pointed first at Grace's breasts in her green bikini top then at Shandra's much perkier breasts in her green bikini top. "Why didn't I think of that?" Syd laughed as he asked himself the question out loud.

Grace looked confusedly between him and Shandra. Why was Shandra wearing a duplicate of her grasshopper bikini?

"Would it really make that big of a difference?" Shandra asked Syd.

"Yes, it could," Kendra responded for him.

Noticing the embarrassed murmur moving through the crew around them and the reddening cheeks of her young and handsome co-star, Grace's patience wore off.

"What are you talking about? Why is she wearing my bikini?"

As the question escaped her lips Grace came to the answer herself.

Syd had used Shandra as her stand-in.

Grace's stomach twisted.

The practice of using a person the same height and size as the star, putting them in the same clothes the star was wearing, and using them as a double so lighting could be tweaked without forcing the star to stand there for hours wasn't new to Grace. Using her ex-boyfriend's new young girlfriend as her stand-in, however, was new.

The twist in her stomach shot heat up into her chest, which threatened to creep up her neck and into her face. It didn't take a genius to see the obvious mistake in using Shandra as her double. Though their bodies and skin tone were similar enough, their busts were like comparing night to day. Or maybe a better comparison would be between firm, ripe cantaloupes and sagging, half-filled water balloons.

Grace didn't need to be informed that she possessed the half-filled water balloons. She could see. Syd could see. Shandra could see. Everybody could see.

Grace stood up, causing everyone around her to pull away like she was about to explode and they were going to get sprayed with debris. Everyone except Syd, who was still chuckling and shaking his head at his faux pas.

"I'll be in my room," Grace said, her voice even and cool. "Let me know when you figure this out."

The crew's half-circle parted to let her walk through. Grace did not look back to see if Syd was still laughing.

CHAPTER 15

*L*incoln opened his eyes, the sound of far off knocking waking him from a deep sleep. He blinked a few times before remembering that he wasn't in his bed, but in the wide hammock on his deck. He'd decided to sleep there last night because of the smell in the house. He had conducted a polyurethane test on the beautiful Mackay cedar flooring the day before, to make sure all was good before he refinished the entire surface.

"Wake up!" Luke hollered as he knocked on the front door.

"I'm back here," Lincoln called out, his voice cracking with sleep. He gripped the sides of the hammock with both hands and turned, sitting up on the edge of it.

A few moments later Luke popped his head around the corner of the house. "What's for breakfast?"

"Keep your voice down. You'll wake the neighbors."

Luke shared his brother's blonde hair and blue eyes, but not his height or his concern for making a scene. He snorted and said, "Not your neighbors. They're sleeping off a long night of cocktail parties I imagine."

Lincoln rubbed sleep out of his eyes and yawned as he spoke, "Speaking of sleeping it off, what are you doing up at this hour?"

Luke observed his big brother for a moment. "Did you sleep in the hammock?"

"Affirmative."

"Didn't you finish the bedroom first so you would have a place to hit the hay?"

"Yeah, but the house needed airing."

"Why?"

Lincoln stood and motioned Luke to follow him as he shuffled sleepily towards the door. Two wild cockatoos landed on the railing of the deck.

"Good morning," Lincoln greeted the birds who bobbed their heads up and down as he opened a drawer on a small side table next to the door and pulled out a tin of unsalted crackers.

"You shouldn't feed them. It makes them bold," Luke warned.

Lincoln shrugged and handed each bird a cracker. "It's Fred and Ginger. Grandad always fed them."

Once inside he led Luke to the corner of the living room where he had set up two sawhorses to hold the pieces of cedar flooring he was testing with stain and polyurethane.

When Luke saw the satin sheen on the two-toned wood he let out a low whistle. "That's a beauty, isn't it?"

Lincoln ran his hand down the smooth surface and nodded. "It's gonna take a lot of work, but it'll be back to its full glory when I'm done."

Luke's eyes wandered around the room, taking in all of the work Lincoln had already done. "You'll make a pretty penny rent–"

"Nope," Lincoln stopped him. He knew Luke wanted him

to use the Hill House as a luxury rental, but that wasn't what he had in mind.

"What are you gonna do to make a living, Link? You should rent this pl–"

"Nope."

Luke shook his head in disbelief. "You're as stubborn as Grandad."

"Grandad didn't want this to be a place for tourists. He wanted it to be a home."

"A fine job he made of it," Luke mumbled.

Lincoln gave his brother a sharp look. "Mind your mouth. He did his best. That's all any of us can do."

Luke's shoulders slumped and he turned away from his brother, shifting his attention to the cockatoos outside on the deck. After a few moments of watching them make a ruckus in hopes of getting another cracker, he changed the subject, "You never said how the Hollywood people were."

Lincoln's throat clenched and he stared more intently at the cedar in his hands. He hadn't shared anything about his time with Grace because he had been trying to get it out of his head.

For two days he had been haunted by the memory of her laugh, the intoxicating citrus scent of her hair, the feel of her hand on his arm, and those hypnotic green eyes. Every time he let his mind wander or closed his eyes to go to sleep those memories swept over him.

He cleared his throat and answered, "They were all right."

Luke looked at him. "Just all right?" He let out a laugh. "Leave it to my big brother to meet some of the biggest movie stars and famous director people out of Hollywood and all he has to say is 'they were all right'."

"It was just her," Lincoln said, immediately wishing he hadn't.

"Who?"

"Grace…Grace Woods."

"It was just Grace Woods? Nobody else?" Luke's surprise was obvious. Lincoln nodded, still looking at the wood. "You're kidding," Luke said. Lincoln shook his head 'no'. "You took Grace Woods on a private boat trip around the islands?!" Luke's voice rose higher and higher with each word.

Lincoln glanced quickly at his little brother and nodded before shifting his eyes back to the wood.

"What was she like?" Luke's inner groupie was making an appearance.

"What was she like?" Lincoln repeated the question to buy time. She was like sunshine incarnate, like a woman who walked out of your dreams and stood in front of you laughing at your jokes and giggling at your attempts to be gallant. She was like every character she had ever played wrapped into one amazing being who had starlight in her eyes. He pushed the images of Grace out of his mind for the thousandth time and cocked his head noncommittally. "She was all right."

Luke hooted with laughter and threw his hands up into the air. "Grace Woods was all right." He used his fingers to make quotation marks for 'all right'. "Grace Woods!?" His laughter turned to mocking concern and he gave his brother a comical frown. "I feel sorry for you, brother."

"Why's that?"

"You don't know how to appreciate the best things in life. How long were you out?"

"On the boat?"

"Yes, on the boat you lummox. How long?"

"About three and half hours."

"Unbelievable. Almost four hours with Grace Woods, one of the most beautiful, sexy, famous, desirable women in the world and all you can say is she was all right."

"What do you want me to say?"

Luke struggled to think of anything, then had a thought, "What's her new movie about?"

Lincoln scowled at him, "That's a stupid question."

Luke tried again, "What's her…favorite color?"

Lincoln rolled his eyes.

"Maybe that's not the best question," Luke said. "But I tell you what, I would have thought of something better over three and a half hours."

Lincoln didn't know if that was true or not. Maybe Luke would have kept his senses dealing with Grace. Maybe he wouldn't have been so taken with her or so distracted by their strange and intimate encounter with the humpback. Maybe Luke wouldn't have looked down into those green eyes and had the crazy urge to kiss her.

"Well, maybe next time you'll take care of your own charter instead of getting tanked," he said gruffly.

Luke grunted. "I don't reckon you booked them again?"

"No, I didn't."

"Why not? You know I need the cash flow."

"It didn't come up."

"Wow, you really didn't talk about anything at all during the whole trip?"

"We talked. There was a lot going on with the whale and all that."

"What whale?"

"A great big humpback surfaced right next to the boat."

"You're kidding."

"I'm serious."

Luke stared at him for a few beats before saying, "Maybe I should do whale tours."

Glad to have him off the subject of Grace, Lincoln said, "I don't know, maybe." He moved to the kitchen and took a shiny new key off of the countertop. "I had to change the doorknob, because the old one, you know."

Luke did know. Their Grandad had been a big, strong man. Even stronger when he was plastered. Many was the night he had picked a fight with the doorknob because he couldn't get his key in the lock.

"No girls," Lincoln warned him as Luke took the spare key and shoved it into his pocket. "I mean it."

"I know, I know," Luke said. Suddenly, his eyes lit up. "Do you think she would do a commercial for the charter?"

"Who?"

"Grace Woods."

Lincoln snorted, "No."

"You could ask her."

"No, I couldn't."

"Yes, you could. You shared a moment of natural beauty together. I'm sure she remembers you. Girls love that stuff."

"You don't know that. Besides, I'm never going to see her again," Lincoln responded, his own words stinging him unexpectedly.

"Yes, you are."

"What are you talking about?"

"They're filming right down on the beach. You could just…you know…stop by."

Lincoln looked at his little brother like he was crazy, because he was. He set his jaw and narrowed his eyes, refusing to be talked into another one of Luke's stupid schemes.

The last thing Lincoln would ever do was saunter up to Grace while she was filming on the beach and try to strike up a conversation. End of discussion.

CHAPTER 16

*P*ain pressed against the inside of Grace's forehead. She almost wished she hadn't sent everyone away in a fit of emotion. Having an assistant or maid or even one of the security guards bring her a cool washrag to put on her forehead might help ward off the sharp stabs of an oncoming migraine.

On second thought, she was glad to be alone in Faye's elite beach house. Even Faye was gone to the spa, thank goodness. The last thing Grace felt like doing was re-hashing everything with Faye. What she needed was peace and quiet and just a few moments to herself.

She sighed and sank further down into the fat reading chair, letting her head rest on its mounded cushions. The chair was situated just inside the glass wall that opened up onto the infinity pool. Grace let her eyes rest on the glistening surface of the pool and allowed the whirring of the ceiling fans high above to calm her nerves.

Still in her grasshopper bikini, because she knew she would have to return to set soon, she pulled a creamy white throw blanket over her body. It was surprisingly chilly in the shadowed room with the breeze coming in the open wall and the ceiling fans. But Grace knew that wasn't the real reason she was covering her body.

Her throat tightened. She swallowed hard to keep from crying.

"Why did I make such a big deal out of it?" she moaned. This kind of body comparison was standard everyday actress stuff. Nothing she hadn't experienced before, so why had she stormed off set and made a small issue seem so big?

Her head dropped all the way back and she stared up at the ceiling. Fans whirring. Forehead throbbing. Throat aching from suppressing her tears. Birds sang to each other outside. Breeze in the palms. The steady liquid sound of the infinity pool.

Nothing else. Nobody else.

Grace tried to take a calming breath to work through her anxiety. That did not help. Her exhale was shaky and unstable. She was all alone and she was losing it.

A single tear welled up in her left eye and released, rolling down her perfectly made up face. That would require fixing. She would have to face the makeup team with a confident smile, trying to pretend she hadn't mussed her mascara by crying.

Another tear. This one in her right eye.

It was too late. Her eyes were most likely bloodshot. She couldn't shoot the scene with bloodshot eyes. Plus her throat hurt so bad…and her head.

The tear dropped from her right eye and rolled down her cheek. Then another. Tears overflowed her attempts to blink them back. She hiccuped a sob, which wrung her throat muscles even tighter. The pain was too much. The force of her sadness too intense. Giving in, Grace put her hands over her face and cried.

Without the possibility of a member of the staff or one of

her assistants walking in on her, Grace held nothing back. Deep, heavy grief rose up from her core. Dark thoughts came with it and before she could regain control Grace found herself curled up in a ball, tucked under the creamy soft blanket, sobbing like a baby into the chair cushion.

She should have never asked Syd to direct. She should have kept him out of her life after he broke her heart and ran off with that Shandra person.

"W-wh-what kind of name is Sh-sh-shandra?" she wailed to the empty room. Nobody answered.

Just as well. Grace didn't want an answer. She wanted to sink into the chair, into the earth underneath the chair, into a cave hidden on the island, and never appear in the sunlight again.

She lifted her head, wiping her tears with the back of her hand, leaving great streaks of black eye makeup. Seeing the makeup brought it all back, the failed first scene of Heart of Mine, the smug youth of Shandra, the mean glint in Syd's eyes, the shock and embarrassment of Zac.

Her tears slowed and she sniffed. Her nose was running from crying and her makeup was ruined.

As suddenly as she had begun crying, she stopped. Grace felt a surge of anger boil up into her chest. She threw the blanket off of her body and stretched her legs out in front of the chair, looking down the length of her body in the green bikini.

This was nonsense. She was being ridiculous and Syd and the others were acting like chauvinist pigs. There was nothing wrong with her body in this bikini. She was beautiful, especially for a woman her age.

A woman her age. There it was. The qualifying statement that was in the back of everyone's mind, especially hers.

"Screw them," Grace spat out as she stood quickly and went to the bedroom where there were several full length mirrors. She turned on all of the lights and stared at her bikini clad body from all angles until her cell phone rang in the other room and she hurried to answer.

Not sure who to expect, Grace was relieved to see it was Ruby. Nobody who had anything to do with Heart of Mine, just one of her oldest and dearest friends.

"Hello!" Grace answered, lifting her voice an octave so Ruby wouldn't know she had been crying.

"Hi! How're you doing? I didn't know if you would answer or not. Thought you might be filming."

"No, no, not right now. I'm taking a break."

"Are you? Is it going well?"

Grace tried to answer, but the painful knot in her throat returned and the pause was too long for Ruby to not get suspicious.

"Grace?"

"Yes?" This time Grace raised her voice too high and, combined with trying to get it past her welling tears, her answer came out more like a squeak.

"Grace," Ruby's voice filled with concern. "What's the matter?"

"Nothing's the matter," Grace managed to keep her voice normal, but was betrayed when it cracked on the last word.

"Something's the matter. Are you okay? What's happened?" Ruby pressed. She continued to press until Grace gave in to the comfort she was offering all the way from America and told her the entire story.

She told her about her bust line being older and saggier than Shandra's, about how nobody would stop pointing out the age difference between her and Zac, about Syd being in control of everything and what a terrible idea that had been.

All of this led to her deeper fears coming to the surface and she confessed those as well. Fears that she was getting old, that her time to be beautiful and deserving of love might be over, that she had wasted her life building her career and getting involved with the wrong kind of men and now she was doomed to be alone forever.

"Now, Grace, I'm not gonna listen to that kind of nonsense," Ruby chimed in. "You are Grace Woods! You have won more awards than Syd or Zac or anybody on that set combined. You are gorgeous. Absolutely gorgeous. And, like a fine wine, you have only gotten better with age."

Grace managed a laugh at the comparison. She sniffled and asked, "You think so? You don't think I should look into getting plastic surgery."

"No, no, no, that's not something you should think about when you're in this kind of mood."

Grace sniffled again. Ruby had a point.

Ruby was on a roll and continued to do what she did best, give awesome advice. "I'm gonna tell you what you need to do. You need to reach inside yourself and remember who you are. Remember all the blockbuster hits you've had, remember your Academy Award and all of your other awards. Think about all the times the biggest and the best in Hollywood have begged to work with you over the years. You didn't waste your time! You've built a career that is the envy of every other actress in the entire world."

Grace laughed again. This time she didn't have to try, it came bubbling out of her.

Sensing she was getting somewhere, Ruby kept on, "And you didn't waste your time on the wrong men. I seem to recall you having a lot of fun with those men. Some of them were the most eligible bachelors around. So you didn't end up with them. So what? If you want to find your forever man that's what you will do. Do you know why? Because you're Grace Freakin' Woods, that's why. And don't you forget it."

"Oh, Ruby," Grace said gratefully.

"I want to hear you say it," Ruby said.

"Say what?"

"Say who you are."

Grace smiled, the depressing sob fest was quickly receding, replaced by a glow of warmth.

"Say it, you'll feel better."

Grace took a deep breath and straightened her shoulders. "I am Grace Freakin' Woods."

"Good," Ruby was smiling on the other end of the call, Grace could hear it in her voice. "And are you going to forget it?"

"No, I won't forget it. Thank you, Ruby."

"Any time. And maybe you should get yourself some kind of getaway from the set…you know, so you can get your mind straight every now and then."

"That's a good idea," Grace responded. It was a good idea. In fact, the thought of it lifted her spirits considerably more than even Ruby's pep talk. "I think I'll–"

A chime sounded, almost like a wind chime, but louder. Grace stopped talking, trying to place what it could be. It sounded again, this time accompanied by a light knock.

"Oh, Ruby, somebody's at the door. Probably one of the production assistants coming to take me back to the set. I have to go."

"Okay, take care of yourself, Grace."

"I will, and thank you so much for the talk. It did wonders for me." Grace clicked off the call just as the doorbell chimed for the third time. "Insistent, whoever they are," she murmured as she went to the door with a new spring in her step. Her mood was improved and she was ready to proceed with filming.

What she wasn't ready for was who she saw when she pulled the door open.

CHAPTER 17

Overall, Zac thought his surprise visit was going really well.

After getting over the initial shock of seeing Grace when she answered the door, complete with puffy red eyes and dried makeup streaks all over her face, he had pulled himself together and turned on the charm.

He felt sorry for her. That whole debacle of using a much younger woman as her stand in shouldn't have happened. Even though Zac wasn't a lighting expert, he could have told Syd that Grace's build was a lot, how would you say, less *full* than Shandra's. Still, she was Grace Woods. Even a big time director who happened to be her ex-boyfriend shouldn't have insulted her like that in front of the whole crew.

"More?" Zac lifted the half empty bottle of sparkling water and began pouring it into Grace's champagne glass before she had a chance to answer.

"Thank you," she said. Since he arrived she had ducked into the restroom and freshened up, cleaning the smeared makeup off of her face and rearranging her mussed hair. She looked a lot more like herself as she sipped the bubbly water.

Zac smiled gently. He wanted her to feel seen without being judged, safe without feeling smothered, and desired without feeling any pressure. In his experience, this system had a 98% success rate to get him to the first kiss. Grace dropped her gaze coyly.

Definitely going well.

A novice may have made his move at this point, less than an hour since she let him into the beach house. But Zac knew there was no rushing the first kiss on any woman, especially someone worldly and experienced. He had to put in the time and earnestly appear to *not* be trying to go in for the kiss.

"So, where were we?" Zac put down the bottle and looked studiously at his script.

Marked with his handwritten notes of the beats of the scene and key words meant to guide him through his character's emotional journey, Zac's copy was messier than Grace's. Hers had the same basic information from her character's perspective, but written in neat, elegant cursive.

He had noticed she left her script behind after she stormed off the set and when she didn't come back right away had decided to grab it and bring it to her. Zac figured practicing the scene in private might get her back into the groove enough to return to the set. Plus it got them alone together for the first time…ever.

"Let's see," Grace's eyes moved down the page. "I think we're at 'Ms. Kensington? *The* Ms. Kensington?'. You know, the part where you can't believe you're meeting me."

Zac cleared his throat nervously and murmured, "I know exactly how he feels." Grace pretended not to hear him, though he saw the corners of her mouth raise slightly.

"You start," she said, positioning herself as if she was sitting on the beach towel looking across the water. In reality they were sitting on the deck next to the infinity pool.

Zac sank into the mind of his character, international spy

turned man falling head over heels in love with Scarlet Kensington, Ethan Wolfe. He furrowed his brow and said his line, "Ms. Kensington? *The* Ms. Kensington?"

Grace slid her eyes towards him, the suspicious eyes of Scarlet, and said coolly, "Do I know you?"

Zac, as Ethan, paused as he looked her up and down in her bikini, grinned rakishly. "Not yet."

Grace, as Scarlet, shot daggers at him with her emerald green eyes. "Not ever."

Zac, as Ethan, put his hand on his heart and feigned being wounded and chuckled when Grace, as Scarlet, turned away from him. He asked, "You're not curious?"

"About what?"

"Who sent me?"

Grace, as Scarlet, turned back towards him, refusing to allow his charms to put a chink in her emotional walls. Her eyes wandered from his, down his chest to his waist then back up. The move was full of such disdain and sexual tension that Zac almost forgot they were in the middle of a scene. She tilted her head almost imperceptibly, but Zac imagined the move blown up on a cinema screen. Brilliant.

"I know who sent you," she said softly. So soft he almost didn't hear her.

Zac stared at her blankly. He couldn't remember his line. For a few beats he didn't look away from her cool, sexy gaze, hoping the words would return to him and he could pass off the lengthy pause as an attempt to portray his character's emotions. Finally, he had to give up.

"Your fairy godmother," he said, breaking character.

Confusion filled her eyes. "Who?"

Zac laughed nervously. "I can't remember my line."

"Oh," Grace shrugged it off, but he could tell she was disappointed. They had just been getting into the scene and he blew it. He could kick himself for getting so distracted. Amateur.

"I'm sorry…I sort of…lost myself there for a second," as he explained he searched her eyes for a glimmer of understanding. If this romance was going to get underway they had to connect. Maybe he could make her believe that whenever he was with her he couldn't think straight. Women loved that kind of thing.

"That line is a little awkward. It doesn't flow," she reassured him.

He held her gaze for a beat then said, "I don't think it's the line."

Her brow wrinkled, not understanding what he meant, but Zac didn't look away. Instead, he ramped up the intensity of his look, hoping she would sense his desire. After a few moments, comprehension moved into her expression and he didn't see any red flags. In fact, Grace let her eyes drop to his mouth, which was a clear indication she was thinking what he was thinking.

Zac moved closer, letting their bodies draw together naturally. That special way a woman leaned into him when she wanted to kiss always got to him. Desire rose inside of him and everything else around them blurred into the background. All he could see were Grace's gorgeous eyes and her mouth moving nearer and nearer.

"Well, hello, darlings!" a woman's voice sounded from the other side of the room.

Grace gasped and pulled away, placing her hand on her chest as if she was having heart palpitations. She looked away from him, her cheeks turning red.

Zac moved away from her, too, but a little slower. He wasn't as keen to hide their moment from the world.

"Faye!" Grace stood and greeted her friend.

"Faye…great," Zac muttered as he, too, stood to greet her.

Faye, blonde and tan, donning a cherry red bikini top and a fringed white sarong with a red fish pattern, stood with her hands on her hips and a mock look of surprise on her face.

"My, my, my! What do we have here?" she asked.

"Not what it could have been," Zac said under his breath.

CHAPTER 18

*P*resley stepped gingerly through the grove of Aspen trees. With her husband's hand firmly holding hers she wasn't truly afraid of tripping, but Hobie had become so careful with her ever since they found out she was pregnant, she felt obligated to take careful steps over the uneven forest floor.

"Honestly, I'm a little worried about her," she said. She had been filling Hobie in on the potential drama playing out with Grace at her film shoot in Australia. Hobie grunted his answer. She stopped walking and asked, "Are you even listening to me?"

Hobie looked back at her, his dark curly hair backlit by the morning sun. "I'm listening. I just want us to get to this spot before we lose the light."

Presley was one of his favorite subjects to photograph before she was pregnant. Lately he was obsessed with capturing her and her growing belly in beautiful surroundings. It was early October and the Aspens in Colorado had turned from green to gold, which made for a magical background. He stopped his forward motion, turned back to face her, and took both her hands in his to show that he was, indeed, listening.

"Tell me why you're worried about Grace," he said.

Presley looked up into his earnest dark eyes and giggled. "Oh, you don't care, do you?"

"I care," Hobie argued, though she knew he cared more about the light changing.

"Well, Ronnie thinks Faye may be interfering in Grace's love life. Right when Grace is trying to film. She gets so stressed when she's filming. And you know how Faye can be."

Hobie nodded gravely. "I do."

Presley pushed him playfully away from her, "Stop. You don't want to hear about any of this. Let's go take your picture."

Hobie gave her a swift kiss then turned and happily started leading her through the fairy-like Aspens once again. As they walked he spoke to her over his shoulder.

"So is Faye trying to set Grace up or something?" he asked.

Pleased at his attempt to carry on the conversation, Presley smiled. "Zac Foster is starring opposite her in the movie and I think they're an item. Jaxson told me he'd heard they were, too."

"Oh, Zac Foster," Hobie sounded like he knew the name. "And…is that a bad thing?"

"I don't know. Ronnie's all worried about it for some reason and Faye was talking my ear off about the whole thing when we spoke the other day."

Hobie stopped. They were dead center in the middle of the Aspen grove. Both of them couldn't help but pause their conversation and look up into the blinking canopy of gold leaves rustling softly in the breeze.

"It's beautiful," Presley said.

"That's perfect," Hobie said and backed away from her, readying the camera that hung around his neck.

The sound of a large animal rushing through the underbrush nearby startled them, but only for a moment. Before Presley could get overly concerned about bears or mountain lions, their big brown and white fur ball burst out of the forest underbrush, barking his greeting.

"Rocky," Hobie called out to no avail.

Rocky had always had a kind of happy obsession with Presley, which had only grown with a baby in her belly. He made a bee line for her, kicking up fallen leaves and debris with abandon.

"Hi, Rock," Presley leaned into the slobbery muzzle that lifted to greet her. Rocky's great lapping tongue licked her cheek. "How did you get out?"

Hobie peered down the path that Rocky had forged through the underbrush. "The bigger question is, did Sugar Pop come with him?"

Concern pinched Presley's heart. "Oh no, she's too little to come all this way." Small, strange, Sugar Pop was not what one would call the outdoorsy type. "She doesn't even have her sweater!"

Presley was worried and Hobie, as usual, came to the rescue.

"Stay there, I'll go look." He made a move to track Rocky's steps back through the forest to the Monroe mansion where they had thought they left the dogs safely penned, and that's when they heard the distinctive *Yip Yip Yip* of Sugar Pop.

"Come on, Sugar," Hobie strode towards the sound of her yipping. Rocky stopped licking Presley and sat at attention, intensely watching Hobie disappear into the thick grove of trees. He was torn between leaving Presley alone and going with Hobie on this important mission.

Presley patted Rocky's head with one hand and instinctively placed her other hand on the hard round bump of her belly. She wondered absently how on earth both of the dogs managed to get loose. "Thank goodness you found us," she said to Rocky. He wagged his tail at the mention of his name and licked at her hand with his big tongue.

Despite the hulking furry mass of Rocky guarding her, Presley began to feel a little uncomfortable. Just when she was considering doing her own sweep of the surrounding area to help look for Sugar Pop, Hobie emerged with the tiny one-eared boggle eyed dog wiggling in his arms.

"Found her, and she has a sweater on so we're good," Hobie announced.

Sure enough, Sugar Pop was decked out in a bright pumpkin orange doggie sweater with a green ribbon collar. Presley was about to ask the dog how she had managed to get herself dressed when she saw her assistant, Jaxson, following close behind Hobie.

"Sorry, they got away from me, but I thought that one may have caught your scent the way he took off!" Jaxson explained. Rocky barked in greeting and raced towards Jaxson, who held his arms up defensively and let out a high pitched squeal.

"Rocky, down!" Hobie managed to stop the big dog right in his tracks with this command.

Rocky dropped to his belly, his big tail pounding the ground as it wagged. In the past, his double paw leap onto the unsuspecting chests of anyone he was greeting would have flattened poor Jaxson onto the ground. Hobie had been working with him to stop that habit and he smiled proudly at Presley when the big dog obeyed.

She smiled back. He handed her the squirming Sugar Pop and Presley warmed at the reminder of what a good father he was going to be. She took her little bundle of joy gently, but was careful to keep her at arm's length. Sugar Pop was prone to accidents when she got too excited.

"They were having a melt down, whining and carrying on, so I thought I'd take them for a little walk," Jaxson explained. "Also I wanted to try her new sweater."

Presley smiled, "It's adorable."

"Isn't it?" Jaxson beamed then he took notice of the shimmering golden canopy of leaves above them. His mouth dropped open and he spread his arms out wide. "This is *gorgeous!*"

Jaxson's enthusiasm was too much for Rocky and the big dog suddenly leaped up from his down position and pounced. As Hobie lunged to get control of him, Rocky placed two big paws on Jaxson's crisp tweed vest.

"Oh!" Jaxson stumbled backward, but in a testament to his fitness level and balance, did not fall.

"Rocky, down!" Hobie tried again and once more Rocky dropped to his belly. "Sorry, Jaxson."

Jaxson brushed off the front of his vest, unfazed. "He didn't push as hard as he can, so that's improvement," he said, putting the mishap behind them. Turning to Presley he shifted back to his efficient assistant self. "Your phone has been blowing up since you left."

"It has? What's the matter?" Presley's mind raced through the possibilities. Was it the Denver residential development? The factory in Costa Rica? The legal red tape in Toronto? The shareholder meeting coming up in New York?

"It's Faye," Jaxson responded, his voice deadpan.

"Faye?" Presley needed a second to change her mind over from work catastrophe to personal catastrophe. "Is she all right?"

"She's having a Faye kind of emergency, not a hospital kind of emergency," Jaxson clarified.

Relieved, Presley had to ask even though she thought she probably knew the answer, "So what is the Faye emergency?"

Jaxson lifted his gaze up as if he was reading an imaginary bullet point list hanging in the air above them. "She needs to know if you will come to Grace's birthday party. She needs to know if you will help her plan Grace's birthday party. And she wants to know how soon you can get to Australia."

CHAPTER 19

Grace concentrated on keeping her eyes open even though all they wanted to do was blink. The fans off-camera that were meant to mimic a balmy ocean breeze and make the bright orange fabric of her evening gown billow behind her, were also blowing a never ending stream of air directly into her eyeballs. She couldn't blink or look away, because she was supposed to stare down Zac, as Ethan, in his attempt at a first kiss.

It was almost 10 o'clock at night and they were struggling to finish the scene. A few technical issues had delayed them wrapping earlier, along with Zac forgetting his lines several times. There was no way Grace was going to blink and mess up one of the few good takes they had gotten so far.

"You...you're not...none of this is what I was expecting," Zac, as Ethan, stumbled a little as he spoke. Grace and everyone on set knew it was because he was unsure he had the lines right, but Grace could tell the awkward way he was delivering would play well on camera. As long as he didn't break character...again.

"And what did you expect, Mr. Wolfe?" she kept her unblinking eyes on him.

He squinted. Thinking.

Grace begged him telepathically to remember his line so they could be done with the scene already. She was exhausted. Ready to go back to the beach house and collapse. She hadn't slept well last night. Or all week. Since the first day of shooting to be exact.

Every morning had been a fight with fatigue, bags under her eyes, a splitting headache. Some of it may have been the stress of filming, or the stress of sharing a beach house–lovely as it was–with Faye, but mostly Grace thought it was because of her dreams.

She kept dreaming that Syd was standing over her on the beach, or the boat, or at the cafe they had built for the set, or any of the different locations they had filmed at all week. In every dream Syd was doing the same thing, flipping through diffusion card after diffusion card, holding them up in front of her and shaking his head in dismay.

He flipped through the cards so fast they looked like playing cards and he looked like an evil magician. The diffusion cards kept growing bigger and bigger, thicker and heavier, until they were blocking the sun and any outside light. She would cower under the dark cards and Syd's menacing looks then she would hear laughing and see that there was a crowd of onlookers surrounding her, pointing at her, and laughing. When she looked down she was shocked to see that she was naked and that her breasts were limp and hanging down to her belly button.

"Have you told your therapist?" Faye asked when Grace shared these repetitive nightmares.

"I don't really think I need a therapist to dissect the meaning," Grace quipped. Sipping a cup of hot, black coffee with a pink gel mask strapped over her eyes, she looked a little like Zorro, if Zorro was a woman at a spa.

"Well, what are you going to do about them?"

"What can I do about it? I'm dreaming, Faye. Nothing. That's what I'm going to do," Grace's answer was a bit sharp, but lack of sleep always made her irritated.

Faye watched her evenly with cool, grey eyes before deciding to ignore her snarky tone. "Well, I have an idea," she offered with a cheerful twinkle. "What about taking some time for yourself? Don't you get time off during filming?"

Grace nodded. "We get the weekend off, usually. That's funny, Ruby told me that I should take some time off, too, when I talked to her the other day."

"See? It's a good idea, isn't it? You know Ruby always has wonderful advice."

Grace nodded again. It was true that Ruby had a good head on her shoulders.

"Maybe you could go on a date or something," Faye continued.

"On a date?"

"Yes, with that charming Zac."

Grace looked at her friend, confused. "You think I should go on a date with Zac? A real date?"

Faye smiled. "Yes, darling. I saw how…intimate you were the other day when I came back from the beach."

"We were rehearsing lines."

Faye blinked at her as if she was waiting for more information. When none came, she pressed on, "Well, there's rehearsing and then there's rehearsing, right?"

"I don't know what you mean by that," Grace had said. She still didn't know what Faye had meant by that comment…days later.

Suddenly, Grace realized that Zac, as Ethan, had said something, but she had been thinking about that strange conversation with Faye and hadn't heard him. Had he said his line? Was it her turn? She was at a loss and a surge of panic rose in her chest. She blinked.

Her eyes immediately began to water. They had been waiting for the tiniest bit of encouragement and blinking had given it to them. She needed to say her line and finish the scene before it looked like she was crying. Scarlet Kensington never cried. Well, not until the final scene.

Grace opened her mouth to say her line then closed it again. Her brain was coming up blank. She blinked again. Tears welled up in her eyes and she silently cursed the stupid fan.

Zac's steadfast stare began to waver. She could see in his eyes that he was wondering what was going on. They had not rehearsed a long pause before her response. Grace found herself sending him another telepathic message. *Do not break character. Do not ask me if I forgot my line. Just give me a second. One second. Whatever you do, don't speak!*

Something changed in his eyes. Instead of the steely, agitated gaze of Ethan Wolfe, Grace saw the smiling, flirtatious gaze of Zac Foster. He was going to speak and ruin the take. She could feel it in her bones.

"You can look all you want, Mr. Wolfe. So long as you don't look to me for help." The line came tumbling out of her mouth in a rush. Grace, as Scarlet, turned her head haughtily and looked away from him. The move could have been for effect, but it also kept the fan breeze from blowing into her eyes.

Grace looked into the middle distance as if she was taking in a silent, almost wild, beach, when in reality she was staring at the belly of one of the sound guys. He kept his gaze cast at the ground so they didn't accidentally catch each other's eyes, which would read on camera.

Grace hoped Zac was maintaining his Ethan Wolfe

demeanor as they held a few more beats for editing purposes. The fan breeze caught a lock of her hair and she felt it sweep across her face. She fought the urge to lift her hand and tuck it behind her ear as she knew that would be a hard motion to cut around if needed.

"And…cut!" Syd called out. The tension in the air subsided as Grace, Zac and the crew relaxed. Syd approached them, rubbing his hands together like he was at a campfire waiting for a smore. "Excellent. Really good. I think we've got it. Let's wrap for tonight."

"Oh, good." Overcome with fatigue, Grace was suddenly aware of every tiny ache and pain throughout her body. And there were many. "I was worried my eyes were tearing up too much."

"No, no, it looked good. Like you were torn, you know?" Syd told her, a big smile on his bearded face.

"You were amazing," Zac agreed. "I felt it."

"Good…thank you. You were great, too," Grace wanted to be polite, but she also wanted to go to the beach house and get into bed.

Syd put one hand on each of their shoulders. "Let's go get a drink at that beach bar we've been walking by every day. Start our two days off?"

"Sounds good," Zac agreed. "As soon as I change out of costume."

Grace cringed at the idea. "Can I take a rain check? I just want to crawl into bed."

"Sure, sure, we'll say a toast for you," Syd slapped her shoulder like they were already drinking buddies and took off to do whatever directors did at the end of a scene.

Grace didn't care to know. She just wanted to get out of her costume and take a nice, hot shower.

"I'm sorry you're too tired to go out," Zac said.

Grace had almost forgotten he was still standing there, so

strong was her desire to be done with their day. She looked up at him and said, "Oh, I'll be fine. I'm just worn out I guess."

Zac looked a little crestfallen, more than she would have expected given the fact that they had spent all day in each other's face. He shuffled his feet back and forth. Grace's feet were aching in her costume sandals. Shoes were always the hardest part of a costume. There was rarely time to break anything in so it was comfortable.

"Maybe tomorrow?" Zac asked, a boyish hopefulness filling his eyes.

"Tomorrow?" Grace's brain felt dull. She didn't understand what he was talking about. They weren't shooting tomorrow. And she didn't understand why they were both still standing there instead of on their way to the costume trailers to get their costumes off.

"Well, since we can't hang out tonight," Zac made a clownish sad face accentuating his disappointment before continuing, "Maybe we could hang out tomorrow? Spend the day together? See some of the sights?"

Grace squinted at him. Her eyes were still streaming, trying to recover from being dried out for too long. Zac's perfectly muscled body was wrapped tightly in a deep blue military uniform matching the time period of Heart of Mine. His natural good looks were amplified by the crisp uniform, and he appeared sincerely nervous.

Grace had the stunningly crazy idea that he might be asking her out on a date.

Her mood softened, confused by this possibility and not wanting to offend him if he was…or wasn't. She gave him a sweet smile, one that couldn't be taken as sensual or matronly, an in between smile for an in between situation.

"That sounds nice, Zac. How does noon sound?" Noon seemed like a benign time. Not a very date-like time, but not a not-a-date-like time either.

Zac's face broke into a brilliant smile. The kind of smile that had won him hearts around the world in his movies.

"Noon it is...Grace," he said as he backed away from her, tipping his head in her direction as if he was wearing an imaginary hat.

Strange, truly. Still, she didn't want to make anything out of his behavior. All it came down to was that Zac wanted to spend some time together to run lines or just build the kind of camaraderie that would make sex scenes easier later in filming. There was nothing more to it than that, she was certain.

However, try as she might, as Grace made her way to her private costume trailer set up nearby, she could not forget the twinkle in Zac's eye when he said her name.

CHAPTER 20

*L*incoln had spent all week on his knees and he was ready for a drink.

Every inch of flooring in the hill house, except for the bathrooms, was gorgeous Mackay Cedar. All of it beautiful, all of it needing sanding. Even if Lincoln could afford the expense of buying or renting a big mechanical sander, he would have had a time getting it to the island.

His answer to this problem was to throw on knee protectors, get on all fours, and sand each board by hand, making repairs where needed as he moved through the house. This can-do attitude had gotten the job done, but left him tired and covered in a thin layer of sawdust.

As he took the first sip of ice cold beer the barkeep, Henry, poured him, he was glad he'd been sanding quality cedar. He may be covered in sawdust, but he still smelled good.

"Workin' on your Grandad's place are ya?" Henry asked. Henry owned Fitz's Bar and was an old friend of the family. Not quite as old as Lincoln's Grandad's generation, but old enough to have thought of him as a friend.

Lincoln nodded, placing his glass back down on the polished bar top and wiping a bit of beer foam off of his upper lip with the back of his hand.

"Yep. It's been a fair piece of work so far, but it'll be worth it."

Henry agreed with a bob of his head as he busily filled a tray with eight more frothy glasses of beer.

Lincoln looked over his shoulder at the mob of tourists packed into every table and booth in the place. Amelia, the sole late afternoon waitress at Fitz's, expertly maneuvered a tray of drinks to one of the tables near the back.

"Busy today," Lincoln observed.

Henry bobbed his head with even more energy, "It's the movie crowd. Thirsty bunch."

Lincoln sipped his beer again, not wanting to be reminded about the Hollywood crowd that had taken over his beloved island.

"They're all right, though. Nice enough...Americans," Henry gave him a knowing look.

Lincoln nodded, keeping his eyes trained on the disappearing foam in his glass. He knew what Henry meant.

"Have you met any of 'em?" Henry asked as he sent the next tray of beers out with Amelia.

Lincoln lifted one shoulder in an apathetic shrug. "A few."

He took a drink of his beer and turned on the stool so his back was to the bar, pretending to scan the crowded bar for anyone he knew. Really he was hoping Henry hadn't noticed any change in his expression when he admitted he'd met an American.

Of course, he'd only met one American from Hollywood—and he hadn't been able to forget her.

"That's right," Henry kept up the conversation even though Lincoln wasn't facing him. "You've been busy working on the house. It's coming along then?"

Lincoln looked back over his shoulder and smiled, "Oh, it's coming…little by little."

The barkeep laughed. "Well, keep at it, Link. You'll have that place done up right soon enough."

The din of voices in the busy bar rose a few levels and everyone in the place switched their attention to the front door. Lincoln saw a glimpse of a good looking young man entering just before most of the seated bar patrons stood in excitement. A few of the younger women let out high pitched squeals of excitement.

"Let me guess, movie star?" Lincoln asked Henry.

"Yep, that's the star. His name's Zac Foster. You don't recognize him?"

Lincoln sipped his beer and he shook his head. "I don't keep up on the latest teen heartthrob."

Henry chuckled, but Lincoln could barely hear it over the uproar that surged again in the already loud bar. Henry nudged Lincoln's shoulder and pointed at the front door, which was obstructed by so many standing bodies that Lincoln couldn't see who was entering.

"What about her? Ever heard of Grace Woods before?" Henry teased.

Lincoln's stomach tightened. He gripped his beer, afraid for some reason he was going to let it slip out of his hand and smash onto the floor at his feet. Applause broke out amongst the bar full of what must be adoring fans.

At first, Lincoln thought the sound was growing louder and louder. Then he realized his ears were full of a sound that came from within him. His heart pumped so hard that the whoops and whistles for Grace and her date blurred and became indistinct. Instead, all he could hear was a deafening wet crashing, like ocean waves during a storm.

Lincoln froze, another realization hitting him straight in the gut. Grace was here on a date.

He peered through the bodies trying to catch a glimpse of her. He could see the guy, Zac, or at least he saw the top of Zac's head as they moved through the crowd. He couldn't see Grace, though. She wasn't tall enough to stand above the crowd.

Torn between ducking out the back door or making his way through the bodies to find her and say–what, exactly, he wasn't sure–Lincoln stood awkwardly poised to go either way. Soon the enthusiastic crowd pressed up against him and he couldn't make a move to the front or back of the bar anyway.

The top of Zac's head appeared just in front of Lincoln, who was still leaning with his back against the bar. He caught a flash of pure white showing between the bodies of Grace's fans. Then Zac Foster pushed his way through the crowd and ended up just to Lincoln's right. He smiled a leading man smile at Lincoln and Henry then turned his attention to his right arm, which was still stretched out behind him and seemed to be pulling something out of the crowd.

Lincoln's racing heart came to a momentary stop.

Grace.

Dressed in a white flowing sundress with a wide white hat that hid her eyes, she was laughing as Zac liberated her from her delighted fans and pulled her into the space between him and Lincoln. Her arm brushed against Lincoln's and he held his breath.

"Two beers, mate!" Zac called out to Henry in a perfect Aussie accent. Lincoln couldn't decide if he was impressed or offended. "Excuse us…mate," Zac nodded towards Lincoln with a happy swagger that Lincoln hated instantly. A knot of jealousy tightened around his heart.

Grace's white hat moved as she turned to look up at him, apparently previously unaware of his existence. She lifted her face so he could see her eyes, green and gorgeous, underneath the hat. They widened in surprised recognition.

"Oh, it's you!" she said, just as someone bumped her from behind and she was pushed so close her body touched his chest.

Lincoln didn't nod or say anything in return. Conscious thought was gone. All he could manage to do was look down into her eyes and wish everyone around them would disappear.

Grace did not look away either. She held very still and searched his eyes. With every bone in his body he knew she was searching for something meaningful.

He wanted to tell her that he hadn't been able to get her out of his mind since they were on the boat. That he wanted to see her again. That he wished she wasn't who she was or he was someone more important, more like her, so they could meet on common ground and he could simply ask her out.

Instead, he simply tipped his glass in her direction and said, "Hi."

A moment passed before she smiled slightly and half-laughed. Not sure if she was charmed or confused, Grace answered, "Hi."

"Come on, Sheila," Zac called out to her in his perfect fake accent. The man was a complete American. Self-obsessed, loud, certain the world was revolving around him and oblivious to the fact that his date was holding Lincoln's heart hostage. Zac tugged on Grace's hand and continued his socially awkward assault on Australia's culture, "Let's go find some shrimp and throw them on the barbie!"

Lincoln set his jaw, tightened his grip on his beer, and used every ounce of self-control in his possession to keep from popping the bloody idiot right in the mouth.

CHAPTER 21

Grace's exit from the crowded bar full of admirers was less exhilarating than her entrance. When the smiles and cheers and kind comments had risen to meet her and Zac at the front door, Grace had felt the familiar lift in her spirits. There were many things about being an actress that she liked, adulation from strangers was one of them.

All of that had fallen away when she saw Lincoln.

Not simply saw him, but stood directly next to him, just like they had on the boat, bodies pressed together, him looking down into her eyes as if he was about to kiss her. She had lost all ability to think straight, let alone pay any attention to her fans.

'Hi'…that's all he had said, but to hear the sound of his voice again…she hadn't been prepared to see him nor could she have known how the sight and sound of him would make her feel so powerless. Her response to his greeting, a feeble 'Hi' of her own, felt woefully inadequate in hindsight. Comical. Tragic.

By the time she and Zac had finished their beer and made

it back to the buggy and driver they had commandeered from the hotel for the day, Grace was numb.

"That was awesome!" Zac declared as he helped her into the cart. She was glad for the wide brim of her hat so she could shield him from her lack of enthusiasm. "I mean, they were cheering in there," Zac laughed as he spoke, obviously thrilled with their experience.

Grace was less so.

Zac laughed again, high on fame, before noticing that she remained quiet. "You probably get that kind of greeting everywhere you go, don't you?"

Grace turned her head so she could look at him. The comment didn't strike her as jealous exactly, but there was something in his tone that she couldn't quite place.

"Not everywhere," she responded.

Zac laughed out loud, pleased with their shared experience and, apparently, happy how their date was going.

It was a date, too. That was obvious to Grace when he picked her up. Zac had arrived freshly shaved and smelling good wearing dinner clothes even though it was the middle of the day. He had brought her a single red rose and offered her his arm as they left. Definitely a date.

"Are you hungry enough for dinner?" Zac asked after they settled into the cart.

Grace sensed he had something special planned so she said yes, even though her stomach was still in knots after running into Lincoln. What was it about that man? He was handsome, for sure, but so was Zac. So were hundreds of other men that she knew, many of which were on this island with them. Why did Lincoln make her freeze on the outside and fall apart on the inside?

Zac tapped the driver on the shoulder and gave him a thumbs up. The buggy took off so quickly Grace had to put one hand on her hat to keep it from blowing off. She was leaving to have dinner with Zac, but her mind remained at the little bar called Fitz's where Lincoln had watched her walk away.

Dinner was nothing short of amazing.

Zac had pulled out all the stops by setting up a private dining experience for them on a secluded beach. A half dozen lazy palm trees bent over a table draped in a deep coral cloth, fine white china, crystal wine glasses, heavy silver, and a centerpiece of exotic purple, pink and white flowers. Waiters and waitresses in tan slacks and crisp white shirts brought them course after course of salads, seafood, and fresh fruits. They ate in the comfort of the shade while watching the sun sink lower and lower over the gorgeous blue water.

"This is lovely, Zac. Truly lovely," Grace said. She meant every word, too. He had really gone out of his way and she had to admit she was impressed. Though the conversation had been a bit dull, she had to account for the fact that they were eating.

"Wait until you see what's for dessert," Zac said, a mischievous smile on his lips.

The sip of wine Grace had just taken caught in her throat and she coughed uncontrollably into her napkin. The coughing lasted so long that Zac made a move to stand up and assist her. She raised her hand to stop him, motioning him to sit back down.

"I'm fine," she managed to say through a clenched throat.

Had she heard him correctly? What exactly did he mean by dessert? Grace didn't want to ask, because she didn't want to know. Surely he didn't expect...he wouldn't...would he?

She looked at him. He was absolutely gorgeous and had been nothing but charming and wonderful and sexy all day long. But she didn't think she was ready for...*dessert*. Not yet.

"Um, Zac…" she stumbled a little on how to explain what they would and wouldn't be doing on this date.

He shushed her and gestured towards the sunset that was beginning to glow orange and pink in the sky over the ocean.

"You'll see when we get there," he said. "Let's enjoy the sunset..together."

They were seated close enough that Zac was able to lean towards her and slip his hand onto her leg. She jumped at his touch, but relaxed after his hand found hers and took it. He wanted to hold hands. That was all. For now anyway.

Without much conversation between them during the sunset, Grace's mind wandered back to her brief encounter with Lincoln at the bar. He hadn't been clean shaven or dressed in fresh going out to dinner clothes, which made him all the more attractive. Rough around the edges, holding his beer with calloused hands, smelling like sunshine and wood shavings, the sensation of standing next to him and pressing into his chest would not leave her senses.

Zac squeezed her hand and she returned to the beach, to the sunset, to her date with one of the most eligible actors in Hollywood. Zac's hand was warm and strong…his skin soft as a baby.

"You seem a thousand miles away," he said, gazing into her eyes with longing.

Grace fought the sudden urge to laugh. Something about Zac made it difficult for her to take him seriously, especially when he spoke in cliches.

She swallowed hard and got her giggles under control, then met his gaze with a friendly smile though she couldn't think of a response to his comment.

"Are you ready for dessert?" he asked, his eyelids lowering into what she assumed he thought was a seductive stare.

Grace pulled her hand from his to adjust her hat. "Oh, I don't know. It's very nice right here."

Too late, Zac had already motioned to the staff that they were ready to leave. "We can't have it here, unfortunately. But don't worry I have something even better set up for us. Trust me, you've never seen anything like it."

Grace thought she probably had, but sighed and let him lead her back to the buggy to advance to the dessert stage of their date. Maybe she was wrong. Maybe he had set up an ice cream bar on a seaside cliff that they could only reach by rappelling or some other over the top experience.

Soon they were buzzing up a narrow road that snaked up a steep hill, moving away from the beach and leaving the deepening sunset behind. Grace had to keep one hand on her hat so it wouldn't fly off and her other firmly gripping the handle on the inside of the buggy so she wouldn't fly out while going around the hairpin curves.

Zac had one hand on his handle and the other wrapped firmly around her waist and he laughed as he said something that was lost in the wind.

"What?" Grace shouted back at him.

"Crazy!" he yelled, laughing again into the wind.

Grace didn't feel much like laughing and she wasn't sure she was up for whatever he had planned for the rest of their date. When they finally arrived at their destination, she was certain that she wasn't up for it.

The dessert Zac had planned for them was being served at a private dance party. Set up under a huge white tent with sides open to the surrounding jungle, the party was complete with loud music, hordes of their cast and crew plus many locals Grace didn't know all jammed together on a temporary dance floor. There were black lights that made everyone's white clothing glow blue in the night and a gigantic disco ball casting its blinking lights over the inside of the tent and everyone inside.

"I hope you like chocolate," Zac whispered into her ear.

Once again she got the feeling he was trying to be seductive, but his whispering didn't send tingles across her spine. It made her feel a little squeamish. A feeling she would experience even more intensely once he led her to the pièce de résistance.

"A chocolate fountain…" Grace said flatly. She was so stunned at the sight of five–no, *six*–tiers of burbling liquid chocolate pouring in thick streams from the smallest container on top into the next biggest directly below until it all ended up in a massive base container sitting on a wide table, that no other words came to mind.

As the chocolate swelled up and over the sides of each tier and dropped in a sheet over the edge, a party goer shoved a stick with a piece of fruit on the end into the melted chocolate to collect the liquid candy. When his little treat was covered in a sloppy mess of chocolate he popped the whole gooey blob into his mouth and went back to the dance floor.

"I couldn't believe they had one of these," Zac said excitedly into her ear.

"I can't believe it either," Grace answered, less excited.

Despite the loud thumping of the dance music, she swore she could hear the sucking sound of the pump in the base container as it pushed all of the unused chocolate up the tiers to be recycled through the fountain again. Her stomach turned at the thought.

"Pretzel stick?" Zac offered her an oversized straight pretzel stick.

"No, thank you," she said, stepping back as yet another party goer approached the chocolate fountain.

This one had two marshmallows stuck on the end of her stick. Grace didn't recognize the young woman, must be a local. She was quite young and very pretty, wearing a barely there white sheath mini-sundress that ended just below her rump. As the girl leaned in to cover her marshmallows with recycled liquid chocolate, Grace averted her eyes to avoid seeing anything she didn't really want to see.

She noticed that Zac did not look away. His attention remained on the girl, but not on her rear end…on her eyes. She was blatantly staring at him as she let the chocolate drain all over her double marshmallow stick. Grace found the obviousness a little crude, but Zac didn't seem capable of looking away.

Grace didn't know if she should be offended or amused. The whole visual was too bizarre. The girl's white sundress glowing under the black light as her marshmallows collected too much chocolate for any one person to eat in one bite and she made eyes at Grace's date. For one awful moment Grace wondered if the girl was going to try to stick both chocolate drenched marshmallows in her mouth while Zac stared. Suddenly, Grace was struck with a different thought.

She, too, was wearing all white.

She looked down at her long flowing sundress, which in the light of day was elegant and graceful, but under the black light was a garish glowing blue-purple. With her big floppy white hat she must look like a neon ghost. An ancient lady ghost from discos gone by haunting the very energetic, very young crowd in the tent.

"Wanna dance?" Zac thrust his pelvis around in rhythm to the music and moved his shoulders and neck like a broken robot, a dance move with which Grace was unfamiliar.

"Oh, I don't–"

"C'mon, I'll teach you," Zac interrupted, moving his writhing pelvis closer, so close she could smell his pretzel chocolate breath.

"No, thank you." Grace put her hand up and placed it firmly on his chest. As nicely muscled as his chest was, Grace still didn't want him to move closer. "I'm a little tired. I think I'll sit out dancing for a while."

A little surprised at her refusal, Zac backed up. Talking was impossible with the noise and the crowd so he gave her a confused smile and offered his hand to lead her to the edge of the tent where a seating area had been set up along the cool edge of the jungle.

"No," she said, a little more kindly, like she was speaking to a boy instead of a man. "You stay here and have fun. I'll be fine by myself."

Then Grace turned away from him and took her glowing ghost-like form out from under the black lights and into the quiet relief of the island trees.

CHAPTER 22

"Of course you want to help, darling. You want Grace to be happy, don't you?" Faye asked Phoenix, after cornering Grace's waif producer at the hotel spa.

Faye was leaving the spa after a marvelous massage and facial and wasn't sure why Phoenix was there, though it was obvious by her clothes, a black tank top, and a pair of baggy cargo pants with a walkie talkie clipped on the waistband, the poor thing was working.

"I'm afraid I don't understand what it is you want me to help with," Phoenix said quietly, her big eyes blinking behind thick glasses.

Faye sighed, utterly exhausted at the idea of having to explain again to Grace's meek little producer about the lovely surprise birthday party she was trying to organize in secret.

She smiled as sweetly as possible, as if she was addressing a very young child. "Do you understand the basic concept of a surprise birthday party?"

Phoenix nodded, keeping her eyes on Faye even though the phone in her hand was vibrating nonstop.

"All I need you to do is help me find a place to hold the party where it will be a complete surprise to Grace…and keep the secret from her…and probably keep it secret from almost everybody else just so they don't let it slip…and make sure we get everyone she loves at the party…and make absolutely sure Zac is there," Faye paused for breath and watched Phoenix's face for some flicker of excitement, or a flicker of anything.

"Why Zac specifically?" Phoenix asked.

The question threw Faye's focus for a moment. Wasn't it obvious? Anyone watching Grace and Zac over the first few weeks of filming could not miss the sparks between them. Could Phoenix really be so disconnected?

The producer's cell phone buzzed anew. Faye glanced down at it, trying to contain her annoyance. "Do you need to answer that?"

Phoenix gave her phone a brief look. "Not yet. I want to get clear on this first."

"Oh, okay," Faye felt a little bit better. At least she had the girl's full attention.

"You need a location for Grace's surprise birthday party," Phoenix verified.

"Yes," Faye answered.

"Will you need help with craft services…I mean, catering?"

Faye smiled, the little producer had been paying attention. "No, when we have the place I will handle the catering."

Phoenix nodded in understanding. "I will keep it under wraps and make sure everyone on set gets the invite. You'll be inviting Grace's family and other friends?"

The efficient turn in their conversation pleased Faye immensely. "Yes. And you'll make sure Zac is there?"

Again Phoenix paused, a question in her innocent owl eyes. Faye took a breath, ready to explain the fledgling romance that she wanted to support between Grace and Zac, but whatever Phoenix's question was, it remained unvoiced. She simply continued with her rapid fire planning.

"I can do that. And I will find a place for the party," Phoenix said.

"Okay…great," Faye responded. Not sure what else needed said about the matter Faye searched for a kind comment to share with the girl to convey her appreciation. Taking in Phoenix's small, lithe form and the delicate bone structure of her face, Faye was struck with an idea. "And as a thank you for helping I'll have Antoinette give you a makeover!"

Phoenix didn't seem to grasp the momentous gift Faye wanted to bestow. Antoinette was absolutely the best with hair, makeup, and fashion and if anyone needed the absolute best to bring out her natural beauty it was the mousy producer.

"What days do you have off during the week?" Faye wanted to know.

As the phone in her hand continued vibrating with unanswered calls and texts, Phoenix's reserved exterior crumpled a little bit, "None, really."

Faye waved her answer away like it was nothing more than a bothersome gnat. "Nonsense, everybody has a day off. Surely you'll have one before the birthday party?"

"I don't know…"

"You must take one, darling. I'll fix you up with Antoinette and you'll be gorgeous!"

Phoenix seemed to make up her mind and stepped back, holding up her phone to indicate she needed to get back to work. "That's very kind of you, but it's not necessary. I'm happy to help with Grace's birthday."

Faye put her hand on the girl's forearm, stopping her

retreat. "You're such a pretty thing, I insist you at least get the basics from Antoinette. My treat."

"It's not the money. I don't think I'll have ti–"

Faye squeezed Phoenix's arm warmly. "We'll make time. With Antoinette's touch you will be breaking hearts all over Australia."

Pink rose in Phoenix's cheeks and Faye knew she had struck a nerve. It made perfect sense. People pleasing, super organized, always working, plain Jane Phoenix didn't think of herself as beautiful or glamorous or the object of desire of all of the handsome leading men who surrounded her.

A tiny, sad twinge wrung Faye's heart. Always one to help the lowly and despaired, she grew even more excited at the idea of throwing Grace's party and giving Phoenix the makeover she deserved. Who knew? Maybe there was someone already working on the film with Phoenix who was a perfect match. Faye smiled at the idea. Maybe she could bring two happy couples together during her little getaway on this island.

As she watched Phoenix walk away, Faye thought about the men she knew were working on Grace's film. Rigby. No, he was not a good match. What about the Assistant Director? Faye couldn't remember his name and upon reflection decided he didn't have enough charisma.

Yes, someone with good looks and charisma was who Phoenix needed to make her come out of her shell. Faye's mind turned to the actors. Actors had charisma and they were, overall, extremely good looking. Zac certainly had both characteristics.

"Tut-tut-tut," Faye said to herself as she breezed towards the hotel's gourmet restaurant to grab a bite to eat. "Sorry, Phoenix, Zac is already taken. But not to worry, there are plenty of other fish in the sea."

CHAPTER 23

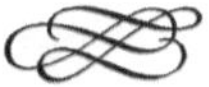

Zac's arms and legs burned as he held two 40 pound dumbbells in the air while maintaining a deep lunge. Checking his form in the mirrored wall of the hotel's elite gym, he was pleased with what he saw. He rarely skipped a workout and it showed.

Compared to Rigby's older, flabbier, reflection next to his, Zac felt especially well formed. Not that it was the old man's fault, he was a producer and didn't have to hold himself up to the same rigorous physical demands of being a movie star.

"It's time to push even harder," Rigby said, slightly out of breath.

Zac raised up out of his lunge, lowered the weights to hip level, then switched it up, lunging with his other foot forward and lifting the weights again high over his head.

"With Grace?" he asked, making sure Rigby wasn't talking about the workout.

"Yes," Rigby put his 20 pound weights back on the rack as if he was finishing up, which Zac found amusing. Zac was just getting started.

"What do you suggest?" he asked. After his perfect date with Grace ended a little flat, Zac was legitimately confused about how to proceed. "My normal moves haven't really gotten me very far."

"Normal moves?" Rigby scoffed, wiping the sweat off of his forehead and face with a towel he kept hooked into the back of his gym shorts. "We're not talking about some starry eyed girl who can be swept off her feet by the fact that you're in the movies, Zac."

Zac raised up from his lunge and lowered his weights, spread his feet apart for balance and lifted the weights up and down in front of him without bending his elbows. Rigby watched him with what Zac thought might be jealousy.

"That's why I need your help," Zac continued, his voice tense from the strain of the exercise.

Rigby moved closer and lowered his voice, "I think we need to push the idea out into the public, for real this time. Grace likes to please her fans. We need her fans to think that you and her are already together. They'll go crazy for that."

Zac didn't know why Rigby was speaking so quietly, there was nobody else in the hotel gym.

"I'm game for that," he said in his regular voice.

He had no qualms about nudging Grace into their romance. The vibes she was sending out were unmistakable. She wanted him just as much as he wanted her. It was bound to happen eventually and he needed it to happen as soon as possible. They had some intimate scenes coming up and he would feel a whole heckuva lot better if he and Grace were a couple by then.

"I trust you, Rigby. You know her better than I do."

Rigby nodded, agreeing with Zac's take on his plan. "Great!"

"So what do you want me to do, exactly?" Zac put his dumbbells down and went to the pull-up bar.

Rigby followed him, his own workout forgotten. "I've scheduled a live interview for you and Grace with New York Today tomorrow morning," he explained.

"Okay." Zac wiped his palms on the front of his shirt and hopped effortlessly up, grabbing hold of the bar. As he counted off 50 pull-ups in his head, Rigby explained his plan for their appearance on New York Today.

When Zac dropped back down to the floor, he grinned at the producer. "That's genius."

Pleased at the praise, Rigby smiled back. "Well, kid, I've been doing this for a long time."

Zac was so happy with the plan he had to reach over and shake the man's hand. "That's obvious, my man. Count me in."

CHAPTER 24

Grace wished she could keep her sunglasses on for the interview. Not only were the lights for the interview glaringly bright and making her squint, she knew she didn't look her best.

She was tired. Quite tired.

Though she was hitting the mark on every scene they shot, remembering her lines, for the most part, making sure to eat well and get enough rest, Grace felt like everything around her was thick, like she was moving through water. The air sat heavily on her skin and any sound seemed to enter her ear through a filter that made it slow and echoey.

She had felt this way for days.

Ever since she got home from her dissatisfying date with Zac. Ever since he had tried to kiss her goodnight and she had managed to duck away from him and escape into the beach house door guarded by one of Faye's silently present security guards. Ever since a motherly Faye, who was waiting up to hear all of the details, gave up and sent her to bed when she wouldn't disclose anything romantic between her and her co-star.

Nothing was right. That's all Grace could think as the producer of New York Today spoke into her earpiece.

"I've got your mic's live now, just fyi," the producer's voice said.

In the high backed chair next to hers, Zac nodded curtly. They were linked to the same audio. He looked over at her and smiled. Grace managed a weak smile back.

"Um…Ms. Woods?" The producer's voice vibrated through her head.

"Yes?" She sat up straighter in her chair, trying to look like she wasn't listening to everything through a wall of water.

"Your sunglasses?"

"Oh, right," Grace removed them, handing them to a nearby PA. It was 10 o'clock at night on Hamilton Island. A brutal time for an interview, but New York Today was live every weekday morning in New York City and the time difference couldn't be helped.

She smoothed her hair, glancing at the makeup and hair team for their nod of approval. Getting it, she glanced down at her dress, a simple chiffon Gucci sundress in teal, to make sure everything was in place. "Am I good?" she asked the disembodied voice in her ear.

"You look like a star," he answered.

Grace took the compliment with a grain of salt. It was his job to make her as happy and relaxed as possible before the interview, after all.

"You nervous?" Zac asked.

"Not nervous, no," she said. Maybe she would have expanded on that and told him that she was actually feeling a little bit numb and disconnected, if they had been given the time.

"All right, 30 seconds folks," the producer's voice interrupted.

"Hi Grace, Zac, this is Jason," another voice came through the earpiece. A few moments later the image of Jason Rodriguez, the popular host of New York Today appeared on a large monitor in front of them.

"Hi Jason, it's great to be here," Zac said.

"It's great to have you both. We're at commercial break right now, but when Frank gives you the countdown I'll greet you like we haven't spoken yet. Sound good?"

"Yes," Grace replied.

"Sounds great!" Zac replied.

Grace gave him a curious sideways look. He was awfully chipper even after their long day of filming.

"Here we go folks," Frank the producer interrupted again and Grace turned her attention back to Jason's gleaming smile on the monitor. "10-9-8-7-6-5-4-3-2-1- and we're live."

"Welcome back," Jason greeted the audience with his deep soothing baritone. "And do we have a treat for you this morning. Straight from location in Australia, Zac Foster and Grace Woods are here to talk to us about the movie they're filming, Heart of Mine."

Grace stiffened. Why would he say Zac's name before hers? She wasn't just the star, she was the executive producer.

"Good morning you two. Well, it's not exactly morning where you are, is it?" Jason laughed oddly loud at his own joke and the sound of it sounded slow motion in her ears.

"Good morning, Jason!" Zac was practically wiggling out of his chair like a toddler.

Grace ignored him and kept her eyes trained on the monitor. "Good morning, Jason," she hoped she wasn't speaking too loud or coming across as aloof or doing anything off putting.

Her eyelids were heavy like she really just needed to close

her eyes for just a moment. Not good. Falling asleep on live television was a big no-no in the interview world. Grace giggled at that thought, then remembered she was on a hot mic and regained control.

"You two must be tired. What time is there anyway?" Jason asked. Which was ridiculous. He was basically a reporter, he knew exactly what time it was on their side.

"It's late, Jason. That's what it is," Grace quipped. Zac shot her a nervous look and Jason paused for a millisecond before filling their ears with his slow motion laughter again.

"Right you are, Grace. While we're still sipping our coffee you have been filming all day already, haven't you?"

"Yes we have, Jason," Zac volunteered.

Annoyance popped into Grace's body and she fought to control her facial features so nobody would see.

"Can you tell us how filming is going?" Jason asked.

"Oh, it's going great, Jason, really great," Zac chimed in again.

Grace decided to let him talk since there was no controlling his bubbly over-the-top responses. She focused on maintaining an attractive yet normal smile and wished this whole thing would be over soon. Through her peripheral vision she caught a glimpse of who she thought was Phoenix and an idea popped into her head.

She needed to ask Phoenix to get her away from everything for a few days. Or a few hours at least. Nothing felt right and Grace didn't like it. She wasn't sure what was the matter, but she thought it might have something to do with the pressure of filming and all of the attention Zac was paying to her...or maybe...maybe she was distracted.

"Is it a case of art imitating life or life imitating art?" Jason asked.

Grace came back to the moment, realizing she hadn't

been paying any attention to what Zac was telling New York Today.

"What would you say?" Zac turned to her, a glint in his eye that made her uncomfortable.

Without missing a beat her instincts kicked in and she answered, "I don't think I can say right now. Time will tell."

Jason's eyes lit up like a reporter who had just gotten a big scoop. A few of Grace's hair and makeup crew 'oohed' and nudged each other.

Grace smiled coyly, ducked her head down as if time would actually tell. She really wished she knew what in the heck she had commented on.

"On that piece of news we will wish you both the best out there in that beautiful part of the world and maybe we can touch base again soon?"

"Absolutely," Zac said enthusiastically. "We look forward to that."

Grace was so glad the whole thing was over. Cheeks burning from forcing a smile she didn't feel, she waited for Jason to say goodbye and Frank to tell them they were off air.

That's when it happened. Zac, whether from inexperience or too much excitement or sheer idiocy she wasn't sure, did the most bizarre thing.

He reached over and slipped his hand over Grace's, squeezing it intimately and leaning in towards her ear as if they were not broadcasting live to New York City and the whole wide world.

"We're not going to be able to keep *us* secret for much longer," he said softly. Not soft enough to go unheard by the wildly sensitive LAV mics clipped to their clothes.

Grace's first reaction was to yank her hand away, but she managed to maintain a calm and collected exterior even though Jason's eyes on the monitor had popped open in surprise. Before she could think of an excellent zinger response to quell the rumor mill that must already be turning, Zac made another move. This one was unthinkable.

He lifted her hand to his mouth and, while staring deeply into her shocked eyes, pressed his lips sensually against her knuckles.

"Not that I want to keep us secret," he said. "I never have."

Grace's mouth dropped open. She was so stunned she could not form a thought.

Jason had a thought, however, and he voiced it live on New York Today, "You heard it here first everyone. The secret love affair that is, apparently, no longer a secret, brewing on the set of Heart of Mine between Zac Foster and the extraordinary Grace Woods."

There was a short pause then a beep before Frank's voice popped into her ear again, "And we're clear, that's a wrap for you two. Danielle will be there in a moment to take off your mics, thank you for your time." He was using his best producer voice, but Grace swore she heard a note of amusement.

She snatched her hand away from Zac and glared at him. "What are you doing?"

He smiled with a confidence she knew he shouldn't feel and reached for her hand again. Grace pulled away from him and stood up. Someone who must be Danielle rushed up to her and unclipped the LAV mic from a fold in the front of her sundress then began pulling the length of wire that had been secured by tape down her side and back so it wouldn't pop out during the interview.

"Seriously, Zac, what in the heck were you thinking?" Grace demanded, anger bubbling up as the insult of his actions formed clearer in her mind.

"I–" Zac began, but before he could finish his thought Rigby bounced up to them.

"That was brilliant!" Rigby exclaimed, holding his arms

out like he was giving them both a giant air hug. "Perfect timing, this is gonna take off like wildfire."

Zac looked at her sheepishly and suddenly it all became clear. Rigby had put him up to this for publicity. Created a fantasy romance between them to build up buzz over the movie.

In a flash, the anger that had been bubbling boiled over and Grace turned her ire onto her longtime producer and friend.

"Who do you think you are? How dare you do this without consulting me first?" She flung her arm out towards Zac, who was getting his mic removed by a hurried Danielle. "How dare you involve him in this mess?"

Rigby was only mildly phased by her anger. "Now, now, Gracy."

Grace narrowed her eyes. "Do not call me that."

Rigby's good mood faded even more under her look. He shrank back from her and added, "This will be great in the end. Trust me."

"Trust you? I can't even speak to you," she spat the words at him and stalked away.

Fuming, Grace made her way through several crew members who were tactfully averting their eyes before she ran into Phoenix who appeared to be as incensed as Grace felt.

"What can I do to help?" Phoenix asked.

"Get me away from them. All of them," Grace motioned her hand behind her to encompass the entire film crew. "I need to get away, Phoenix."

Phoenix nodded, understanding, "Okay, I'll find somewhere."

Grace's mind was whirling, trying to think of where she could go on this tiny island where she could figure out what to do. Suddenly, she had an idea.

"Get me another boat trip with that charter, the one I went on when we got here," Grace said.

Phoenix nodded again, "Right. I can do that. When?"

"First thing in the morning." As she said the words a rush of anticipation moved through her, so strong it overpowered her anger and allowed a smile to touch her lips.

CHAPTER 25

Grace could not decide what to wear. After days of being told what to wear, where to stand, what to say, she sometimes stumbled when given the freedom to choose. It didn't help that she was trying to get dressed at six in the morning.

Phoenix had booked the boat at the earliest possible time – 7:00 am–and Grace didn't want to be late.

She had slept fitfully. Thoughts of Lincoln kept drifting through her dreams and waking her. Though she would never admit it to anyone, she was excited at the idea of seeing him again, of being on the open water with him. At four in the morning Grace gave up on getting any more sleep and decided to take a shower.

The problem was, nothing was going her way.

"What's the matter with that one?" Faye asked, rubbing her eyes and face to try and stay awake.

Grace had knocked on her door in a panic after realizing she had nothing appropriate to wear. Faye was dutifully laying on Grace's bed with different outfits strewn in front of her, giving her best half-asleep fashion advice.

Nerves building, Grace stood in front of the mirror in an A-line navy Ralph Lauren dress. Fun, flirty…formal. She screwed her mouth into a frown. "It's too much."

For all intents and purposes, Faye was sleep walking. 6:00 am was not her best time to shine. She flopped back into the pillows on the bed and threw her hands up into the air in frustration. "Where are you going at this hour?"

"I told you, Phoenix arranged a…a kind of a private boat trip for me."

Faye perked up a little. "Will there be a special someone on this boat trip?"

The nerves in Grace's stomach flipped and twirled as she concentrated on peeling off the Ralph Lauren dress and avoiding looking Faye in the eye. "You could say that."

"Hmm," Faye raised her head from the pillows and watched her carefully for a few moments. "You're blushing, darling."

"I'm not blushing. I'm trying to get out of this dress."

"Who arranged this little boat trip again?"

"Phoenix," Grace tossed the navy dress aside and looked at her remaining options spread out across the bed.

Faye's sleep deprived brain seemed to chew on this information for a long moment then she sat up with a burst of energy. "These," she reached out and grabbed a pair of Tommy Hilfiger navy blue anchor print shorts. "Aaaaannnd…" she scanned the bed again, spied what she wanted and grabbed a white loose fitting spaghetti strap tank top, "…this."

She tossed them to Grace who put them on obediently and surveyed the look in her mirror. Fresh and youthful without trying too hard. Faye, even straight out of a dead sleep, could be a genius.

"Wear your navy bikini underneath in case you go swimming and this in case you get cold," Faye instructed as she grabbed a waist length fat knit navy sweater from the pile of clothes.

Grace put on the ensemble and topped it off with a wide brimmed straw hat that Faye wrapped a navy and white cotton scarf around for flare.

"Not bad," she said. Her comment was met with a soft snore from Faye who, her fashion advice complete, had fallen back to sleep.

Grace still felt good as she hopped out of the buggy that delivered her to the pier. A tiny thrill moved through her when she realized she already knew the way to the boat. Something about that fact gave her a sense of intimacy with its Captain. An intimacy she hoped to build on this little trip today.

There was a spring in her step knowing that she looked cute, casual, youthful even, and Grace hummed a little tune to herself as she made her way down the pier. The memory of Lincoln racing past her on her first time there came back. Their abrupt meeting and the immediate, overwhelming attraction she had for him also came back.

Grace picked up her pace, eager to lay eyes on him and see if those feelings returned. She really wanted to feel that way again–light, sexy, swoony. The feelings of falling in love.

When she got to the Lady Jane, Grace paused. She had been so involved in her emotions she hadn't taken a moment to appreciate how beautiful the morning was dawning. Glimpses of pink and orange clouds over a bright blue ocean between the shining white boats docked at the pier lifted her spirits even more.

Another memory of her first morning with Lincoln came to her. The indescribable sensation of looking into the eye of that humpback whale wrapped around her heart and soul again. Living in Los Angeles and making movies rarely afforded her a chance to connect with nature, not really. But to connect with such an amazing creature had been truly awesome.

A clanking sound came from aboard the Lady Jane. Grace's heart skipped a beat. He was here. She was about to see him again. Sail with him again.

Grace took a deep breath and boarded the Lady Jane, calling out across the deck towards Lincoln who was at the helm and silhouetted against the beautiful sunrise.

"I'm here! Ready for another whale sighting!"

The man's silhouette turned, waved to her, and moved in her direction. Her heart raced as she took a step towards him, impatient to see his face. But the morning sun was bright as it lifted off of the horizon and it shone into her eyes, blinding her briefly.

"Hello," the man answered.

Grace stopped moving forward. The man's form seemed similar to Lincoln's, but not as tall as she remembered. And his voice. It was familiar, but was it Lincoln's? She couldn't decide.

"Nice to have you onboard," he said as he moved to her side and out of the path of the blinding sun.

Grace could finally see him–and he was not who she was expecting.

CHAPTER 26

"It's so nice to meet you, Ms. Woods. I'm a huge fan," the man reached out his hand to shake hers and Grace took it, confusion overwhelming her ability to respond. "I'm Luke, Captain of this fine vessel and your guide for the day."

"Luke?" Grace still couldn't grasp what was happening. This man looked eerily similar to Lincoln except he was shorter and appeared to be younger. He was handsome, but not the level of handsome Lincoln was, still she recognized Lincoln in his features.

For one horrifying moment Grace thought she might be losing her mind. Had she imagined Lincoln? Had she been so tired on that first boat trip that she misunderstood his name, created a taller, better looking version in her mind and hallucinated their time together? She gasped. Had she really seen a humpback whale?

"But, I…uh…" she stumbled over her thoughts as Luke waited politely. Finally, Grace blurted out, "Where's Lincoln?"

Luke laughed, a good humored sound, "My brother, right.

He took you on the first go around, I know." Luke offered her his arm and she allowed him to lead her to the cushioned seats up near the helm. "I have to apologize to you for that. Link takes over for me every now and again when I am too…*busy*…to sail. He's a bit rough around the edges, I know, but no worries today, Ms. Woods, I've got everything under control and we have a full day of fun and relaxation planned for you."

Grace plopped into the cushioned seat, disappointment washing away all of her previous excitement.

"You're his brother," she stated, not sure why she decided to say it out loud.

"Yes, younger brother. I hope he wasn't too much of a surly old man with you. Link's charm doesn't always come across," Luke said this like it was a joke, but there was a twinge of concern in his eyes.

"No, not at all. He was quite…enjoyable, actually."

Pleasantly surprised, Luke stepped back and gave her a half-bow. "Good to hear. Now, can I interest you in a mimosa while we cast off?"

Grace nodded absent-mindedly. Lincoln's absence had dealt a blow to her expectations and she needed a moment to adjust. She might need more than one mimosa to get through the melancholy that was swiftly moving through her.

As she waited for her drink Grace's mood fell to an all time low, a low she hadn't experienced since Syd told her he was breaking up with her, a low that was too low given the circumstances. Lincoln wasn't her boyfriend. They had never been on a date. They barely knew each other. So why was her reaction to not seeing him so intense?

"Here you go," Luke handed her a champagne flute full of orange juice and bubbly champagne.

"Thank you," she took it and, as soon as Luke turned his back on her to manage the casting off, she drank the whole thing down at once. Grace put the back of her hand against her lips as she swallowed the last of it. The sharp bubbles of champagne burned the back of her throat. For some ridiculous reason she wanted to cry. "Stop it," she whispered. "You're overreacting."

"What's that?" Luke's head popped around the corner at the sound of her voice.

"Oh, nothing," Grace hiccuped.

Luke's eyes fell on her empty glass and he hurried over. "Another one?"

Grace nodded, bleakly ashamed of her desire to drink away her feelings of hopelessness, yet unable to stop herself. She took care to sip slowly on the second mimosa as Luke maneuvered the Lady Jane away from the pier and into more open water.

"Do you feel like swimming?" he asked in a shout over his shoulder as he steered past a few other pleasure boats.

Grace thought of her navy bikini under her clothes. It was well cut to her shape and one of the more flattering suits she owned. She had hoped to show it off to Lincoln during their day together. She sighed and answered, "Not right now, thank you."

Grace watched as the Lady Jane cut through the blue water and left a swirling wake behind. The waves were mesmerizing and she allowed the champagne to do its work, warming her body and fuzzing her thoughts. The movement of the boat on the water relaxed her a little and she tried to enjoy the gorgeous view.

At least she wasn't back on set. She had a few scheduled days off and after the fiasco that Rigby made Zac pull on New York Today she was going to take full advantage of all of those days.

"What a colossal mess," she said under her breath, speaking more to the ocean water than anyone else.

"Is everything okay?" Luke asked, he had arrived unseen at her side and Grace jumped a little at the sound of his voice. "I'm sorry, didn't mean to frighten you. Would you like another drink?"

Grace looked down at the almost empty champagne flute in her hand. "No, I should slow down on these." She looked out over the water and said, "It is truly beautiful here, isn't it?"

"Yes, it is," Luke answered, a smile in his voice.

Grace turned to look up at him. "Did you and your brother…Link…did you grow up here?"

"Yes, well for the most part. Our Grandad worked here his whole life. He built a nice place up in the hills with his own hands. Link and I came here all the time when we were kids, then we moved in with him permanently when our parents passed on."

"Oh, I'm sorry. I didn't mean to pry," Grace sincerely meant that, but couldn't help but be drawn into the details of the childhood Luke had shared with Lincoln.

Luke shrugged off her comment with the same casualness that she had noticed in his brother. "No worries. Nobody's life is perfect and this isn't the worst place in the world for two little orphan boys to end up, now is it?"

She smiled. "No, it's not bad at all." Something he had said popped out to her and she asked, "Are there many places up in the hills?"

"A fair bit."

"Are they private? Secluded I mean."

"A lot of them, yes." Luke had a thought, "Are you in the market for a private, secluded hill house?"

"I've been looking for someplace I could go on my time off from shooting while I'm here. Nothing to buy, just rent."

Luke's face broke into a wide smile. "Look no further, I've got you fixed for that."

A flutter of excitement raced through her. Was he saying what she thought he was saying? "Do you mean…?"

"You can have a go at my Grandad's house. It's a beauty, and Link's got it all fixed up. It's the perfect getaway on the island. And I'll cut you a deal, too." Luke gave her a salesman's wink.

Grace blushed, not so much from his wink, but at the idea of staying in a house that Lincoln had been working on. That Lincoln had grown up in. Would she see him? Could this be considered stalking?

Before she had a chance to chicken out, Grace put on her most gracious smile and answered, "That sounds lovely. I'll take it."

CHAPTER 27

*P*hoenix hit the send button and transferred the money for Grace's rental. Like almost every transaction she had these days, paying for the movie star's getaway was all done on her phone. Quick. Easy. And the answer to her dilemma.

Ever since Grace's friend, Faye, had set her the task of finding a secret getaway to hold Grace's surprise birthday party, the pressure was on. Phoenix was a doer who had a hard time saying no to the requests of any of their above the line talent. Especially Grace, or her friends apparently.

Phoenix had never been enlisted on such a personal level by anyone like Faye. Wealthy beyond belief, beautiful, commanding, unapologetic, in a way Phoenix found her intriguing. She didn't seem like the kind of woman who liked being disappointed.

Not that Phoenix disappointed people. That was not her norm. Usually she was way ahead of what someone wanted and managed to wrangle it for them before they had the chance to ask. She kind of prided herself on this trait. She thought of it as her superpower.

Phoenix's fingers flew across the face of her cell. Texting was preferable, especially when dealing with someone who made her nervous. She hit send on a text to Faye.

I think I've found an out of the way place for you know who's party.

There. Done. Hopefully, Faye would agree and she could tick that off her never-ending list of to-dos. Surprisingly, a response came almost immediately.

Wonderful! I knew you would do it. It's a place she likes?

Phoenix thought about it for a second, then answered.

She just had me book it for this weekend break so she could go there and relax. So, yes, I would say she likes it.

Another half of a second passed before Faye responded.

Excellent! Let's book the date for the party and get you an appointment with Antoinette right away!

Phoenix cringed. She was glad this conversation was over text and Faye couldn't watch her discomfort at the idea of a makeover. She understood the lady thought she was being generous, but all of the glam stuff wasn't Phoenix's style. However, she had to say something in response.

Send me the date you want for the party. I will have to get back to you on a good time for Antoinette.

There. Done. Makeover successfully pushed off into a dateless future.

Phoenix ticked the 'Book Party for G' entry on her notes tab and went on to the next item on her agenda for the day.

CHAPTER 28

Lincoln was finally done sanding the cedar floors. A job well done, if only half done. The staining would have to wait until morning, because his shoulders were aching.

"Not a young buck anymore," he muttered to himself as he popped the cap off of a bottle of beer and took a pull.

"Have a go, mate!" Fred called out to him from where he was perched on the far corner of the deck.

Lincoln eyed the big bird then tipped his beer bottle at him. "You stay out of it. Where's your missus anyway?"

Fred bobbed his head up and down vigorously then squawked again, "Have a go, mate!" before flying away.

Lincoln watched the grand white bird float off into the tops of the gum trees further down the hill and took another drink of his beer. The wild bird friends of his Grandad's weren't always talkative, but when they did say something, they said it loud.

He placed his beer down on the railing and hunched his shoulders forward and back, trying to stretch out the kinks that he had built up hand sanding all day. As he stretched he took in a deep breath and tried to relax. Once he started the staining he needed to finish it, so he could take off the rest of the day and rest up to begin that job in the morning.

Normally, Lincoln might go down to one of his regular hangouts for a drink and a few laughs, but nothing was normal anymore. Not since that movie had taken over the island.

Lincoln picked up his beer and took another drink, a long one. This whole gorgeous movie star in his midst had already taken over too much of his energy. It seemed like he spent half of his time working hard to try and not think about her, only to have her pop into his head the moment he slowed down.

"Like right about now," he scoffed in disgust at himself. He'd worked his fingers to the bone all day and all he wanted to do was relax, but here he was thinking about how he couldn't stop thinking about Grace. "Get a grip," he said out loud.

He couldn't go out or he risked running into someone from the movie or, worse, Grace herself. He couldn't work anymore, because he was exhausted. He couldn't even call Luke and take the boat out for a spin to get his mind off things. First, everything on that boat would remind him of Grace. Second, Luke was driving him nuts and Lincoln didn't want to talk to his troublesome little brother at the moment.

He had texted him earlier in the day saying he was out on a charter and he needed to talk to Lincoln about renting out the Hill House. This was a hard no, which Luke already knew, so Lincoln hadn't even bothered answering him.

Lincoln had been so busy sanding that he got fed up with the constant buzzing of his phone with texts and calls from Luke, no doubt trying to convince him to make their Grandad's house an Airbnb. Or maybe to take over another charter for him because he was hungover. Lincoln didn't want to bother with any of it while he was sanding. He had turned down the volume on his phone and thrown it into the kitchen drawer.

He almost retrieved it as he went back into the kitchen to get another beer from the fridge. When he opened the drawer he saw the latest text from Luke front and center on the screen.

This could be huge, Link. Big money for both of us.

Lincoln grunted and shut the drawer with his phone still in it. Instead of arguing with Luke, he grabbed the rest of the six-pack in the fridge and took it back out to the deck. He would spend his evening relaxing on the hammock and enjoying the cool night air. With any luck, the noisy cockatoos wouldn't return until morning.

CHAPTER 29

*B*y the time Grace arrived at the Hill House getaway night had fallen. The deep jungle surroundings were thick with chirping night insects and much darker than the wide open night skies of the beach. Grace found the deep, damp night rather peaceful. And it was certainly far from the prying eyes of absolutely anyone, which was her highest priority.

The plan had been for her to arrive sooner in the day. However, convincing Rigby and Syd that she needed to get away, didn't want or need bodyguards, didn't want to tell them where she was going, and didn't legally have to, had taken her a while. As the buggy driver, who had been summoned by the hotel concierge, took her higher and higher into the hills, Grace thought about how long it had been since she could do whatever she wanted without having to check in with anyone else.

Her life was wrapped up in assistants and producers and security and she realized how much she missed this kind of freedom. She had experienced it for the first time in a long time on her first boat trip with Lincoln. Then again, on a lesser scale, with his brother, Luke.

But when Luke had offered her this quiet rental high in the hills of Hamilton Island, Grace had felt a new sense of freedom. Somewhere to go that was all her own, unknown to anyone else, where nobody was watching her or waiting for a reaction.

It sounded perfect.

The driver pulled to a stop at the end of a long drive, turned to her and said, "This is it."

Grace peered into the darkness. There wasn't one light on in the property. A thrill of excitement went up her spine and she grabbed her overnight bag.

"No, no, I'll drive you," he said.

"Don't bother. You're sure this is it?"

"Yes'm, this is the Reeve's Hill House."

"I'll walk. I don't mind," she insisted.

About midway between the road and the dark house Grace wished she had allowed the driver to take her to the front door.

The chirping and buzzing of night insects grew louder the deeper she got onto the property and they sounded more and more ominous. The house wasn't mansion sized, but its completely darkened windows made it look like a huge stone looming in her path.

Grace fumbled for the key Luke had given her earlier with simple instructions, "When you go in the front door the living area and kitchen are on the right and the bedrooms and baths are on the left. Oh, and watch out for the cocka-toos. They can be a bit overly friendly."

"Overly friendly cockatoos," Grace whispered to herself as she used the light of her cell phone to fit the key into the door lock. In retrospect the warning sounded a little weird.

With a satisfying click the key turned in the lock and

Grace pushed the door open, eager to be inside and away from whatever might be lurking in the jungle. Once inside she was just as blind as she had been outside. The only light in the place was a ghostly dim glow coming from a row of windows on the opposite side of the room. The scent of cedar drifted to her through the dark emptiness. At least it wasn't an unpleasant smell. In fact, it smelled familiar.

Grace ran her hand along the wall next to the door until she came to a switch. She flipped the switch up. Nothing happened. She flipped it down. Still nothing. With some frustration she flipped the switch up and down quickly. Nothing.

"Great," she murmured. No light bulb or no electricity? What had she gotten herself into? Maybe the lights would work in the bedroom. "Bedrooms to the left," she repeated Luke's instructions and felt her way along the wall until she came to what must be a hallway. "So far, so good," she said softly. The sense of adventure she had felt earlier returned. "Nothing like feeling your way through the dark in a strange house to give you a few thrills," she continued with a small laugh.

Her hand felt a doorway. She pushed the door all the way open and felt blindly for the light switch. Finding it, she flipped it up and was immediately washed in light. So much light she had to squint until her eyes adjusted.

When she could finally see she found a clean, fairly straightforward bathroom.

Nothing luxurious. Noted.

With the light from the bathroom spilling into the hallway Grace easily saw the other three doors. Following her intuition, she went to the last door at the end of the hall, believing that would be the master suite.

When she flipped the switch, she was surprised at the lackluster decor and small size of the master bedroom.

A Queen sized bed, no headboard, no pillows, no decorative touches at all, stood against one wall. The comforter was a drab olive green and there was only one nightstand with a simple lamp. Several blue rugs covered most of the floor, but didn't match the comforter.

"Hm, roughing it I guess," she said, a little disappointed, but too tired to do anything about it. The place seemed clean enough and she would check out the other rooms in the light of morning. "Right now I just need some sleep," she told the room then laughed at her need to say everything out loud even though she was completely alone.

She quickly washed up and got into her most comfy pajamas, a pair of slouchy soft striped pajama bottoms and a white cotton tank top. This getaway was all about being quiet and comfortable, not necessarily being pampered. If the rooms weren't entirely five star accommodations, she hoped the privacy and seclusion would make up for it.

As she sank into bed, Grace was completely happy with the mattress and comforter. They were soft and cozy and within a few moments she was fast asleep.

CHAPTER 30

Grace flew over the ocean, blue water swirling with white sand underneath. Her toes skimmed the top of the water releasing sparkles of light that trailed behind her like the twirls released from a fairy's wand.

Her toes were warm from the water. Her cheeks were cool from the breeze. In the near distance she saw something floating on the water and she willed her flying form to veer in its direction. Almost instantly she arrived at the object and discovered it was a small raft, the kind of raft that Gilligan himself may have built from pieces of driftwood lashed together with dried palm fronds.

Grace smiled inwardly. She didn't know why it was here, but its shabby tropical vibe was charming. A small cup made out of half of a tiny coconut sat in the middle of the raft. Grace reached down to pick it up, expecting to find a delicious fruity cocktail. When she went to take a sip, however, she recoiled in disgust.

"What the-?" she exclaimed. In shock, she realized that the gross smell of whatever was in the coconut cup had taken away her ability to fly. She screamed as she felt her body plunge into the ocean water.

Grace sat up with a jolt and cried out. Heart pounding in her chest she looked wildly around the room, unsure for a moment where she was. After she took several calming breaths she remembered.

The Hill House.

Two large windows let in the soft light of early morning and Grace could see the outline of the plain furniture along with her leather overnight bag in the corner where she had left it last night.

"Right, I'm here," she said out loud, partly to settle her nerves. She took another breath in through her nose and the disgusting scent from her dream was back. This time in real life. "What in the world?" Grace's nose wrinkled and she coughed into her hand, fighting back her gag reflex. "Oh, gross!"

She flung the comforter off and made her way to the door, keeping her hand tightly cupped over her mouth and nose like a makeshift filter. In the hallway the smell grew stronger. It seemed to be coming from the living room area that she hadn't been able to see last night when she arrived.

"Ugh!" she cried out, bravely moving towards the source of the stench. "Did something die in here?"

She didn't really expect to find a dead animal. She expected to find, perhaps, a burst pipe or a broken window that was letting in some type of horrible jungle smell.

What she didn't expect was to find a person at the source of the disgusting smell. And she did not expect that person to be Lincoln Reeves.

Standing up from a crouched position at the far corner of what was a very large open living, kitchen, dining room, Lincoln turned towards her, a look of shock that equaled her own on his face.

Dressed in torn jeans and a long sleeved T-shirt, he had deep red and brown stains all over him and was holding the source of the stains in his hand, a wet, wadded up rag.

Despite recognizing him instantly, Grace screamed out of pure instinct. The sound surprised both of them and they paused, staring at one another before both of them spoke at the same time, asking the same question.

"What are *you* doing here?"

They paused again, waiting for the other to make their excuses. When no excuses came they both spoke once more, again asking the same question.

"What am *I* doing here?"

Fed up with the confusion Lincoln raised his hands in front of him, palms down, and lowered them in what Grace supposed was meant to be a calming gesture. She couldn't take her eyes off of the gorily stained rag in his hand and the stench had become unbearable. Instead of calming her, Lincoln's hand movements sent her into somewhat of a panic.

Lincoln saw the change in her eyes and glanced down at his hands and chest. He looked back up at her and started an explanation, "Grace, I–this isn't–"

Too late, her flight instinct kicked in and Grace took a few awkward steps back from him then turned and bolted towards the door that led out to a deck to her left.

Lincoln called out after her, "Grace, it's fine–it's only stain–wait! Don't open the–"

Too late, Grace found the knob and flung open the door, charging through it, desperate to get a breath of fresh air– and get away from whatever Lincoln was doing.

Before she could get all the way out the door, she was attacked from the front by a fantastic flurry of white feathers accompanied by deafening screeches.

Grace threw her arms up in front of her face to block the

blows and screamed. Her screams added to the screeching and somewhere behind her, she heard a man shouting. She turned in a circle, unable to escape the flock of angry birds whose beating wings, scratching talons and impossibly loud squawks overwhelmed her senses.

"Fred! Ginger! Get back!"

Lincoln's voice mixed in with the screeching and her screams. He was right there next to her, fending off the flapping.

A different voice called out, "Have a go, mate! Have a go, mate!"

Grace's bewilderment was complete.

Suddenly, she felt strong hands gripping each side of her waist and yanking on her–hard. Defenseless against his strength and desperate to get away from the bird attack, Grace let Lincoln pull her back into the house.

Once inside she pulled away from him and backed up against the nearest wall. Lincoln slammed the door, leaving two peeved cockatoos pacing back and forth on the deck. Grace scanned the rest of the deck and the treetops she could see through the wall of windows.

Both breathless, she and Lincoln locked eyes for a long moment.

Finally, her exasperation getting the best of her, Grace broke their silence, "Two!? There's only *two* of them!?"

CHAPTER 31

*L*incoln couldn't catch his breath–and it wasn't because of fighting off the bloody cockatoos.

Grace Woods was in his living room. She was in her pajamas, backed up against the wall, her hair a crazy mess, her eyes a little wild, but it was still her in the flesh. Everything about her took his breath away.

As they stared at each other, recovering from their battle with Fred and Ginger, Grace found her voice, "Two!? There's only *two* of them!?"

Lincoln glanced at Fred and Ginger bobbing up and down in front of the glass door, waiting for him to go outside and give them a treat. He looked back at Grace, alarmed and disheveled, bearing his handprints in wood stain on her white tank top where he had grabbed her to pull her back inside. The whole scene was so bizarre it was funny.

"Yes–" he began to explain that cockatoos, when agitated, can become aggressive, but instead of giving her a careful account of the natural tendencies of the cockatoo...he laughed.

He knew it was probably not the gentlemanly reaction,

and from the shocked look on Grace's face it wasn't the reaction she was expecting from him either, but he couldn't help it. From deep in his belly, the laughter overcame every effort he made to speak coherently until his sides hurt and he was even more out of breath.

As hilarity overtook him he continued watching Grace's face and what he saw wrapped around his heart and wouldn't let go. Her beauty shone through no matter what the expression, but beyond that beauty, Lincoln saw her face change from shocked disbelief to guarded amusement to, finally and gloriously, a bright eyed merriment that burst into laughter of her own.

Her joy lit up the room and Lincoln thought his heart might explode at the sight of it.

When he did finally catch his breath and speak, he looked her square in the eye and asked, "Really, though…what are you doing here?"

This sent them both into another fit of laughter until they were spent, holding their sides and half bent over, Grace leaning on the wall and Lincoln leaning on the back of the sofa.

Grace wiped tears of laughter from her eyes and answered, "I am renting this place. What are *you* doing here?" Her eyes moved down to the stains on his clothes. "And what is that all over you?" Her nose wrinkled and she scanned the room. "And what in the world is that awful smell?!"

A twitch of irritation interrupted Lincoln's good humor at the word 'rent'. Luke. He knew it had to be his brother that set this up. What an idiot. He turned his attention back to Grace, who must be the target of some kind of con by his little brother.

"This is my house. Well, it was my Grandad's house and now it's mine…ours technically, I guess."

Grace's brow pinched in confusion. "Ours?"

"My brother, Luke. Is that who rented it to you?" Grace nodded and Lincoln shook his head in disgust. "I'm sorry for the confusion, but he didn't have any right to." He stretched his arms out wide to encompass the great room in one large gesture. "Does this place look like it's fit to be a rental?"

Grace looked past him and took in the construction supplies stacked on the kitchen counters, the vast unfinished floor, and finally flicked up to the non-existent light fixtures above.

She shifted her gaze back to him and looked once again at the brown and red stains all over his clothes. "And that is…?

"Wood stain. That's what the smell is, too. I got up early to get started on it and get it all done in one day." He decided not to mention that he had gotten the permanent stain on her tank top during the earlier chaos. That would come up eventually.

"Wait, you slept here?" A new puzzlement came over her. "*I* slept here."

A swift spark of attraction surged through him, but he managed to keep his cool. "You–you slept here? Where?"

"In the bedroom. Where were you?" Her eyes narrowed as she eyed him.

"Me? I wasn't in the bedroom," Lincoln felt the need to defend himself, but the idea of Grace sleeping in his bed had him momentarily flustered. He pointed at the deck where the crazy cockatoos were preening on the railing. "The hammock. I fell asleep in the hammock last night."

An awkward silence hung between them. He wondered if she was contemplating what might have happened if he had not decided to sleep in the hammock, because that particular thought was heavy on his mind.

She cocked her head to the side. "So…I'm trespassing?"

Lincoln opened his mouth to answer, but didn't say

anything. The polite thing to say wouldn't come to him. The flirty thing to say wouldn't come to him.

Finally, he settled on, "I suppose…technically…you are." He winced at the sound of the words as they came out of his mouth.

Grace put her hands on her cheeks, her eyes wide. "I'm so embarrassed. Your brother–he gave me the key when he took me out on the boat again–I thought it would be you…" her words trailed off and she dropped her gaze. Suddenly, she gasped and looked down, realizing she was in her pajamas. "Oh my goodness." Then, seeing his wood stain handprints for the first time, she grabbed the bottom of her tank top and pulled it out to look at the stains better, exclaiming, "Oh my goodness!"

Heat rose in his cheeks as he pointed weakly at the handprints, trying hard to ignore the fact that as she held out the tank top he had a great view of her belly button. "Yeah, sorry about that. I was trying to get you away from Fred and Ginger."

"Fred and Ginger?"

"The birds."

Grace shot a look at the cockatoos just in time to watch them take flight off of the deck. She pointed at them. "They're loose!"

Lincoln grinned. The layers of shock and discovery she was going through were pretty amusing to observe. "They don't live here. They just visit."

"Oh." Her hand dropped to her side and she kind of slumped against the wall again, exhausted.

"Can I get you a cup of coffee?" he asked.

Grace caught his eyes again and Lincoln was glad he was still leaning against the back of the couch or he may have wobbled a bit at the sight of them. Intensely green in the morning light, no makeup, naturally gorgeous, he really wanted to have more time to gaze into those eyes.

"No, thank you, I should go," she said, rousing herself from the wall.

"You don't have–" Lincoln stood, too.

"This has been a huge mistake. I didn't mean to invade your privacy."

"That's not your doing. That's on Luke."

"Still, I should go," she glanced down the hallway as if she was already deciding what to pack.

Lincoln stepped forward. "I insist," he said. "The least I can do is make you some coffee after all of this." He waited, heart beating fast, hoping she would agree.

Grace averted her eyes demurely and Lincoln's stomach dropped. She was going to be polite about it, but she was still going to leave.

"Please," Lincoln said, not pleading, but close to it.

A slow smile spread across her lips and his heart leaped in his chest. He had those green eyes all to himself, for one cup of coffee at least. Lincoln vowed silently that this would be the best, and longest, cup of coffee he would ever make in his life.

hat was supposed to be one cup of coffee turned into breakfast.

Grace didn't mind at all. Lincoln, apologizing profusely for the messy kitchen and his stained hands, washed up as best as he could to fix her a delicious, French poured, cup of coffee, and the rest of their morning just fell into place.

"You've gotta eat, haven't you?" Lincoln asked as he watched over a pan of sizzling bacon.

"Yes, but I don't want to put you out."

"You're not putting me out. It just so happens I've got an urge for a big fry up, and it's no fun cooking a big fry up for only one."

Grace was convinced, easily, to stay for breakfast. Lincoln cooked some baked beans, fried tomatoes, fried mushrooms, fried eggs, and bread toasted in the oven to go along with the bacon. Though the food wasn't her normal fare of plain yogurt or grapefruit and hard boiled eggs, watching him move around the kitchen and tell her funny stories was worth it. She had always believed that one of the sexiest things a man could do was cook. This morning proved her correct.

"This'll stick to your ribs," he told her as he put a plate heaping with the fried morning goodness in front of her.

She clutched her coffee cup with both hands and looked at all of the food. "More like stick to my hips, you mean."

"Ah, your hips will love this stuff. It's power food," he encouraged. He swept her plate up again and grabbed his own, nodding towards the deck. "It's a beautiful morning. Shall we?"

She grabbed his coffee cup for him and followed him out the door, keeping one eye open for any return of the crazed cockatoos.

Lincoln noticed her squinting into the sky. "No worries, Fred and Ginger only come by in the morning and in the evening. They've got better things to do all day than hang around with the likes of me."

Grace smiled. "They are quite the eccentric companions."

Lincoln shrugged one shoulder, digging his fork into the baked beans. "They came with the house. I suppose I sort of inherited them."

While he was cooking, Lincoln had filled her in on the project that was his Grandfather's house. Though it was in ample disarray, she could understand what Lincoln saw in the house. Quality that had gotten a little run down and could be restored to its original glory with a little elbow grease. Plus, she liked how his eyes lit up when he talked about his Grandfather's craftsmanship.

"It's quite a legacy your Grandfather left you," Grace noted as she took a bite of toast he had toasted in the oven. Quaint and delicious.

Lincoln nodded as he chewed and washed his baked beans down with a swig of coffee. He watched her chew for a few moments, then asked, "What's your house like?"

"My house?"

He grinned as he picked up a piece of bacon. "Yeah, someone like you must have a big Beverly Hills mansion or something like that?"

Grace did have a big Beverly Hills mansion and a few other mansions around the world. She tried to come up with a list of them in order of when she usually used them and a strange emptiness came over her.

Lincoln waited patiently, taking robust bites of his bacon as she pondered how to answer his question. Finally, he swept his non-bacon holding hand in front of his face as if erasing a chalkboard. "That was a rude question. You don't have to answer that."

"It wasn't rude," Grace said as she let her eyes wander across the deck that Lincoln's Grandfather, or Grandad as he called him, had built by hand. Her gaze returned to Lincoln eating his bacon in the morning sunlight, golden hair, jaw flexing as he chewed, eyes brilliant and blue, open and unguarded, and something sweet and loving squeezed her heart. "I do have a house in Beverly Hills, among other places." Lincoln's gaze dropped to his plate and she hurried to explain, "But, what I was just realizing is that I don't have any place quite as inviting as this house. Your house."

Lincoln looked back up at her, a smile spreading across his face and into his eyes. Grace had to focus on not swooning.

"Thank you," Lincoln said.

It was Grace's turn to look down at her plate. She tried not to blush as she answered, "You're welcome."

"And you're welcome...to stay, I mean...if you want to," he fumbled his words.

Grace lifted her eyes just in time to see his cheeks redden and she couldn't help but smile. "I would love to stay, but I think I would be in the way, wouldn't I? With all the work you have to do?"

"Right, the work. You wouldn't want to be here with all the staining," his gaze flicked to the handprints on the stomach of her tank top.

She could still feel his hands gripping her waist and her skin tingled at the memory. The tingle moved from her stomach to her back and up into her shoulders giving her a delicious shiver, but then a sense of gloom overtook her.

She would have to pack up after breakfast and call for a driver from the hotel to retrieve her from the Hill House. A wave of sadness rippled through her chest. Her whole day stretched out in front of her. Maybe she would go to the spa with Faye…or run her lines…or lay in bed and stare up at the ceiling fan.

Grace sighed.

"Not hungry?" Lincoln asked, eyeing her rapidly cooling breakfast.

"Oh, no, I was just thinking." She picked up her fork and took a bite of fried tomato to prove she was enjoying the meal.

"What were you thinking about?"

"I was thinking that I don't really have any plans for today. And maybe…if you really don't mind…I could stay here and…sort of…help."

"Help?"

"Yes…maybe?"

"Help with what?"

"With some of the work. Since you're letting me stay and it seems like you have a lot to do."

"I couldn't let you do that."

"But I want to. I want to be useful. Surely there's some-thing I could do that's useful?"

He paused. Grace looked as earnest as she knew how.

"Really?" he asked, not quite believing.

"Yes, really. It would be good to get my mind off the movie and…everything." Syd using his girlfriend as her double. Zac's stupid on air comment. She pushed all of it out of her mind and waited for Lincoln to give her permission to continue her escape here with him.

He squinted through the windows into the great room. After thinking for a few moments he asked, "Can you paint?"

Relief. Something she knew how to do. In college she had excelled in all of her fine arts classes, including painting. Grace nodded with confidence. "I can."

"Okay, well, after we finish breakfast I'll get you set up to paint the kitchen."

"Oh…right…good," she said, slowly comprehending that he needed help with construction painting, not fine artwork. Chuckling at her misunderstanding, she picked up her fork and dug into her food. She was going to need a good breakfast to keep her energy up.

"What do you mean you don't know where she is?" Zac could not believe what he was hearing.

"She didn't give me all the details," Phoenix responded curtly.

Zac let out an exasperated sigh. Sometimes trying to deal with the always busy and usually serious little producer drove him crazy.

"But I booked all of this for her," Zac swept his arm backward encompassing the sleek grey helicopter behind him. He had done all of the research and the romantic air tour of Whitehaven Beach and the Hill Inlet was one of the Top Ten Romantic Things to do on Hamilton Island'.

Phoenix leaned over slightly so she could look past him and see the helicopter, then straightened and peered up at him through her thick glasses. She had come to the air terminal at his request, but had left out the most important part of the request, which was to bring Grace along.

"She's gone until tomorrow, Zac," Phoenix said simply.

He threw his hands into the air. "Where could she

possibly go? It's a tiny little island! Can't you get her and bring her here?"

Phoenix pursed her lips together at his show of emotion and answered calmly, "She wanted some privacy on her days off."

"Privacy?"

She nodded.

"Privacy?" he asked again. The word wasn't sinking in.

Phoenix, unchanged by his confused disbelief, nodded again. Then, perhaps because he seemed undone by this information, she added, "She's been pretty tired lately. I think she just needed a break from everything."

If Zac had readied a crestfallen lover expression, he would have used it, but the sudden jolt of rejection left him momentarily without words. Without a planned response.

"I thought…" he started to tell Phoenix that he thought he and Grace were at least close enough for him to plan an impromptu romantic excursion, but then thought better of it. He wasn't sure Phoenix approved of his romancing Grace, not the way Rigby approved.

"You were going to take her on a helicopter ride?" Phoenix guessed the obvious.

"Yeah, I thought she would like it."

Phoenix paused, thinking. She leaned around him again to look at the helicopter then asked, "Did you clear this with Rigby or anybody else?"

Zac didn't understand. "Clear it?"

"With the insurance. With Syd. With the company."

Zac still didn't get it. He just gave her a mute look.

Phoenix sighed, the burden of having to explain tightening her lips even more. "You can't take Grace Woods flying through the air without clearing it with our insurance at least. Let alone Syd. If something were to happen to her…" she paused and locked her eyes with his, "If something were to happen to either of you, it would be a catastrophic loss to this production."

Zac raised his eyebrows. "Oh, right." He glanced back at the helicopter, its blades beginning to turn as the pilot prepped for the trip. He hadn't thought about that. He hadn't thought about anything except how to make the biggest impression possible on Grace.

"Maybe it's best that she couldn't make it this morning. So she wouldn't have to be disappointed," Phoenix said, trying to fix the whole mess with logic.

His initial irritation and subsequent let down fell away as a new feeling rose from the center of his being. He, Zac Foster, was considered as essential to the production of Heart of Mine as Grace Woods, mega-movie star. If he died in a helicopter crash it would be considered a catastrophic loss. His star meter had raised to a new level.

A smile he could not contain spread across his face and he wanted to plant a celebratory kiss right on Phoenix's tense little mouth for bringing this to his attention.

She blinked up at him. "You're good now?"

A woman from the helicopter rental company approached and asked, "Are you and your guest ready to go, Mr. Foster?"

The look on Phoenix's face was priceless. Surprise, alarm, and dismay mixed together as her cheeks pinked. She was flustered. Zac grinned.

Feeling cocky at his newly realized stardom and at Phoenix's guard dropping, Zac offered his arm to her and said, "Shall we, babe?"

Eyes wide, she shook her head. "Me? No, we can't."

"You're not afraid, are you sweetheart?"

Phoenix narrowed her eyes. "It's not a matter of being afraid, Zac."

The way she said his name reminded him of his first girlfriend in elementary school and he was encouraged. He kept his eyes, which he knew could weaken the resolve of most women, set on hers and let them do their work.

Finally, behind the thick glasses and the producer resolve, Zac saw a flicker of interest.

"C'mon…babe," he winked at her and her cheeks pinked again. "It'll be fun and," he leaned in closer to her, whispering, "I won't tell if you won't tell."

A tiny smile cracked her stern facade and she glanced around like she was checking to see if anyone would stop them. Nobody but the airport personnel were nearby.

Without saying a word, Phoenix slipped her slender hand into the crook of his arm. Zac thrilled at her touch, which confused him for a moment, but only a moment. Knowing they were bucking the system and taking a risk together would make walking arm and arm with anyone more exciting. There was nothing to see here except a big time movie star and his producer breaking the rules.

The chopper's blades were whirling, creating a strong wind current. He dismissed any possible attraction to Phoenix, putting it down to the forbidden adventure they were about to have together. Zac put his hand over hers so he knew she was hanging on tight and they ducked down together, making a run for the helicopter and their impromptu grand romantic air tour.

CHAPTER 34

$\mathcal{L}$incoln had not led a sheltered life. Though most of his formative years were spent mainly on an island, he had seen his fair share of celebrity types, politicians, and mega-rich come and go. He knew how to sail a boat, fly a plane, deep sea fish, and was a certified scuba instructor. He had helped run his Grandad's business, made a lot of good friends, and fallen in and out of love a few times, too. The point being, he wasn't naive—he had seen a few things.

One thing he had never seen, nor expected to see, however, was a world famous movie star painting his kitchen in her pajamas.

After refusing his offer of a change of clothes since those she had on were already stained, Grace got busy painting the kitchen side of the great room.

She seemed to be enjoying herself, surprisingly. And she wasn't half bad at it either, once he showed her how to tape off the cabinets and the best way to get solid coverage with the roller. After that she went to work. He even had to force her to stop and eat something for lunch.

"Come on, you've got to take a break," he insisted, holding up a plate with a chicken sandwich on it as bait.

"Okay, I'm almost done with this corner. I'll be down in one minute."

She was working at the top of a 12-foot ladder, carefully painting the corner where the two walls and ceiling met. When she was satisfied that everything was perfect she joined him for lunch on the deck.

"Thank you!" she said with delight at the sight of the sandwich.

"No, thank you," Lincoln answered, and he meant it. She had made quick work of painting the kitchen and having her around had sparked his energy. The stain job was complete everywhere except the kitchen floor, which he would do next. "The work's gone faster with you here."

She smiled at him before taking a big bite of her sandwich. Lincoln thought he might not be able to eat his, the sight of her sent flurries of excitement through his stomach and his appetite was quickly disappearing.

Her hair was pulled roughly back into a ponytail and pieces of it had come loose, falling sensually around her face and neck. A few flecks of the off-white paint had joined his wood stain handprints on her tank top and a few had ended up on the smooth skin of her shoulders and arms. She had washed her hands before eating so most of that paint was gone, but there was one small, adorable smear of paint on the side of her nose where she must have touched her hand to her face without thinking.

He tried to think of the last time he had been as attracted to someone as he was to Grace. Nothing came to mind.

"You were a great teacher," she said. "Painting's kind of fun. Relaxing, you know?"

He nodded. He did know.

"And the background music is nice," she added with a grin.

His Grandad's old radio still picked up stations and Lincoln had tuned it to an oldies station while they worked. When 'Livin' La Vida Loca' had come on, Grace had danced as she painted.

"That's an oldie?!" she had asked incredulously.

"I guess so," he answered with a laugh.

"Where has the time gone? Oldies songs are Elvis and the Four Seasons, not Ricky Martin," she said.

"Doesn't he have a couple of kids?" Lincoln asked.

Grace moaned. "Four. He has four kids."

"Oh, wow," Lincoln chuckled.

Later, when they had moved on to another topic of conversation, 'Oops I Did It Again' came on. It took a few moments for the song to register with both of them, then they each paused and turned to each other in disbelief.

"Britney Spears is an oldie song?!" Grace had exclaimed.

Lincoln shook his head slowly in mock resignation. "You can't argue with the oldies station. They have final word on such matters."

Lincoln smiled and took a bite of his sandwich at the memory as he watched Grace eat heartily. The radio was still playing and he recognized Pink's voice. He chuckled and looked at Grace for her reaction, but her eyes were wide and focused on something just behind his shoulder. Lincoln turned to see Fred already on the railing and Ginger landing next to him.

"They're back," Grace whispered, not taking her eyes off the birds.

Lincoln laughed, which triggered a coughing fit caused by the remaining crumbs in his mouth. Grace looked at him quickly, noting that he might be choking, but kept flicking her gaze back and forth between him and the cockatoos, not sure which emergency needed her attention the most.

He tried to wave away her concerns about the birds and him, knowing that he wasn't exactly choking, just unable to control his laughter, but she didn't know that. She also didn't know that Fred and Ginger were relatively harmless, they just weren't acquainted with her yet.

Lincoln finally swallowed then sucked in a breath and tried to speak, but to no avail. His coughing fit was not over yet. Meanwhile, Fred hopped off the railing onto the deck and waddled towards them.

"It's coming over!" Grace squealed in a whisper, pushing away from the table with both hands and watching with growing alarm as Ginger flapped down to join Fred on the ground.

Unable to reassure her through his coughing, Lincoln pulled a few pieces of crust off of his sandwich and tossed them across the deck. The cockatoos waddled after them, giving him a few precious moments to recover.

Finally, he managed to choke out, "They won't hurt you."

Grace, still poised to jump up and run, gave him a pinched look and asked, "Are you all right?"

"I'm fine." He took a drink of water to prove it then tossed more bread to the birds. "They just want a bite." Her eyes widened even more. "Of bread. They want a bite of bread." He tossed them some more of his sandwich and the cocka-toos raced after it, their black leathery feet making scratching sounds on the deck floor.

"Oh, right," she settled cautiously into her chair again.

"They'll make friends with you if you give them some-thing," he suggested.

Grace broke off some of her crust and tossed it to the birds who rushed and snapped it up unceremoniously. "Oh!"

she chirped out the sound in surprise then giggled and tossed another piece to them.

Lincoln watched.

As he watched his heart warmed and the warmth moved through his chest and stomach, then down his arms and legs, until his whole body tingled with longing. Not simply a desire for the beautiful woman lunching with him on the deck, but a deep longing for the pleasant camaraderie they had shared all morning. He wanted more of that, more of her.

Lincoln cleared his throat and tried to think of something benign to say, something that would get his thoughts back on track. "You made fast work of that kitchen."

Grace turned her attention from the cockatoos back to him. When those green eyes locked onto his Lincoln's mind went blank for a second and he couldn't remember what he had just said.

Pleased at his compliment, she smiled. "What else do you need me to do?"

Abruptly, as if a rock had fallen from the sky and hit him on the head, Lincoln saw how he had been acting the idiot. A true moron. He had asked her to paint his kitchen. Paint his kitchen!? What a great way to impress a woman, especially a woman like Grace.

"I can't ask you to do anything else," he said.

She sank gloomily into her chair. "So I have to go?"

"No, no, that's not what I meant."

He wanted to explain, but he couldn't tell her what he was feeling. How creepy would it be for him to confess how he got lost in her eyes, how she filled him with longing, how sometimes when he looked at her he didn't see a movie star, but a woman he was falling for–falling hard.

Maybe he couldn't speak what was in his heart, but he could at least not ask her to retile the bathroom or whatever other nonsense might pop out of his mouth. Panic pumped through him. He knew he didn't want her to leave.

"How about you take a break? Chill out. While I finish the floor." The panic subsided. That hadn't sounded too needy.

"Chill out?" She paused, soaking in the suggestion, then she glanced down at her paint splotched pajamas and admitted, "I could use a bath."

"That sounds good. Go relax and take a bath and I'll be done before you know it."

Her mood brightened and she added, "I'll take care of dinner, too. Since you've been working and cooking all day."

"We won't be able to use the kitchen until the stain is dry," Lincoln hated to burst her bubble, but it was the truth of their situation.

"No worries," she smiled brightly at him as she used the slang. "I can have something delivered."

"Sounds good." It sounded very good. In fact, it sounded positively domestic.

CHAPTER 35

Grace stared at her reflection in the bathroom mirror. Spread out on the vanity in front of her were a plethora of skincare products and makeup. Every one of them promised to hide any and all imperfections and enhance her best qualities.

Hair still wet from her long soaking bath, Grace could not bring herself to start her skincare regimen, let alone blow dry her hair. She couldn't concentrate. All of her thoughts were wrapped up in the other room with Lincoln.

The bath had been exactly what she needed. Her arms, shoulders, and back ached from all of the painting. Sinking into the steaming water had been just as satisfying as some of the more expensive spa treatments she had ever experienced, if in slightly more humble surroundings.

No candles, no aromatherapy of any kind, no fizzing bath salts, no pre-warmed towels, no attendant nearby to bring her whatever her heart desired, yet she had managed to have a wonderful bath.

"Who knew?" Grace asked her reflection, chuckling lightly at her own joke.

Of course, part of her wonderful bath had been the knowledge that Lincoln was nearby. Sunk down to her neck in the warm water she had traced her fingers across the surface, watching the ripples and thinking about him. Thinking about the way he moved, the way he smiled, his incredible laugh. Her senses were overwhelmed knowing he was just on the other side of the wall and she would see him again as soon as she was dressed.

Humming softly, she sifted through the lotions, creams, and makeup options on the vanity. She lifted her eyes to her reflection and considered the face looking back at her. Freshly washed, glowing from the exercise of the morning and, perhaps, the time spent with Lincoln, she found that she didn't feel like slathering gloop onto her face. Somehow it didn't seem right.

"I still have to order dinner," she reminded her reflection.

A sparkle of pleasure fluttered through her heart. She didn't normally have to take care of those types of mundane tasks, but she liked the idea of ordering dinner for Lincoln. It felt intimate.

Suddenly in a hurry to finish up and call the hotel, Grace combed her wet hair carefully, lifting it up and back into a bun. Her hair had always been straight as an arrow, but fairly thick. Letting it dry in a bun would give it volume. That was a little trick she had learned on location when she was younger and still making low budget films.

Grace found a light moisturizer, some translucent powder and her favorite mascara then put all of the other toiletries back in her bag. She wondered if Lincoln had any candles in the house that they could light during dinner. Her natural look would go over better in candlelight.

"I'll have the hotel send some," she said to the mirror and made a mental note to do so.

A soft knock on the door startled her, then sent a brand

new rush of sparkles through her body when she heard Lincoln's voice on the other side.

"Do you need anything?" he asked.

Grace, wrapped in one of his navy blue towels and nothing else, put her hand on the doorknob. Did she dare?

"I don't mean to interrupt," he continued.

"It's fine," Grace answered hurriedly, her hand trembling slightly against the cool knob. Her heart thudded against her chest as she wondered what would happen if she opened the door...or if he decided to open it from his side. Swallowing hard, Grace managed to say, "I don't need anything, thank you."

"Okay, I'm all done in the kitchen. I'm gonna wash up in the other bathroom if you're all good."

"Yes..." Her voice came out as more of a croaked whisper, so she said it again louder, "Yes, okay, I'm all good."

For a long moment Grace stood at the door. Her heart kept pounding, her hand on the doorknob. She thought she heard him move away, back down the hallway to the second bathroom, but she couldn't be sure. She imagined him on the other side of the door, his hand on the doorknob, his heart pounding in his chest.

Grace leaned her forehead against the door and closed her eyes. She felt a little dizzy, a little disoriented, just like the first time she had seen Lincoln and he ran past her on the dock, sending her heart spinning.

She took in a slow breath, trying to steady herself, trying to wrap her mind around what was happening. The feeling was familiar, falling in love. But the intensity of what was happening with Lincoln was like nothing else she had ever known...especially considering their short acquaintance.

"Get a grip, Grace," she whispered. "You're just a little light headed. You're not falling in love."

Before she could spend any more time overthinking

things, she threw on the little makeup she planned on wearing, cracked open the bathroom door to make sure the coast was clear, and hurried to her bedroom to get dressed and order dinner.

***

THE HOTEL SENT CANDLES. The hotel sent gourmet food. The hotel sent everything they needed for a perfect meal, because that's what Grace ordered.

"We need china, stemware, wine…oh, a wine opener," Grace had told the concierge on the other end of the phone.

"I understand, Ms. Woods, everything for a wonderful evening."

"Yes, everything."

Two men, one short and one tall, driving two buggies packed to the gills with pre-cooked food, candles, candlesticks, several bottles of wine, a complimentary bottle of champagne, bags of ice, she hadn't even thought about needing extra ice, all arrived as she and Lincoln were admiring their work in the great room.

As Lincoln greeted them to have them take their dinner around the house instead of through the great room on the newly stained floors, both of the men gave him an odd look. Lincoln ignored them and ushered them around the corner.

From her position at the open front door, she overheard the tall one ask,"Ay, Link, hungry for some posh grub?"

All three of the men disappeared from her view. There was the sound of the tall and short staffers laughing raucously then Lincoln said something she couldn't quite make out and they went silent.

She hadn't thought about him knowing the staff at the

hotel. Maybe she shouldn't have gone so overboard on the dinner. Grace bit her bottom lip, a knot of anxiety twisting in her stomach. She decided to stay near the front door instead of following them to the deck to make suggestions on where to set up the candlesticks.

She didn't have too long to be anxious. Within ten minutes the two hotel staffers tromped back around the corner carrying empty bags and keeping their eyes averted to the ground in front of them.

"Thank you," she said cordially as they passed.

"Enjoy your evening, Ms. Woods," the short man said and they were gone.

Nerves still fluttering in her stomach, Grace stepped out into the darkening jungle that surrounded the house and made her way around to the back deck. She wondered what kind of rumors were already starting about her staying up here with Lincoln, and she wondered how far they would spread. She should probably let Rigby know that he may have some public relations to work out, especially if he was trying to pitch her and Zac as an item.

"Ugh," she whispered under her breath. She hated this part of celebrity. This carefully curated information feed to the public. For decades she had gone along with whatever her producers and marketing departments thought would be best for the films, but she was growing weary of the whole mess.

As Grace stepped around the back of the house, the glow of candlelight greeted her and she forgot all about any gossip that might be swirling over her and Lincoln.

"Good evening," Lincoln came down the short set of stairs leading up to the deck and offered her his hand.

Grace stood dumbfounded for a few moments, taking in the sight.

He was showered and shaved, that much she had seen

already, along with the white slacks and deep salmon shirt he wore that contrasted those brilliant blue eyes. The surprise was that he had slipped on a tan linen jacket since guiding the hotel staff to the deck, and it added a level of finery to their evening meal. Grace wore a simple turquoise sundress with silver jewelry and white sandals. She hadn't been planning on going out during her stay so she had kept her wardrobe simple.

The other surprise was that the stairway and deck above had been transformed with garlands of white flowers and candles. There might have been over a hundred candles in all.

"What–?" she started to ask, but Lincoln took her hand in his before she could finish and led her up the stairs.

The sun was setting on the island, filling the sky with deep pinks and reds. White flowers and thick white candles flickering in the perpetual ocean breeze were on every single flat surface available on the deck. White linens with white china, shimmering crystal glasses, and gleaming silver utensils covered the simple table they had eaten chicken sandwiches on earlier in the day. In the center of the table were silver domes covering several dishes.

"It's something else, isn't it?" Lincoln said proudly.

"It is…and the view…" Grace's attention was drawn to the amazing sunset.

"This old place has never seen such a spread, that's for sure. My Grandad would have loved it."

She heard the hint of sadness in his voice and turned to him, looking up into his eyes and wishing she could take away the pain of his loss. "That's so sweet," was all she could think to say.

Lincoln ducked his head, bashful all of the sudden. Then he seemed to see her for the first time. He allowed his eyes to wander up her body, taking in her dress and the silver necklace resting on her collarbones, and her hair, thick and wavy after drying in its bun.

He sucked in his breath and said quietly, "You look beautiful."

Undone by his attention and the compliment she tried to giggle coyly, but it came out more like a choked laugh. Lincoln didn't look away at her embarrassment, he simply smiled.

"Don't you think we should dig in...before Fred and Ginger show up?" she asked.

Lincoln laughed. "That's a good point. But I thought we could have a dance before we eat...if that's okay with you?"

It was her turn to blush. She nodded, then looked around, wondering if there was a violinist or something hiding in the corner.

"Great," Lincoln stepped away and bent down to retrieve something off the floor next to the table. "I've got the music," he declared happily, lifting his Grandad's radio up so she could see.

Grace clapped her hands, applauding his idea. "The oldies?"

"What else?" Lincoln said, turning up the sound. "Saturday is Elvis night!"

The funky drumbeat of 'A Little Less Conversation' filled the air and Grace laughed in delight as Lincoln grabbed her hand and pulled her to the center of the deck to dance.

CHAPTER 36

Faye was almost as excited to hear about Grace's romantic getaway dinner than she might have been to have one of her own. She called Presley almost immediately to share the news.

"I'm absolutely thrilled for her, darling," Faye cooed into the phone.

"He is certainly a good looking guy," Presley said agreeably.

"He's quite charming in real life, too," Faye reassured her.

"Hmm," Presley seemed distracted.

"What?"

"I'm just surprised all the gossip outlets got it right, that's all."

"Is it in the news?" Faye hadn't been paying attention to the press since on the island, she had been focusing on getting her friend Grace into a wonderful romantic relationship. Priorities.

"I just saw a piece on the entertainment section about them. It seems they let something slip about their romance during a live interview."

"That was fast," Faye was rather impressed at the intense interest the public had in Grace.

"Well, that's Hollywood I guess," Presley said.

"So when will you and your little bun in the oven be joining us here?" Faye asked, then added, "And Hobie, of course."

"I have a few things to wrap up here first."

Faye sighed. She had grown a little bored with all of the sand and water, and since Grace and Zac were happily romancing at some private estate on the island she wouldn't have anything fun to think about except Grace's surprise birthday party.

"When will that be?"

"Not for at least a few weeks," Presley said firmly.

"But what about the party?" Faye pouted, though she knew pouting didn't work on Presley. The woman was basically a workaholic even though she was expecting.

"That's the best I can do, Faye. Ronnie said she might come earlier. She needs a beach break."

"So do you. You're going to work so hard while you're pregnant that your baby is going to pop out a tiny little uptight businesswoman–or man!"

Presley laughed, "I doubt that." There was a pause then Presley added, "You're not going to get too nosy with Grace and Zac are you?"

Faye gasped at the suggestion. "I"m offended."

"You know how you can get, Faye," Presley warned.

"I most certainly do not know how I can get. I'm merely helping their romance along, that's all. The whole dinner went on without me."

"Okay…" Presley didn't sound convinced.

"Grace doesn't even know that I know. I found out from the concierge when they billed the beach house."

"Oh…and you know for sure she's with Zac?"

"Who else would she be with?" Faye sighed the frustrated sigh of a person who was paying attention when everyone else was daydreaming. "Zac called the beach house looking for her early this morning and I told him to contact Phoenix. That girl keeps track of everything. When I was talking to him he said he had a big surprise planned for Grace...and now we know what the plan was!"

Satisfied with her answer, Presley stopped grilling Faye about intruding on Grace's love life and they topped off some plans for the big surprise birthday party.

"How big is the venue?" Presley asked.

"It's a private home, that's all I know right now. What I really want to talk about is what do you think Grace should wear?"

Presley paused then asked, "Don't you think Grace can dress herself?"

Honestly, Faye wasn't so sure. Since starting filming Grace had been so flaky about things like that.

"The other morning she woke me up at an ungodly hour to help her pick out a boating outfit. I think it would be nice if we removed that stress...it will be a lovely part of the surprise."

"All right..."

"Besides she has costume people right here who know her measurements. I'll ask Phoenix who's the best."

"They are probably busy doing costumes for the movie."

Faye waved her hand in the air, shooing away Presley's negativity like it was a pesky mosquito. "Don't worry about that. What we need to decide is what the design of the whole evening will be."

Silence on the other end.

Faye sighed again. "Or I'll talk to Ronnie about it?"

"That might be best," Presley agreed.

They finished their conversation by agreeing to rope Ronnie in on Grace's dress design.

Once off the phone Faye strolled to the edge of her infinity pool and looked out over the beach and ocean beyond. She took in a deep breath and exhaled, dropping her head back and looking into the blue, blue sky.

"I'm soooo bored!" she groaned to the sky.

The success of her matchmaking between Grace and Zac left a void in the pit of her stomach. A void that could normally be filled by parties or shopping, but none of those things were readily available on this tiny island. There were mostly tourist shops here. Some luxury and art shops, but nothing that interested her.

"I certainly don't want a sea turtle beach towel," she muttered.

If only Grace would come home and tell her about her wonderful date, but if that happened the date wouldn't be going very well. Faye would need to be patient.

She groaned again. She hated being patient.

Reaching out to Ronnie would also have to wait, Presley had insisted that she be the one to contact her sister first. The only thing remaining was to reach out to Phoenix again.

"Phoenix," Faye said her name thoughtfully as she moved from one edge of the infinity pool to the other, pacing of a sort, in an extremely relaxed and graceful manner. She tapped her fingernails on one hand against her fingernails on the other as she thought about Phoenix and her drab appearance.

Within just a few minutes of considering how many ways Phoenix's look could be improved, Faye was invigorated again. A fresh burst of energy and interest filled the void in her stomach. She had made a decision. Until Grace and Zac needed her involvement again, she would zero in on Phoenix's much needed makeover.

CHAPTER 37

*L*incoln could not go to sleep. He was overheated, uncomfortable, and preoccupied. The stars blinking above him could not soothe his mind and the cool night breeze did nothing to bring his temperature down. This was an internal thing.

It was late–nearly two in the morning–and Grace had just gone to bed–in his bed.

Being a gentleman, he hadn't even tried to press anything more and had opted to camp out on the hammock again, thinking that if he put as much distance between them as possible he would be able to get some sleep.

He had thought wrong.

He cursed as he flipped over one more time in the hammock and almost spilled out onto the deck. Growling in frustration, he pressed the base of his palms against his forehead.

The woman would not get out of his head. The way she talked, the way she laughed, the way she danced. A pang of yearning shot through him and he sucked in his breath, holding it and counting to ten, hoping that would help him forget.

It didn't.

How could he forget holding Grace in his arms? How could he dismiss how soft and light she was, how her smile dazzled him, how perfectly she fit against him as they swayed to the music?

He couldn't.

"No, no, no, no..." he told himself harshly. Obsessing would do him no good. Nothing would. The yearning twisted around inside of him, emptying him of everything except loneliness. He hadn't realized how lonely a man could be until he watched the door to his own bedroom close with Grace on the other side. She was so near and still completely unreachable. Untouchable.

He needed a drink.

Lincoln untangled from the hammock and made his way past the remains of their dinner. Melted candles, wilting flowers, crumpled napkins, all of it lost its magical sheen without her there. He felt like the last guest at a wedding when everybody had gone home and the lights were turned off. Left with nothing but his own company and a big mess to clean up.

His mates from the hotel would be back in the morning to take everything back. He had moved the leftover food and dirty dishes inside after Grace went to bed to keep unwanted critters from showing up during the night. He passed the mostly empty silver dishes of grilled prawn with mango chutney, bitter greens salad, and one half empty bottle of leftover wine, and went straight to the liquor cabinet. He needed something stronger to wipe his brain clean for the night.

With a glass of straight whiskey in his hand, wearing only his pajama bottoms, Lincoln stood at the living room window. As he looked out into the night their dinner date ran through his head.

He felt safe calling it a date. Even considering the strange circumstances that had put them together, the evening had turned into a date.

He grunted and took a sip of whiskey, letting it burn the back of his throat as it went down.

"Maybe it wasn't," he wondered out loud.

Grace was a movie star, immensely wealthy, used to all of the finer things in life, and used to the glamour of Hollywood, maybe their dinner had simply been an average Saturday night to her.

He took another drink of whiskey. Clicking through the events of the evening in his mind he couldn't pin one moment down where Grace had said or done anything to him that was an open invitation. Being beautiful and sexy didn't automatically mean she found him attractive. Or even if she did, it didn't automatically mean that she wanted a relationship with him.

He looked down the hallway where he knew she was sleeping in his bed.

What had she said when he walked her to the door? "Thank you, I had a lovely time."

And how had he responded? "Me too."

Me too?

Lincoln dropped his chin towards his chest and shook his head, "You're an idiot, Link."

Alone in the night staring out at the stars shining down on the jungle and ocean beyond Lincoln could think of hundreds of things to say that would have better expressed his feelings.

'You're an amazing woman.'

'I've never had this much fun, this much to talk about, this much to dream about, with anyone else.'

'I can't believe you appeared like this in my life. It feels like destiny.'

Any of these would have been better than 'Me too'. But there was no going back. That's what he had said and then she had smiled softly and closed the door in his face. He shook his head again with a wry laugh and dropped his gaze to the amber liquid in his hand.

"Bottoms up, you mug," he said under his breath and swallowed the rest of the whiskey in one gulp.

The next morning his head ached, almost as much as his heart. Watching Grace follow the hotel driver carrying her suitcase to the buggy that had come to pick her up was excruciating. He didn't know what to say and knowing that he wasn't good at speaking his heart, Lincoln stayed quiet.

Grace was quiet, too, which was even more disheartening. From the moment she emerged from his bedroom she seemed far away.

At one point she seemed to want to apologize for leaving. "I have to get back. Shooting starts up tomorrow and I have a lot to do."

"Of course, the show must go on," he replied, trying to make a joke but somehow his words had a bite to them and she looked down at the floor after he spoke.

In the end, he let her go without saying much more than formal pleasantries, not so much as a handshake, and was left, once again, on his own.

Emptiness roiled into irritation in his gut as Lincoln dove back into his construction project.

First on the agenda was removing all remnants of Grace painting the kitchen. He wasn't crazy about the fact that every time he looked at the crisp newly painted walls he would be reminded of her on the ladder laughing down at him. However, he could clean up the paint cans and drop cloth and put the ladder away, and at least try to forget.

By mid-morning every bit of leftover mess from the painting and staining was out of sight, leaving the room in a nearly complete state–minus the new light fixtures he hadn't hung and the new hardware on the kitchen cupboards. Still, it looked nice. Lincoln wished he could enjoy it.

For a long moment he stood in his Grandad's great room, the bulk of its facelift complete, and thought about all the years after his grandmother passed. The grief in his Grandad's piercing blue eyes, exasperated when he was liquored up, Lincoln always knew when he'd been drinking hard. As the oldest he had tried to shield Luke from it, but Grandad's pain lashed out at both of them when it was fueled with whiskey

Lincoln knew the feeling, both the urge to use the blinding heat of whiskey to dull his pain and the uncontrollable anger that sometimes erupted afterward. He'd told himself a long time ago that he would never follow in his Grandad's footsteps…not those footsteps anyway.

Lincoln moved to the liquor cabinet that he'd opened the night before, took out the partly full bottle of whiskey, and dumped it unceremoniously down the drain. He didn't need the stuff calling to him when he was down in the dumps about Grace. May as well get rid of it while he was still thinking straight.

"That's no way to treat fine whiskey," Luke's voice chimed in from behind him.

Lincoln didn't turn around as the last of the liquor glugged out of the bottle and into the sink. "What are you doing here?"

"Oh, I don't know," Luke scanned the room, looking for signs of his surprise house guest no doubt. "Just wondering how my big brother's doing."

"A head's up would have been nice," Lincoln said. He grabbed the only other bottle of liquor in the cabinet, an unopened fifth of vodka, twisted the top off and poured it down the drain.

"A head's up?" Luke tried to look innocent, but unable to conceal his curiosity any longer her leaned towards Lincoln and whispered, "Is she here?"

Lincoln shot a look at his brother. "No, she's not here. Not anymore."

The vodka empty, Lincoln tossed it into the trash with the whiskey bottle and the other remains of last night's dinner and bundled the bag up to take outside.

"So it all worked out? She stayed?" Luke followed Lincoln outside to the trash can.

"No, it didn't work out," Lincoln threw the bag roughly into the can, slammed the lid back down, and turned to face Luke. "What were you thinking? You don't have any right to rent this place out."

Luke raised his palms in front of him, signaling Lincoln to back off. "Hey, I've got a part ownership of this house. Just like you have a share of the boat. We're partners."

"Partners? Partners in what?"

Luke grinned. "Now that Grace Woods has stayed here we could turn this into a high level rental."

Lincoln stared at Luke, unable to process his inane plans. He scowled and stalked back into the house, Luke on his heels.

"She liked it, didn't she?" Luke glanced around at the newly painted kitchen and stained wood floors. "I mean, you've got the place looking really good, Link."

Lincoln turned on him, all of his frustration boiling over, "I was in the middle of staining the floor when she wandered out of my bedroom, Luke. She didn't know I was here. I didn't know she was here. The whole place was a total mess." He could see Luke didn't understand the seriousness of the situation. "She could have called the authorities, told them I was an intruder!"

"Did she?" Luke was almost worried, but not really.

"No," Lincoln admitted.

"What did she do?"

Lincoln looked down at his feet, not wanting to give Luke any credit for anything. He sighed. "She painted the kitchen for me."

Surprise then amusement registered on Luke's face while the words sank in, then he let out a belly laugh, "What?"

"She wanted to help so I let her paint the kitchen," Lincoln tried to downplay the odd situation with a dismissive wave.

"Grace Woods painted Grandad's kitchen?" Luke was still laughing. "What else did she do?"

Lincoln looked out the window at the deck. "Then she bought me dinner."

Luke's eyes widened and he slapped his knee, bending over laughing.

"I'm glad you think this is funny," Lincoln scolded him, but he was beginning to see the situation from an outside view and had to admit, it was kind of funny.

Luke wiped tears of laughter from his eyes and said, "You should be thanking me."

Lincoln grunted.

"Come on, you can't stay mad at me for getting Grace Woods to buy you dinner," Luke chuckled.

Lincoln grunted again, then said, "You can't just send someone to the house without any warning, Luke."

"I did warn you! I texted and called all day…answer your phone why don't you?"

Lincoln thought of his phone in the kitchen drawer. It was probably dead by now. He rubbed his face with his hands, ready to move on from this strange weekend.

"All right, but I don't want this to be a regular thing," Lincoln stated. Luke looked down at the floor and shuffled his feet. Lincoln shot him a look. "What did you do?

"They called and wanted to book the place again. For the next three weekends."

Lincoln groaned.

"What was I supposed to do? Turn down the money?"

"Who's renting it?"

"Grace Woods. It was her producer that set it up."

Lincoln hadn't expected that answer. His stomach clenched at the thought. "Grace is coming here again?"

Luke nodded, then a smile slowly emerged and he winked. "Maybe she'll buy you dinner again." Laughing, he added, "Or maybe you could have her paint the bathroom!"

Lincoln ignored him, a new thought coming to him. He knew his brother could be a relentless salesman and he didn't want him harassing Grace. "I'll make sure everything here is fine for her. But you stay out of it."

Luke pretended to be hurt. "What would I do that's so terrible?"

"Oh, I don't know, you'll do almost anything for a buck."

Luke shrugged, but didn't argue.

Lincoln narrowed his eyes and asked, "What else did you try to sell her when you had her alone on the boat?"

"Nothing, I swear."

"I don't believe you."

"No, really, I didn't. Only this rental and only because she said she needed to get away from all the stress and everything."

Lincoln watched for a crack in Luke's exterior, something that showed he was covering something up. Nothing came. In fact, Luke's face softened slightly as he thought back to being on the boat with Grace.

Finally, Luke shrugged and said, "It didn't seem right to try to sell her on anything."

Lincoln was surprised at his little brother's answer. "Why?"

Luke considered the question for a moment before answering, "I don't know. She seemed kind of lonely."

CHAPTER 38

From her seat on the high backed makeup chair, Grace could see every nuance of the transition her hair and makeup team were conducting. She had rolled out of bed at 4:00am and settled into the chair just forty minutes later in order to give them enough time to work their magic. And magic it was.

Bags under her eyes from lack of sleep…gone. Oily, limp hair that she had not washed yesterday and slept on all night…gone. Broken soul of a woman who felt like she had abandoned something beautiful over the weekend…that part was still there.

"How's it going in here?" Max stuck his head into the trailer. "It's 6:45."

"We'll need another hour for the wig and her dress," Anne Marie, her hairstylist and wig master extraordinaire answered.

"Got it," Max replied and was gone.

Today they were filming the elite party scene, the part of the movie where Scarlet and Ethan experience a moment away from the drama surrounding them when they get unexpectedly invited to a chic party. They drink champagne, eat fine food, and dance the night away until they share an intimate moment staring into each other's eyes. Then, because of their character's emotional walls, they both back off.

Sounded eerily familiar.

Grace looked down at the script in her lap. She'd been reviewing her lines as the team worked on her appearance. She wished she had had a script over the weekend. Screenwriters came up with some of the best lines. It would have been magical to have their words on her lips when she and Lincoln danced and had that wonderful dinner on his deck. Just magical.

Left to her own communication skills, however, Grace had found herself more and more tongue-tied as the night wore on. As her attraction to Lincoln increased, her ability to make conversation had decreased. By the time he had walked her to her room–his room in reality–she couldn't think of one sexy, charming or witty thing to say.

She had been a real dud.

It was no wonder he retreated and bid her a welcome goodbye in the morning.

"Are you ready to be the life of the party?" Anne Marie asked as she carried the styrofoam head holding Grace's, or rather Scarlet's, ultra-chic and elaborately done hairdo.

"If only," Grace mumbled, then she smiled sweetly and allowed the gluing and tugging process of fitting the wig to her head to begin.

Once the wig was on, Grace stood and her team removed her pink silk robe. Then she held her hands out to the side and they dressed her. By the time she was done and they turned her around to have look in the full length mirror, Grace had become Scarlet in every possible way.

"This is gorgeous," she slid her eyes towards Anne Marie and the others, afraid if she nodded in one direction or the other the wig would slip, even though she knew it was held securely in place. The wig was quite heavy and it would take her a few minutes to get used to the way it felt balancing on her head.

The look was over the top, as if her hair had lengthened by several feet and been braided and piled on top of her head then pinned with tropical flowers. The flowers were white in the center and yellow, pink, and orange on the outside, which matched her tight, shimmering dress with the plunging neckline. With the bright colors, shimmering fabric, and massive wig hairdo, Grace thought she looked like a blend between a mermaid, a popsicle, and a Jane Austen character.

"It's really going to pop," Syd's voice came from the doorway.

Grace turned slowly towards him, careful to display the full glory of the costume. "Do you like it?"

He nodded. "Wait till they light you. And you should see Zac. He's all in blues and greens. It's going to be tremendous." Syd glanced around at the team who had prepared her for the scene. "Great job, kids. Let's go, Grace."

She took his hand and allowed him to lead her down the steps of the makeup trailer. Her trailer was parked in the driveway of a tropical mansion where they were shooting the grand party scene. Various buggies and a few larger battery operated vehicles that looked more like mini-trucks were parked willy nilly along the drive. The whole cast and crew were here for this big shoot, plus about a hundred extras they had recruited as background party goers.

The buzz of excitement was palpable and when Syd led her from the driveway through the foyer and living room of the great house, Grace straightened her shoulders and held her head high. She was no longer Grace Woods, a quickly aging Hollywood actress, she was Scarlet Kensington and she was about to fall in love with the mysterious and incredibly handsome Ethan Wolfe.

With one hand firmly grasping onto Syd's hand, Grace clutched her script with the other, running her lines over and over in her head even as she nodded regally at all of the extras and the production assistants who were wrangling them. The awe and delight she saw in their eyes added to her feeling of strength and purpose.

Heart of Mine was an excellent script and it was going to be an excellent film and she was its star. There was no getting around that.

"We'll get you into position out here just to figure out the blocking then you can wait in your trailer," Syd told her.

She smiled at him. She liked when he was sensitive to her needs.

Two crew members opened the vast double doors that led onto the veranda and Syd led her through. The view was fantastic. The beach, the sky, the turquoise water beyond.

"Isn't this something?" Syd asked, noticing her reaction.

She nodded, "It's really beautiful, Syd."

"I couldn't agree more. The best view on the island, that's what it is. Nobody can step out of their house and see anything better."

Grace twitched. The image of Lincoln reaching out his hand to lead her up the stairs, the view from the candlelit deck, the Elvis music, all of it flashed through her mind. Unable to shake her head to erase the memory, because of the unsteady sensation of her wig, she blinked hard several times in a row to try and get Lincoln's face—that smile—to disappear.

"We're right over here," Syd said, indicating the mob of crew and equipment that had taken over the far end of the veranda. They would shoot the scene right on the edge over-looking the beach.

Grace's feet kept moving and she continued to smile softly at anyone and everyone who looked her way. Syd kept hold of her hand as they stepped over heavy electrical cords taped to the tile and walked through a bank of tall stands that held lights, screens, and filters.

Syd was still talking, but he had turned his head away from her and Grace couldn't quite make out what he was saying, but she didn't speak up. All of her focus remained on keeping the smile on her face. Her heavy blinking had not helped much and even as she carefully maneuvered her perfectly made up and costumed self through the set, Lincoln would not leave her mind–or her heart.

The air around her seemed warmer, probably the lights or maybe the sun was easing up into the sky and heating up the veranda. She thought about asking for some water, but just wanted to get to her mark so she could settle in and run her lines again from the top.

Her hand felt sweaty in Syd's, like it was about to slip out of his and she would be left standing alone in the sea of lights, melting into a puddle like a popsicle left out in the heat. She squeezed the script in her other hand. The paper was limp and wet.

They finally broke through the wall of lights, stands, and crew, and came upon Zac leaning against the white stone railing. For an instant, as he turned towards them in his bright blue suit, Grace had the crazy idea that he was Lincoln. She hesitated for a mili-second and watched as Lincoln's smile dissolved into Zac's and suddenly she couldn't catch her breath.

Syd sensed that she was no longer moving forward with him and turned to her, a question on his heavy brow, "You all right?"

A tiny switch deep in her stomach flipped and Grace's insides plummeted to the ground. Everything strong and proud that had been Scarlet walking to meet her lover suddenly darkened and fell down, down, down, shattering on the veranda tile.

She trembled, fragile, encased in a shell made up of a shiny popsicle colored dress, a too-tall top heavy wig, and layers upon layers of makeup. Her breath came in short gasps and she watched as Syd's expression grew even more concerned over her not regaining control of herself.

Grace dropped her script and raised her hand to her chest, feeling at once the pounding of her heart and the panic over being nothing–nothing but an aging actress who happened to have enough money to buy the starring role in her own film–nothing but a lonely woman who was too weak to tell the man she was falling for how she felt.

"Grace!" Syd called out, but his voice sounded far away. There were other voices, all shouting, but growing more and more muffled by the second. Then…nothing…only quiet, mummifying darkness.

CHAPTER 39

Zac felt like an idiot.

He had requested the clove cigarettes because he didn't smoke, but Ethan Wolfe did. They had given Zac a choice of what he would smoke and, unlike someone from Ethan Wolfe's time, Zac had a wide variety of options. From organically grown and hand rolled pure tobacco to the tobacco-free clove variety he had chosen, they all looked like cigarettes, but the clove type didn't have all of the nicotine or toxins.

What it still had, however, was smoke.

He tried another drag on the thing and even though he only took in the tiniest, most infinitesimal amount of clove smoke his lungs rejected it wholeheartedly. They seized in his chest as his throat muscles tightened, bulged out, and tried to push everything out of his lungs and mouth in a massive cough. He suppressed the fit for a few moments, the pressure made his face go hot and his eyes tear up. He pressed his lips together, which only succeeded in his cheeks puffing out like two red balloons.

Finally, he couldn't hold it in and Zac hacked out a cough.

Then another. He hacked and hacked, trying to catch his breath as he held the smoldering fake cigarette as far away from his body as he could.

Irritated, he flicked the lit cigarette over the edge of the railing to the beach below. He had spent weeks trying to get used to these stupid things. So far no luck.

"Do you need some water?" Phoenix asked. She was standing to the side, going over something on a clipboard with the assistant to the assistant director.

He waved her away, but couldn't speak from the coughing. Phoenix said something to a production assistant nearby and in the blink of an eye the guy was standing in front of Zac with a bottle of water.

"Thanks," Zac managed to squeak out between his clenched vocal cords and red, puffed out face.

"You're welcome," the guy said. He leaned over the railing where Zac had tossed the burning cigarette, zeroed in on its location, and took off, presumably to retrieve it from the pristine sand.

Zac felt a little guilty for throwing it to begin with, but forgot about that as he took several sips of the water, calming his freaking out lungs.

He looked around. Nobody except Phoenix seemed to be paying him any attention. That was good, he guessed. He wondered if his makeup would need touching up before the scene since his eyes were tearing from the coughing fit. Then he wondered how they would cut around him smoking and coughing so he didn't look like an idiot.

"You okay?" Max asked. He was eyeing Zac from his position next to the empty director's chair.

"I'm fine, not sure how I'm gonna smoke that stuff during the scene," Zac worried aloud.

"We'll take care of it," Max reassured him. "Syd and Grace will be here in a minute. We'll figure something out."

Zac nodded and took a deep, cough free, breath as he looked out over the ocean. Through his peripheral vision he could see Phoenix watching him and wondered what she was thinking. It was hard to tell with her. She had such an unemotional response to everything, especially since their secret helicopter ride. He had thought maybe she would loosen up after that, but it seemed to have made her even more uptight.

He sighed. It didn't matter. What did matter was Grace was on her way and he needed to get his head right. He glanced down at his suit. He hadn't rumpled anything while coughing. Though he still wasn't sure about the look they had put him in for this scene.

Dressed in a bright, so bright, blue suit with an emerald green shirt and white tie, he both stood out from the landscape and perfectly blended with it, like an exotic sea creature turned into a man and plopped onto a veranda to sip cosmopolitans, smoke cigarettes, and make love to fancy ladies.

A low murmur moved through the crew and Zac looked up. He knew that murmur. It was the sound that happened whenever Grace entered a space. The sound of fame.

"Look cool," he said under his breath.

After she ghosted him on Saturday, Zac had decided that his heated pursuit of Grace might be putting her off. He would need to play harder to get with someone like her, someone who was used to men falling all over her.

Zac turned away from her approach and looked out over the ocean view, pretending to take in the beauty of the sparkling ocean. He would wait until he had some clue Grace was almost to him before turning around and giving her a killer smile. Maybe this sea creature blue suit would give his blue eyes extra punch.

He heard Syd say, "We're right over here." Zac decided he

could start a super slow turn in her direction. He had to choose an expression from his repertoire and landed on one he called The One That Got Away. It came from his first heartthrob role where he had played an ex-boyfriend returned from the military. He had used it a lot since that role, but not on Grace. Not yet.

Zac was taken aback by the sight of her in full costume. He had seen the dress before and the bright colors were arresting, but he had never seen it combined with the wig and makeup. He was literally stunned by the sight of her and almost let The One That Got Away slip off of his face.

Grace's eyes lit up when she saw him and Zac felt a flutter in his chest. He had heard people talk about heart strings, but never experienced the sensation before. He started to move towards her, automatically drawn to her presence, when something on her face shifted.

Grace's glittering smile that greeted him abruptly dulled and dropped into a frown. All of the color washed out of her cheeks, he could see it happening even through layers of makeup, and it left her a strange, indescribable pallor. She looked like she might be about to throw up.

Zac hesitated, not wanting to get too close if that was the case.

Syd turned and said something to her, but Grace didn't respond, she kept looking at Zac in the most unnerving way.

As if in slow motion, the script she was carrying dropped to the ground. Zac watched in horror as pain flickered through her eyes and then, unbelievably, she dropped.

The faint was so undramatic, so blasé, Zac wasn't quite sure that's what had happened. The only reason he knew Grace had just passed out was that Syd, Max, and everyone else, started shouting. The whole crew erupted into action, racing to gather around Grace's colorful crumpled form.

He started forward, too. An automatic response. A

slender hand on his arm stopped him. He looked over to see Phoenix, drawn and concerned, holding him back.

"Don't, they'll need room," she said, her voice worried and tense.

"Right," Zac stayed and allowed the pressure of her hand on his arm to center him. An emergency medical team arrived and the crew parted to let them through. "Has this ever happened before?" Zac asked in side whisper.

Phoenix shook her head, obviously distraught, but steadily holding herself and him back to let the professionals do their job. "No, she's always been in perfect health," she said quietly.

Zac would agree that Grace looked in perfect health, but looks could be deceiving. Especially when age was a factor.

Phoenix moved at his side and he looked down to find her squinting into the rapidly rising sun. Her brow furrowed with concern and she tugged on his arm, moving him the long way around the lights and the team working on Grace.

"We should get you out of the sun and the heat," Phoenix said.

Glad he had her looking out for him, Zac followed obediently.

CHAPTER 40

"It was the wig glue," Faye declared with conviction for the fourth time so far during lunch.

Ronnie gave Grace a sympathetic look. When Faye latched onto an idea as the truth it often remained true to her even if was proven to be untrue by others.

Grace returned Ronnie's look with an exasperated one of her own and Ronnie decided she would intervene. Grace had been on her own with Faye for a while down under, she deserved a break.

Ronnie cleared her throat and said, "I'm sure they've got it figured out now, Faye. The doctors said it wasn't an allergic reaction to wig glue, probably low blood sugar from not eating breakfast. Nothing more to worry about."

"They had better have it figured out," Faye complained. "Imagine, sending our Grace into a fainting spell. It's unacceptable. And I'm telling you it was the wig glue."

"Why don't you tell me what else you've been up to here on the island," Ronnie tried to change the subject.

Faye widened her eyes at her, not wanting her to spill the

beans about Grace's surprise birthday party. Ronnie wasn't planning on bringing up the party, but she did think it was time to talk about something other than Grace fainting on set.

Faye decided to focus in on another one of her favorite topics, disliking Syd. "Well, Grace has been working like a maniac, you know. Syd is an absolute beast about it. Hardly giving them any time off."

Ronnie took this with a grain of salt. Faye didn't understand anything about working, let alone working on a project as large as a movie, but for someone who had little experience with such matters, she had strong opinions.

"We have time off," Grace said weakly.

Ronnie couldn't tell if Grace was still tired after her episode or just tired of Faye, but she did seem very, very tired.

"It's been no more difficult than any other film I've ever been in," Grace added.

"You do have scheduled time off, don't you?" Ronnie asked, just to make sure.

Grace looked around at the table spread with tropical salads, roast chicken, sweet rolls, and a pitcher of strawberry margaritas as proof. "I have this afternoon off."

"And I'm glad about that," Ronnie smiled.

She had flown in on the pretense of getting away for a bit and touching base with her friends. In reality she was here as an incognito support person to help Faye plan Grace's birthday and, most importantly, design the dress she would wear at the party. As luck would have it Grace happened to have the afternoon free. Apparently, they were shooting Zac's individual scenes and she wasn't needed for the rest of the day.

"Do you have any full days off?" Ronnie pressed ever so gently. She needed more information on when she could sneak off and create a gorgeous dress without raising Grace's suspicions.

"She had a few days off this last weekend," Faye answered, then added with a sigh, "Though she doesn't want to share exactly what she did."

Grace put her fork down. Ronnie noticed she hadn't eaten a bite of the food on her plate.

Faye leaned over and picked up the pitcher to pour more strawberry margarita for herself. "I think it had something to do with Zac Foster, but nobody's talking about it with me," she added a tiny pout for emphasis.

"I just had to get away from everything, that's all," Grace explained as her attention drifted out the glass wall over-looking the infinity pool.

"Sounds reasonable," Ronnie answered.

"Reasonable? There's nothing here to get away from!" Faye scoffed. "Really, Ronnie, there's only so much sand and water a person can take."

Ronnie understood. She had declared herself addicted to New York City for most of her adult life. Still, only Faye could find something to whine about while vacationing in paradise.

Grace, still staring out the window, started talking again, "It's strange. I've been thinking about this movie and making movies in general…and all of this." She waved her hand limply towards the food and drink. "Everything has gotten so easy." She turned back to her friends, her eyes meek and sad. "We have all of these experts and skilled craftsmen and the movies are so technical, you know. And so much can be done CGI or fixed in post production. It's not as challenging as it used to be for me."

Grace looked between Faye and Ronnie for a response, but they had none. Ronnie had not expected to arrive for a surprise birthday and find her life long actress friend questioning her career.

Grace shrugged and looked down at her hands in her lap. "And don't even get me started on growing older in front of the camera. I've always told myself I wouldn't fall into the plastic surgery trap…but sometimes…I don't know." She shook her head and her bottom lip quivered as she spoke. "Something's different. It's almost like it doesn't feel real anymore…does that make sense?" She looked up at her friends for an answer.

Faye thought about it for a nano-second, then said, "I suppose it's not really real because it's a movie, darling."

Ronnie was pretty sure that wasn't what Grace was aiming at. Was this a mid-life crisis? Was Grace old enough to have a mid-life crisis?

She reached out and put her hand on Grace's shoulder. "Maybe you've grown too used to making movies? Maybe you need to try doing something else for a while?"

"For heaven's sake, Grace, just take a break," Faye chimed in, raising her margarita in a toast. "You've been acting for a long time."

"A very long time," Grace mumbled, just loud enough for Ronnie to hear.

From Grace's gloomy demeanor it was clear to Ronnie that her friend may need more than a party to cheer her up.

CHAPTER 41

*E*ver since her fainting spell everybody was treating Grace like she was about to crack. Every day she was surrounded by a pack of assistants watching her every move and offering her hundreds of different fixes for whatever they perceived to be her problem.

"Water, Ms. Woods?"

"Are you too warm? Would you like an icepack?"

"Protein bar, Ms. Woods?"

"Vitamin shot?"

"Would you like to sit, Ms. Woods?"

"Are you ready to stand?"

"Are you tired, Ms. Woods? Do you think you should lay down?"

It was enough to drive someone over the edge. She finally had a moment to speak her mind during a production meeting on Thursday evening in Syd's hotel suite.

"I'm not a porcelain doll, Syd," she argued when he suggested they redo the shooting schedule to give her three days off instead of two, starting the next day.

"I know you're not," he told her, but she could see doubt in the back of his eyes. "It's just a precaution. We can work around it and maybe extend our stay here by a few days… more or less." He could see she was still incensed at the suggestion and looked at Rigby for help.

"Gracy," Rigby started. Grace narrowed her eyes at him, causing a moment's hesitation before he began, "Three days off would do you wonders. You could get more rest, make sure you're eating healthy. You could take in some of the sights."

She glared at him. "I'm here to work on the movie, not be a tourist."

"Maybe Zac could join you on some excursions," Rigby suggested, looking to Syd for encouragement.

She glared at him. "Why would that make a difference?" Rigby squirmed a little under her gaze, which just made her angrier. "That's another thing. You need to dial back this ridiculous idea you have that Zac and I are an item, or will ever be an item. Talk about stressing me out. What was that stunt you had him pull on the morning show all about?"

Rigby touched his hand to his chest as if she had just stabbed him in the heart. "I don't know what you're talking about. I think you and Zac have excellent chemistry." Again he looked to Syd for encouragement. This time the director nodded in agreement.

Grace clenched her jaw so she wouldn't scream at them. When she spoke, it was through gritted teeth, "I am not talking about on screen chemistry. That's all fine for the film. I am talking about your purposeful lies that make it seem Zac and I are a couple off screen. I want you to stop them right now and stay out of my personal life."

Rigby's smile flattened. They had worked together long enough for him to tell when she meant business.

Syd either wasn't aware she was irritated or he wasn't bothered by it. Shandra sat next to him on the loveseat, popping her gum and thumbing through her cell phone. Phoenix was the only other person in this meeting and she remained quiet.

Grace had a throbbing headache. She didn't know why she was fighting so hard about having extra time off. Hadn't she been the one questioning whether she wanted to continue her acting career? Why couldn't she just take this extra time? Maybe she could relax, think about her future... go up to the Hill House for the weekend and be with Lincoln.

The thought of him wrung her stomach into a knot. It was a good thing she had skipped breakfast or she may have thrown up right on Syd's lap. That wouldn't give much strength to her 'I'm fine, let me work' argument.

"Fine, we won't reschedule the rest of the weeks," Syd stood as he spoke, he was making the final decision for them. "But tomorrow is already done." Grace opened her mouth to argue and Syd raised his finger to stop her. "Doctor's orders."

As she was leaving, Phoenix followed her to the door and asked in a low voice, "Would you like me to book your rental one day earlier?"

Grace's heart leaped at the idea. Bless Phoenix's little mind. It was always working.

"Yes, please. That would be nice," Grace replied, trying not to sound too overly happy.

Back at the beach house Grace packed her own bag for her extended weekend. Faye had people to help, but Grace didn't want to explain her three day plans to anybody. In fact, she didn't really know what the weekend would look like so she brought a variety of clothes. Some she wouldn't mind getting paint on, some that were more casual date outfits, and one fancy nightie...just in case.

The thrill of it all overtook her thoughts, which was why she was utterly surprised to see Ronnie lounging by the infinity pool when she brought her packed bags out from her bedroom.

"Oh, Ronnie!" she exclaimed. "I forgot you would be here." Grace glanced around. "Where's Faye?"

"She's at the spa, thank goodness. If there wasn't a top notch spa on this island I think Faye would have washed her hands of it long ago." Ronnie said with a giggle.

Grace laughed a little awkwardly. She was glad she didn't have to face a thousand questions from Faye, but not sure how to explain where she was going to Ronnie–and the fact that she wanted to go alone.

"Where are you off to?" Ronnie asked, taking in the packed luggage.

"Oh, there's this little place I found…in the hills…it's very relaxing. I go there to relax."

Ronnie looked confused. "You're staying the night? Aren't you filming tomorrow?"

"No, no, I'm not. Syd rescheduled things. He wants me to take an extra day off this week…because of the whole fainting thing." Grace rolled her eyes and laughed again, even more awkwardly. "It's so silly, really."

"That sounds like a good idea, though, Grace. Maybe you need some down time."

"Thanks," Grace started towards the door, but couldn't leave it at that. She turned back around and said, "I'm sorry I'm leaving. You just getting here and all."

Ronnie dismissed her concern with a shake of her head. "Don't worry about it. You're coming back on Sunday night?" Grace nodded. "I will find something to amuse myself until then…and something to amuse Faye as well. Go enjoy yourself."

Grateful for Ronnie's laid back attitude and filled with excitement at the idea of seeing Lincoln again at the Hill House, Grace didn't even wait for a bell hop. She took her luggage and walked out the door.

CHAPTER 42

Lincoln was almost done remodeling the bathroom. The project had been top on his list after finding out Grace was returning this coming weekend and he'd made great headway. He hadn't been prepared to replace the bathtub, but he did replace the sink, vanity, mirror, and all of the fixtures. He had also retiled the whole room including the floor. All of that he'd gotten done by Thursday and the only thing left to do was paint.

On a whim, he had purchased a new comforter and sheets for his bed when he had been at the home goods supply store. The comforter set was light turquoise with a pattern of white and tan ribbons that tied into bows every now and again. He had caught a glimpse of them out of the corner of his eye when he was looking over a display of dishware. He thought maybe he should replace his random, chipped dishes since Grace would be a regular guest for at least a few more weeks.

As he ran his hand over the comforter he noticed how his callouses caught on the pillowy softness of the bedding.

"Redecoratin'?" Mindy, the store owner, old school mate

of his and well known flirt, had sidled up next to him while he was distracted.

Heat rushed up his neck and Lincoln felt like he had been caught doing something he wasn't supposed to do. He took a deeper look at the comforter as if inspecting it for flaws, then said in a serious voice, "I'm just looking. Getting the place straightened up."

"Mm-hmm," Mindy inched a little closer to him, eyeing the comforter. She traced the fabric with one finger right along the edge of his hand. "This is a little feminine for a single man." She let her finger slip and touch his pinky. Lincoln nonchalantly pulled his hand back and put it in his pocket.

"You think?"

"Yes, I would think someone like you, someone tall and masculine, might like something like this." Mindy pulled out another comforter, this one dark grey with a black and white geometric pattern down the middle.

Lincoln tried to imagine Grace Woods sleeping under that pattern. He couldn't see it and thinking about it with Mindy giving him her over the top bedroom eyes made him even more uncomfortable.

"That's nice, but I think I'll take this one," Lincoln gathered up the blue ribbon pattern with matching sheet set. "For the guest room," he added as he moved quickly to find a cashier.

The comforter and sheets were freshly laundered to get the crisp out and neatly folded on his dresser. He would change all of that tomorrow before Grace arrived in the evening.

"Right now I need a drink."

He dropped his head to his chest immediately after the words left his mouth. After working hard all week his body was sore and he was tired, but that didn't mean he needed a shot of whiskey or a beer or any other kind of alcohol.

"What you need is a long sleep, mate," he muttered to himself.

Lincoln wandered out to the hammock and started to sit down just as a breeze caught him at the right angle and he got a good whiff of the dried sweat and grime that had built up on him during the day.

"And maybe a swim," he added.

A quick trip to the nearby water hole on the property and an almost skinny dip in the cool, fresh water that bubbled up from a spring below was enough to finish him off. He had barely enough energy to throw his shorts back on, make his way back to the house, and crawl into the hammock to relax in the cool evening air. He was asleep almost before he closed his eyes.

Sleep enveloped him, wrapped around him like a dark, soft blanket as the sun dipped below the ocean beyond and the buzzing of night insects filled the surrounding jungle.

Lincoln slept calmly, the fatigue in his muscles translating to a deep, much needed rest. As he slept the temperature dropped and the moon rose. A three quarter moon, it was still bright and white and seemed closer than normal.

Lincoln opened his eyes and the moon's shining face turned into Grace's beautiful face looking down at him. The sight of her warmed his heart.

"Grace," he mumbled.

"I'm here," she said.

He smiled, pleased that she was here. Pleased that she was with him.

"C'mere," he said sweetly and reached out towards her beautiful moon face.

"Lincoln," she pulled back, but he had gotten hold of her moon body and wanted to hold her against him. He wanted to kiss her. He figured that was okay, because it was his dream.

"C'mere," he made smooching sounds with his lips as he brought her into him and felt her warmth against his naked chest.

"Lincoln, you're asleep," she said.

"Yes, I'm asleep," he murmured into her beautiful black hair. "And I'm holding you in my arms." He hummed a little tune as he wrapped his arms around her and squeezed.

"Lincoln…Lincoln…wake up!"

CHAPTER 43

"Lincoln, wake up!" Grace cried out again.

Locked in his arms and twisted inside the unbalanced hammock, this was not how she had envisioned their first embrace. Her face squished into his naked chest, her rear end hanging off the edge of the hammock, his right leg flung over the top of her left, his mouth in her ear, humming and murmuring incoherently–until she called out his name again.

"Wha—? Grace?" Lincoln pulled away from her with a start, which further destabilized their already precarious position. Grace felt the hammock lose its patience with them and with one mighty flip it tossed them out.

She squealed. Lincoln shouted. The hammock dumped them into a pile on the deck with a thump, still entwined, still in a state of confusion.

"Grace! What?" Lincoln was laying on top of her trying to disentangle his limbs from hers.

Grace couldn't move. The weight of his body on hers, the closeness of his undeniably gorgeous chest, it was a lot to manage. She could see the muscles flexing in his shoulders and pecs. Quite impressive. And she could smell him. He smelled like wood shavings and sunshine and earth with the tiniest bit of musk. Heavenly.

"I'm so sorry," he lifted off of her, carefully moving his legs out from between hers so as not to disturb her too much. "Are you all right?"

Flat on her back, staring up at Lincoln, his hair haloed from the light of the shining moon in the sky behind him, Grace felt like her whole world had toppled over.

Not in a bad way and not in a good way, more like in an extremely real way.

"Hang on, hold on, my foot…" Lincoln was still over the top of her, though he had lifted up off of her body, push up fashion. It was difficult to ignore his physique as he held this stance. She could feel his foot tugging out from underneath her calf and tried to move her leg to assist. "Hold on one second…I think I've got it…" he said.

His foot came loose just as she was able to move her calf, which sent her knee up into what she hoped was his stomach.

"Oof," he let out a sound like he'd been kicked in the gut… or worse.

"I'm sorry, did I hurt you?"

He shook his head, but was holding his breath as he gingerly moved his body next to hers and lay flat on his back.

She rolled onto her side to look at him. He was breathing carefully in and out. Grace put her hand on his bicep and apologized again.

"I'm sorry, I didn't mean–" she began.

He turned his head to face her, eyes twinkling. "No worries, you didn't hurt me."

"Oh, good!"

"You were close, but you missed," he grinned as he said it.

Grace smiled back. Then she giggled. Lincoln chuckled in

response. Pretty soon they were both cracking up laughing. Belly laughing. The kind of laughing that caused stomach cramps.

When their laughter died down, Lincoln looked at her again and said, "I'll say one thing, you really know how to make an entrance."

She gave him a matter of fact look and said, "I am a star, after all."

This sent them into another wave of merriment until Lincoln got it together enough to stand up. He stood above her and offered his hand to pull her up. Blonde hair tousled, bare chested, an Adonis wearing wrinkled cargo shorts, Grace felt like she had been blissfully marooned with an enchanted sailor on a desert island.

Placing her hand in his, she felt an electric shock shimmy up her arm. With zero effort he pulled her to her feet, the momentum bringing her right into his chest–again.

She didn't mind.

From the moment she had spied him sleeping shirtless in the hammock she had experienced waves of attraction so strong that she hadn't exactly been thinking straight. For one, if she had been thinking straight she might not have leaned over a sleeping man and tried to wake him up. One never knew how somebody was going to wake up, although grabbing for her and trying to kiss her was not a response she was expecting at all.

Between the attraction and the surprise of being pulled down into the hammock with a half-dressed Lincoln while he murmured sweetly into her hair, a far more intense feeling had emerged. Desire.

That feeling came back front and center as they stood only inches away from each other, so close she could feel the warmth of his skin on her cheeks. She couldn't catch her breath.

"Sorry about that," Lincoln said. Placing his hands on her shoulders he held her in place and took one step back. The space between them became feet instead of inches and cooled significantly. Grace took in a breath, then another, and gathered her thoughts.

"I am guessing you didn't know I was coming early?" she asked.

Lincoln dropped his eyes to his feet almost bashfully, "Um, no, I didn't."

Her heart sunk. She would have to go back to the beach house.

Lincoln lifted his eyes to hers and must have read her disappointment. "Not that that's a bad thing. It's good...I mean...I'm–I'm glad you're here."

"Are you sure?"

"It's completely, absolutely, 100% okay," he said. A thought occurred to him and he held up one finger in the air, the signal to wait. "I just need to change the sheets on my bed–your bed, I mean." This time she was sure she saw him blush.

"I'll help you," she insisted.

A few minutes later they were standing on opposite sides of his bed, spreading a sheet with elasticized corners between them, trying to figure out which corner went where.

"These are pretty," Grace commented on the pattern.

"They're new...I thought I should spruce up the place a little...since you were coming back."

Her heart warmed at the thought of Lincoln picking out new sheets for her. She could hardly think of anything sweeter.

They continued to fumble with the corners. "It's been ages since I made a bed with someone," Lincoln said with an embarrassed laugh.

Grace didn't tell him she had never made a bed in her life.

Although she thought he might figure it out. All she was doing was watching him carefully and trying to mimic what he was doing with the elastic corners of the sheet. She did not possess seamless bed making skills.

Finally, it was done and the pretty new bedding made the whole room feel cozy.

Once again, Grace found her eyes wandering down Lincoln's chest to his abs. She caught herself before he noticed and tried to change the subject.

"I suppose you've already eaten?" she asked.

He ran his hand through his already messy hair, "Actually, I fell asleep before I ate."

"Good! I had the hotel pack something. It's not much, but I brought it just in case."

Soon they were picnicking on the deck again eating crab salad sandwiches and sweet pickles. There were some vanilla wafer cookies for dessert. Simple, but delicious.

"I haven't finished the bathroom," Lincoln confessed to her after munching on a few vanilla wafers. "I was going to paint it tomorrow..."

"Before I arrived unannounced...and early, I know," she laughed. "Well, I can help with that."

"Oh, no." He screwed his face into an uncomfortable frown. "You don't have to do that."

"But I want to. I had fun painting the kitchen. And I didn't do a half bad job, did I?"

"You did a great job, but..." He popped another cookie into his mouth and shook his head 'no'.

"Come on, it will be fun and if I'm helping it will go more quickly won't it?"

Lincoln winced. "I don't want you to work while you're renting the place. That doesn't seem right. I stocked up on groceries and thought I could grill up some dinner while you relaxed."

Again, a warm fuzzy sensation squeezed her heart at the thought of him grocery shopping for their dinner. She put her hand out and touched the top of his so he would look at her and know that she meant what she said.

"How about this? We'll paint the bathroom in the morning and then you can grill."

Lincoln looked at her and gave her a reluctant half-nod. "All right...I don't know why doing manual labor is so much fun for you."

She laughed. "Think of it like a dude ranch vacation, except it's remodeling!"

"Okay, if you insist. We'll start first thing in the morning."

CHAPTER 44

$\mathcal{L}$incoln wasn't exactly sure if Grace was interested in doing remodeling work or if she was just enjoying learning how the other half, or other 99%, of the world lived, but he didn't really care. When she was around the air felt lighter and he liked it. If she wanted to roll up her sleeves and do a little work, far be it from him to refuse.

He did insist that they get some sleep since they were going to get up early and paint. Despite the strangeness of their cohabitation, going to bed wasn't too awkward. His bed, the one they made together, was obviously set up for her and he crashed on the hammock again, chuckling himself to sleep at the memory of her confusion over trying to put on a fitted sheet.

"You ready?" he asked when she joined him in the kitchen the next morning, a little bleary eyed, but dressed in her version of painting attire: a pair of loose fitting khaki pants, the white tank top with remnants of his stain handprints on it, and a pink and red plaid shirt she had tied around her hips.

He could barely tear his eyes away from the handprints–his handprints–on her slender waist.

"I'm ready, just need a little coffee," she said as she slipped in next to him.

Lincoln focused his gaze on his own coffee to avoid staring at her as she casually pulled a mug out of his cupboard and helped herself.

The space between his skin and hers sparked as the memory of her laying underneath him after they fell out of the hammock popped into his mind. He cleared his throat and took a sip of coffee. How was he going to make it through a whole morning of being in a small bathroom with her if he couldn't handle standing next to her in the kitchen?

An hour into painting he was sorry the room was so small, because it would be done too soon.

"You've done a really good job on this bathroom. It's lovely," Grace had started off the work with a compliment. She ran her hand along the new antique white tile he had installed, "Where did you get this?"

"I ordered it from a place that makes it by hand," Lincoln answered as he opened a can of pale grey paint.

"It's beautiful. It's all beautiful, I love the dark fixtures," she continued as she picked up a roll of blue tape to begin taping off the edges.

Pleased that she liked it, Lincoln started explaining the different changes he had made from the new narrower dark wood vanity down to the updated copper piping. "I'm not a plumber, keep that in mind. I had to make sure I got the p-trap right..." he paused, realizing that he had been talking on and on about plumbing.

"Mm-hmm," Grace murmured softly. Perched on the edge of the bathtub she was focused on the handmade tile, carefully taping off the edges.

"You don't want to hear about the plumbing, I imagine."

Grace's eyes moved to his though she remained poised in her taping position. "I don't mind. You obviously love this house."

"Yes, I guess I do."

"What are some of your favorite memories here with your Grandad?" she asked, turning her eyes back to the tape.

Lincoln thought for a minute. So many memories flooded through his mind, he didn't know which one to choose. He sorted out the rough ones, the ones where his Grandad was drinking, and tried to zero in on something good and wholesome, a memory he wanted her to know.

"I've got one," he said.

"Good, tell me."

"He had a magic trick he used to do with a ball. Any regular sized tennis ball would do the trick. Anyway, he told Luke and I that he could throw the ball so high into the sky that it would never fall back down. It would just disappear."

"Did it?"

Lincoln chuckled, "Yes, it did." He paused, more of the story returning to him. "He would do a few test throws, you know, so we would know what to expect...or not expect. We watched him so carefully. He'd throw it straight up and it would come straight back down. He'd catch it. Then again. Then again. Then he'd say 'Ready, boys, don't look away' and he threw that ball so high into the air I could swear it disappeared into the clouds." He shook his head and laughed again. "Luke and I would stand there for ages staring up into the sky...and that ball never fell back down."

He looked at Grace, she was smiling warmly at him. Suddenly a knot in his throat kept him from talking. He turned his attention back to the paint at his feet, fiercely focusing on pouring it into the roller pan.

"That's a sweet memory," Grace said carefully.

He swallowed hard and managed to answer, "I guess it is."

He looked up and her gaze caught his as another thought hit him. "When we got older I would find the ball later somewhere around and I realized that it hadn't disappeared at all." He grinned at her. "But I never told Luke, didn't want to spoil it for him."

Grace laughed. "That's what a good big brother does."

"Do you have any brothers or sisters?" he asked. He'd had enough of being the center of attention.

"No, I'm the one and only," she said as she turned back to her taping. "I had some really close friends growing up, though. They're kind of like my sisters."

"You went to school together?"

"Yes…and art camp…and college."

He raised his eyebrows, "Wow, you must be close."

"Sometimes too close," she laughed.

Done pouring paint, Lincoln grabbed the other roll of tape and joined Grace sitting on the edge of the bathtub to help her by taping off the other side.

"Are they actresses, too?" he asked, curious about her personal life.

"Oh, no. I'm the only one who took that route. Though one is a fashion designer."

Lincoln grunted his understanding. He noted that his thick fingers fumbled more with the tape than Grace's smaller, slender fingers.

"Have you always wanted to be an actress?" he asked.

She thought about it for longer than he expected and he turned to find her staring at the tile without seeming to see it. When she noticed him looking at her she smiled, but there was no joy in it.

"I didn't mean to pry," he said.

"No, no, it's not you. I just…I always thought I wanted to be an actress. Well, from as early as you can remember those kinds of things." She dropped her eyes again to the tile and confessed, "It's just lately I've been wondering if I really enjoy it anymore."

Her answer surprised him. "Oh…well…what would you do if you weren't acting?"

She laughed, but again there was little joy in the sound. "That's the crazy thing. I don't know!"

It seemed to him that someone in her financial position wouldn't have much to worry about. Maybe he was wrong. He decided to make a suggestion.

"I don't know your business, but I would think you can do whatever you want to do. Can't you?"

Grace looked back to him with eyes full of confusion and sadness. It broke his heart to see those gorgeous eyes in such a state.

"That's the thing. It's been what I do for so long…the fans, the deals, Hollywood, everything…it's kind of who I am."

Sitting on the edge of the bathtub, looking into each other's eyes, blue rolls of tape in their hands and paint sitting ready to put on the walls, she was just another person. Not Grace Woods the famous actress, not a celebrity who belonged to her fans, but a woman looking for happiness. A beautiful, desirable woman for sure, but a woman nonetheless.

Lincoln's heart wrenched. He had been doing exactly what the rest of the world did to her, thought of her as something other than simply a person. He, too, was guilty of looking at her through the lens of her fame and fortune instead of her personality and character.

He nudged her gently with his elbow. "That's just your job. I mean, I know it's a big deal and you're famous and everything, but it's not you. You're you without your job… aren't you?"

Grace's eyes shone wet with tears. Her bottom lip trembled slightly. Lincoln shifted so he was facing her and she did the same. A few strands of black hair had fallen out of her ponytail. Lincoln reached up and moved them gently out of her eyes, letting his fingers graze her temple as he did. She didn't pull away from him and her gaze dropped to his mouth then back up.

Heart thumping in his chest, the tips of his fingers tingled at the feel of her soft skin, Lincoln had only one thought. He was going to kiss her. He leaned towards her, she tilted her head ever so slightly so their lips could touch, and–

A blast of music sounded in the tiny bathroom and they both jumped, pulling away from each other.

Grace gave him an apologetic look and fished her phone out of her pants pocket. She lifted the phone to her ear. "Phoenix?" She kept her eyes on Lincoln for a few moments, but soon her attention was taken by whatever this Phoenix person was saying. "This weekend?" Grace sounded disappointed. Then she looked at him again, surprise in her voice, "Now?"

CHAPTER 45

Zac refused to lose focus again. He stared at his reflection in the makeup mirror, his mind reviewing everything that had happened since Grace fainted.

The quick rescheduling of filming had basically made him the center of attention as they shot whatever scenes he had without Grace. The sudden dependence he developed on Phoenix to help keep him on task during the whirlwind filming. The absence of Grace as she escaped to whatever secret haven she had been using to avoid the world—and him—over the past few weeks.

All of it had thrown his plans into the dumpster.

"We all usually hang at the beach bar on our days off, if you want to join us next time," his makeup guy, Federico, said.

The invitation broke through Zac's concentration. "Hmm?"

Federico sat back casually in one of the extra makeup chairs lined up in front of the long mirror. Zac couldn't turn his head while they were doing his hair, so he shifted his eyes to Federico's in the reflection.

"What was that?" he asked.

Federico grinned at him and continued, "You were saying your plans fell through. You can always party with us, you know."

"Oh, right…" Zac hadn't thought once about prioritizing time with the crew since they started this movie. "Thanks, Federico, I might," Zac answered with a flash of his best chummy smile. He was lying, of course, but Federico didn't know that.

The assistant to the assistant director popped her head into the room and announced, "Twenty minutes."

"Okay, he's almost done," his hairdresser responded.

"Hey," Zac spoke to the assistant as she was closing the door. Keeping his head perfectly still for the hairdresser, he motioned to her with his eyes to come back in.

"Yes?" she entered the room cautiously. This was not part of her assignment.

"Is…um, is Grace okay? I mean, is she feeling okay?"

"Oh," she glanced around at the hair and makeup team, apparently not sure if this was an appropriate topic. "I think so. I haven't heard anything if she isn't."

"Okay, good," he answered.

The assistant left and the room fell silent. Zac sensed his question had peaked some interest in the crew and wondered if he should have kept his mouth shut. He didn't know if it was best to keep the gossip flowing or if the gossip was what had driven Grace away.

His instincts were off. Ever since he had followed Rigby's advice and made his move on the morning show, whenever they had time off Grace was nowhere to be found and his advances seemed to fall short.

Zac suppressed a scowl, keeping his expression neutral as he watched his reflection disappear behind great clouds of hairspray. He was running out of time. There were only weeks of filming left, not months, and the serious sex scenes were coming up. He had fewer and fewer chances to get this right.

"You're ready to get dressed," a voice from behind the hairspray cloud announced.

"Can someone get me Phoenix?" he asked. The air hadn't cleared yet, which sent him into a coughing fit.

"On it," another voice from behind him said as someone else helped him out of his chair and led him to the wardrobe room.

By the time Phoenix arrived he was dressed and Federico had touched up his makeup after all of the coughing caused some tearing in his eyes.

"What's up?' Phoenix asked, her eyes big and serious as she looked up at him expectantly.

"I–I'm a little off center," he admitted.

She looked at him carefully for a few moments then glanced around at the nearby crew. Putting her hand lightly behind his elbow she turned him towards the door and said, "Let's walk."

Movement helped and as they walked Zac was able to articulate his concerns. Phoenix listened patiently, skillfully guiding them out of earshot of anyone who happened to come near.

She stopped him right on the outside of the lighting set up and said, "So let me get this straight. You're worried that Grace is avoiding you and how that will affect your performance in the scenes?"

He nodded, a little embarrassed at the way she put it, but trusting her ability to fix it.

She took a moment to consider her response, looking past him without really focusing on anything. Finally, she lifted her eyes back to his and something in them made Zac's confusion and worry subside.

"It's not just you that she's avoiding, if that makes you feel any better," Phoenix began.

He smiled. Relieved. "That does make me feel better."

"She's been pretty stressed out, it seems. She's spending a lot of time alone up at a private house she rented."

"Oh, I see."

"But I want you to know that nobody has been questioning your performance. Not at all. You're doing great," she smiled.

The smile brightened her whole face, and with the morning sun glinting through her pale blonde ponytail, Zac thought she looked quite pretty. He ducked his head, pleased at the praise, the anxiety in his stomach dissipating.

"I haven't had a chance to tell you, but there's a big surprise party being planned for Grace's birthday in a few weeks," she said.

He lifted his gaze, interested.

Phoenix held his look for just a moment before looking past him again, her attention captured by something on set no doubt.

"Her friend, Faye, is throwing it. She wanted me to be sure to invite you."

"Oh…great, I'll be there," he assured her.

"But it's got to be a secret." She looked back to him as she pulled her constantly vibrating cell phone out of her pocket. "Promise?"

Their clandestine helicopter ride popped into his mind and he smiled. "I can keep a secret."

"Good." The shadow of a secret smile touched her lips then disappeared. "Now, are you okay? They'll be calling you in a few minutes."

"Sure, sure, I'm okay," he said, waving her away to attend to her other duties.

As she walked away he felt a little better about the Grace

situation. Watching Phoenix's frail yet competent frame moving out of view held his attention longer than he expected and Zac forgot about Grace altogether. A curious idea flitted through his mind as something new and unexpected tugged at his heart.

CHAPTER 46

"Don't worry, we changed the wig glue," Anne Marie said reassuringly as she painted a clear goopy substance around Grace's natural hairline.

"You did? I didn't think the wig glue was the problem."

Anne Marie avoided looking her in the eye as she explained, "It wasn't. We've used that glue with you for years and years. But your friend was pretty insistent so we changed it just to be sure."

"My friend?" Grace was confused, but only for a moment. "Did Faye get involved in this?"

Anne Marie nodded apologetically, though she had nothing to be sorry about. Grace's brow furrowed in annoyance. Faye was a dear friend, but honestly, she needed to learn how to stay out of things that weren't her business.

"I'm sorry if Faye caused any problems," Grace said with a heavy sigh. "She is…" Grace looked for a word that fit and came up short. Sometimes Faye defied description.

"Concerned," Anne Marie said with a good natured smile. "And this is a small island, it's kinda hard to stay out of someone's way if they want to run into you."

Grace had to laugh at the idea of Faye marching around the island stalking her wig master and complaining about the wig glue. Anne Marie laughed, which was a relief. At least she wasn't too put out about it. She and the others had already given Grace a talking to about the paint under her normally perfectly manicured fingernails.

"I'll talk to her about that," Grace said. "She shouldn't be harassing you about your work."

"I don't think you could stop that woman with a tidal wave," Anne Marie laughed again.

"True," Grace agreed. "I appreciate your patience."

"It's all good. We have new eco-friendlier wig glue and the show will go on."

Grace turned her attention back to the mirror as she watched Anne Marie and the others set the wig back on her head and ready her for the chic party scene. Phoenix's phone call, the one that interrupted her and Lincoln, had been to get her back to the set to finish the party scene. It turned out they couldn't extend their time at the location to make up for the lost time caused by her fainting spell. They had to work overtime to complete the whole scene by the end of her weekend off. So much for doctor's orders.

"Will you be back this weekend?" Lincoln had asked.

The question was so innocent, but it sent butterflies whirling through her stomach. She wanted to tell him that she would race back to see him the moment she could. That every second she was gone she would think about him. That she would miss everything, his house, his jokes, the sound of his voice, how he smelled so good no matter what he was doing.

Instead, she said, "I doubt it. We have a lot to get done in this scene. We'll probably be working until all hours of the night this whole weekend."

"Oh," was all he said, but Grace swore she saw disappointment in his eyes.

As she was taking her bags out the door she stopped, turned around to look at him, and said, "You should come to the set."

Lincoln's eyebrows lifted at the suggestion. "Me?"

Immediately uncertain that he would be interested, she added, "If you want to. I mean, you could come by and take a look around…you know, for something to do."

Grace almost blushed in her makeup chair thinking about that awkward invitation. Lincoln had said he might drop by, but he may have just been telling her that to be polite. What a strange thing it was, to feel like such a shy schoolgirl at her age.

Still, she had alerted Phoenix and Rigby that Lincoln Reeves was to be put on the visitor's list. They hadn't asked for an explanation and she hadn't given them one. She was the star of the movie as well as the producer, it wasn't unusual for her to add names to the visitor list.

This time, however, it felt monumental.

Fully dressed wig and all, Grace made her way along the same path she had walked previously when she fainted, but she didn't feel weak or strange. She held her head high and kept her back straight using all of the posture and dance training she had ever taken in her life, but deep down she understood something else was making her stand tall.

Ever since she and Lincoln had sat on the edge of the bathtub together there was an electrified buzz zinging through her entire body. She was also infused with a new sense of calm she had brought back with her from the Hill House. These two opposite sensations blended together and created a sort of spiritual strength in her core, making everything around her seem surreal and her own emotions untouchable by mere mortals.

Grace smiled quietly at the crew who greeted her, noticed Rigby waving hello to her from the other side of the set, and could see glimpses of Zac in his bright blue suit waiting at the railing of the grand patio where they would shoot this scene. Suddenly she was overcome by the realization that the only person who could affect her at this point was Lincoln.

Her feelings for Lincoln were more than just sexual attraction. Even though her physical attraction to him grew every moment she was with him, there was something else, something stronger, that rose in her when she was with him—contentment.

What had he said to her? Something about her being *her* even if she wasn't acting. In that one question Lincoln touched on an insecurity she had held ever since she shot to fame in her early 20's. Who was she if she wasn't Grace Woods Superstar, Grace Woods Celebrity, Grace Woods Hollywood Powerhouse? Was just being plain Grace enough?

Somehow, when she was with Lincoln, she felt like it was.

"And here she is," Syd announced to everyone and no-one as she stepped through the last of the towering lights and into the scene.

She smiled, a secret happiness filling her heart. "I'm here."

Zac stepped forward and took her hand, his famous blue eyes glittering. "You look beautiful…amazing."

"Thank you, Zac." She eyed his suit, appreciating Syd and the costume designer's color selection. "That is quite a suit isn't it?"

He grinned. "And that is quite a dress."

Grace laughed, feeling lighter and more at ease than she had in a long time.

"All right, let's get down to business," Syd began.

Grace did a quick scan of all of the crew and equipment surrounding them, peering through them into the outer circle, wondering if Lincoln had taken her up on her invitation.

She didn't see him.

Surprisingly she didn't feel let down. He was busy and she was, too…for now. Soon enough she would be back at the Hill House with him and that thought steadied her.

"Tell us what you want to do, Syd," she said as she turned her attention back to the director. "We're ready."

What Syd wanted, it turned out, was to change up the end of the scene on the patio. Instead of Scarlet and Ethan pulling away from each other immediately, he wanted them to share a meaningful look and their very first kiss before putting up emotional walls and backing off.

"It will play off better if the audience thinks the romance is starting then gets disappointed. They'll be more invested," Syd explained.

Grace and Zac both stared at him.

"Are you guys good with that?" Syd asked, though it was a moot point. He was the director and he could change up anything at any time without their approval.

"Um, sure," Zac seemed embarrassed. Grace understood, she was also more than a little taken aback at this new development.

"It's just a little kiss, nothing huge," Syd reassured them.

Zac looked at her and though he had successfully covered up his initial embarrassment, Grace could feel his nerves. She gave him a comforting smile.

"It's fine, Syd," Grace answered for both of them. "It just would have been nice to have a little warning."

Syd wiggled his heavy eyebrows up and down comically. "That's part of the plan, my dear. If you are actually nervous it will come across better on screen."

Grace rolled her eyes and shooed his comment away with a wave of her hand. "Stop being brilliant, please."

Syd threw his head back and laughed heartily then dove into giving them direction on the changes in the scene. Before they had too much time to worry about it, she and Zac were on their marks and ready for the first take.

Max brought them both an Altoid, which they accepted gratefully. "Everything's ready, are you two ready?" he asked.

"Ready," Grace and Zac answered at the same time.

Grace pushed every other thought out of her mind and focused on being Scarlet. What would Scarlet be feeling right now? How would she react to Ethan at her side?

When 'Action' was called she and Zac were in perfect synch. Their lines came naturally, the connection between them was exactly what Syd had wanted between Scarlet and Ethan. As the scene moved closer to the end, closer to their first kiss, Grace struggled to drum up the desire for Ethan that Scarlet should have. She allowed her anxiety to come through just enough that Syd would think she was manufacturing the emotion.

Still, the pressure was on, the camera was rolling and it was almost time for the kiss. Grace's mind flew through her repertoire. She was a professional, after all. She had so many acting tricks up her sleeve to make this work there was no way she was going to not land this kiss.

Zac moved towards her as Ethan and in a flurry of internal panic Grace had a moment of pure inspiration.

She closed her eyes for just a second and imagined sitting on the edge of Lincoln's bathtub, drawing on the way she had felt when Lincoln leaned towards her, the way she had longed to feel his lips on her own.

She opened her eyes. Zac's mouth was inches away from hers. She tilted her head slightly to the side so their lips could touch and look good on camera. Ready for the sensation of Zac's kiss, Grace tried to think only as Scarlet about to kiss Ethan, nothing else.

But even as Zac put his hands on her waist, even as their mouths came together, even as she knew they had successfully delivered what Syd was looking for in the scene, Grace could not get the image of Lincoln leaning in to kiss her out of her mind.

CHAPTER 47

"Stupid, stupid, stupid," Lincoln repeated the word over and over as he drove back up the winding road leading home. He hit his palm on the steering wheel of his buggy and said it again, "Stupid. That's all you are. What did you expect?"

Yelling at himself as he drove didn't fix anything, but he had to vent somehow. He didn't know for sure if his heart was shattered, but his ego definitely had taken a blow.

The sight of Grace gazing longingly into that Hollywood heartthrob's eyes had wrenched his gut and he hadn't been able to turn away. He had stood in silent agony, watching as they kissed over and over again, take after take, until he had managed to mumble an excuse to Grace's producer and escape.

Trying to push the memory physically out, he ground the palm of his left hand into his forehead as he used his right hand to steer into his driveway. It didn't work. Nothing was going to work. He was stuck with that picture in his mind forever. Not only that, he would be able to stream the film version complete with background music once the movie came out.

"You're an idiot," he said again, pressing hard on the brakes so the buggy came to an abrupt stop. "What did you think was going to happen?" Nothing but jungle around, nobody heard and nobody answered.

Lincoln slammed the front door behind him. Storming towards the liquor cabinet he stopped short, remembering it was empty. Anger and regret surged through him and his first thought was to go back down the hill to pick up a bottle of whiskey. He paused again, tense and unmoving in the middle of his kitchen.

"Pull it together, mate," he muttered.

He had made a decision not to turn to drink every time something didn't go his way like a petulant child and he was going to stick with it. He glanced at the closed doors of the empty liquor cabinet. Whiskey might dull the hurt in the moment, but not long term.

How was he ever going to get the image of Grace kissing another man out of his head?

Lincoln scowled and went to the wall of windows in the living room. He stared out over the trees, considering his options.

Keen to see her he had thought taking her up on the offer to come to the set was a banger of an idea. Not so much. Being treated as a possibly dangerous superfan to begin with hadn't done much for his confidence. Once his identity had been confirmed and they found him on the guest list he had been handed off to Grace's producer, Rigby, a too tan salesman type whose prodding questions had gotten under Lincoln's skin. Then…Lincoln shook his head sharply trying to avoid thinking about that bloody kiss.

"Hey, brother!" Luke's voice called out behind him.

Lincoln turned at the sound, not surprised Luke had let

himself in, but startled out of his thoughts by the sound.

"Hey," he answered unenthusiastically.

Luke grinned. "Don't get too excited to see me, it might go to my head."

Lincoln turned back to look out the window. He wasn't in the mood to exchange jabs.

"So…" Luke sidled up next to him, craning his neck back and forth to see out onto the deck then back inside down the hallway. "How's everything going?"

"She's not here," Lincoln said.

Luke's face fell. "She canceled?"

Lincoln sighed. "No, she got here early, but was called away to film…something."

Luke was silent for a few moments then asked, "Is she gonna want a refund?"

"I don't know," Lincoln said crossly. "She was needed on set. She's a movie star."

Luke gave him a long look. "Don't get bent at me. I have a financial interest in this place, you know."

Lincoln dropped his head down and pinched the bridge of his nose, wishing Luke would be quiet.

"I have to remember to tell people there's no refunds if they leave early," Luke continued with his concerns out loud.

"I don't think money is an issue, Luke," Lincoln snapped. "She's got plenty of money. And fans. And fame. She's got everything." Including a co-star who seemed right at home kissing her. Lincoln clenched his teeth together to stop talking.

Luke gave his brother another long look. "What's the matter with you?"

"Nothing."

Luke grunted. "Well, I guess this little place wouldn't hold someone who has everything's attention for long. Still, it was nice while it lasted."

Lincoln continued staring out the window without answering.

Luke looked down at the stained floors. "You've got the place looking good. That's something."

Lincoln glanced at his brother then around the main living area and kitchen. The place was looking good. In fact, since completing the bathroom most of the main renovations were done.

"And who else can say that Grace Woods painted their kitchen, right?" Luke chuckled.

A pang of sorrow moved through Lincoln's chest, pushing away some of the anger that had been roiling around inside. He didn't like the way Luke was talking, making it sound like Grace was never coming back to the Hill House.

"I don't think she's canceling the rest of her visits," he said, more for his own reassurance than Luke's.

Luke brightened. "That's good news, then." He nudged Lincoln's arm with his elbow. "Maybe come up with a few more projects she can put her stamp on before she leaves the island for good. We could rename the place the Grace Woods House."

Even as Lincoln dismissed his brother's joke with a shake of his head a tiny spark of an idea lit his dark mood.

Maybe he needed to approach Grace with something more than just helping him remodel his house.

He almost laughed out loud at this realization. He really was an idiot. How could he expect to catch the eye of someone as wealthy, worldly, and famous as Grace Woods with a bucket of paint and a few picnics on his deck?

He couldn't.

Seeing the error of his ways, Lincoln's dark mood disappeared completely. His heart lifted because he had an excellent idea of what he needed to do to fix the problem.

CHAPTER 48

Not everybody looked good in green, Faye knew this. However, as she stood admiring the rich green dress Ronnie had created for Grace, Faye also knew down to the tips of her toes that her friend would look splendid in it on her birthday.

"You've really outdone yourself, darling," she said, pleased and somewhat in awe of what Ronnie could do with a few yards of fabric and a little time.

Ronnie beamed. "You like it?"

"Like it?" Faye held the shimmery silk between her fingers, pulling out the skirt and letting it fall back against the mannequin Ronnie had borrowed from Grace's costume department. "I love it!"

Ronnie fussed over the dropped shoulders. "I was going for something between Cleopatra and jungle goddess."

Faye laughed, delighted. "That's exactly what this is. It's perfect." She stepped back and imagined Grace moving around her birthday in this dress, laughing, talking, flirting. "Simply perfect."

"Good," Ronnie responded. "How are the other preparations going? Did you find the band?"

"Oh, yes! I forgot to tell you. The Kismit's are playing in Sydney the week before and Randall said they would love to do a private show for Grace."

"Good! They're really good."

"Yes, Grace loves them. And the hotel will do the food. There's a local baker who does these marvelous firecracker cakes that's going to do the birthday cake."

"A firecracker cake?"

Faye smiled knowingly, "They're gorgeous. Lots of gold and sparkle. You'll love it."

Ronnie stepped back next to Faye and eyed the dress. "Sounds like you have everything under control."

Faye's heart swelled a little bit. Given the reduced resources here on the island and the fact that she had a lot of time on her hands, she had done much of the legwork for this party herself. She knew that her friends didn't always believe in her organizational abilities, at least without the help of several assistants and a butler. Ronnie's praise was flattering.

"The only thing I have left to do is convince Indigo Lee to come."

Ronnie gave her a questioning look. "Indigo Lee? Wasn't she going to star in this movie?"

Faye nodded. "Yes, it was a big to-do when Grace fired her."

Ronnie blinked, waiting for some kind of explanation. When one did not arise, she asked, "Why would Grace want Indigo Lee at her birthday party?" Before Faye could respond, she had another question. "Didn't she used to date Zac?"

Faye grinned. Ronnie had inadvertently stumbled across

the exact reason Faye was inviting the waif actress to fly across the world and attend Grace's surprise birthday party.

"Yes, she did. They broke up before filming began," Faye answered. Ronnie continued to stare at her, oblivious to the genius in Faye's plan. "Nothing makes the heart grow stronger than a little old fashioned jealousy," she said, punctuating her statement with a wink.

"What are you talking about?" Ronnie's voice raised in pitch.

Faye gave Ronnie the look of someone burdened with the everlasting job of explaining how things work to people who just couldn't understand.

"Grace is in love, that's obvious," she began.

Ronnie paused before answering, "She does seem a little distracted."

"She's distracted because she is falling in love with Zac and he is falling in love with her and they need a little…push."

Ronnie was still gawking in disbelief. Faye felt a little sorry for her. How could someone be such a talented designer and artist and still not see the way love and relationships worked. It was no wonder dear Ronnie, though gorgeous and successful, was still single.

"Faye…I…I don't think–"

"I got your sister married off, didn't I?" Faye interrupted. "And that was an achievement nobody thought possible, wasn't it?"

Ronnie closed her mouth and seemed to reconsider what she was about to say. She opened her mouth to speak, but Faye was compelled to explain.

"Not that I think Grace and Zac should get married. I'm not delusional, you know." Faye chuckled at the thought. She had always had a very clear mind. She reached out and touched Ronnie on the shoulder reassuringly. "I just want Grace to have something...*nice* for her birthday."

"I'm not sure this is the way to do it," Ronnie said weakly.

"I am," Faye smiled broadly, confident in her little plan and glad to see Ronnie's opposition to it was fading.

"Have you talked to Presley about it?"

Faye frowned. "I don't have to clear everything I do with Presley."

"I know...I was just wondering what she said about it."

"Well, I haven't told her yet. I haven't told anybody except you."

Ronnie perked up. "She might have some good advice. I'll call her." Ronnie picked her cell phone up off the small sewing table.

"I've already sent Indigo an invitation."

Ronnie's hand paused midair. "You did?"

Faye nodded, dismissing Ronnie's concern. "We don't need to call Presley and get her permission. I've got everything under control. Trust me."

Ronnie put her phone back on the table and didn't ask for any more explanation, which was fine because Faye didn't see that any explanation was needed. She was fully aware of Grace's feelings for Zac, even though her friend had tried to keep them under wraps. She could see the melancholy in Grace's eyes when he wasn't around. She had turned into a mooning teenager for goodness sake.

There was a reason Faye had stayed on in the Whitsundays this whole time. She had sensed Grace needed help getting through the making of this movie and was happy to be the catalyst to her finding love. The movie was almost done filming, but Faye wasn't about to let her friend down when she needed her most.

Faye smiled quietly to herself as she looked at the green

dress again. Not everybody looked good in green, but Grace did. When Indigo arrived at the party it would trigger the spark of jealousy needed to get her to act and get Zac to react. Then–voila–her matchmaking work here would be done.

CHAPTER 49

"You can fly?" Grace laughed as she asked the question and watched Lincoln climb into the pilot's seat next to her.

"Yep," he grinned. "Are you surprised?"

She nodded, her heart beating hard in her chest. They were about to go up in a small four passenger plane to take an air tour of the island and sights beyond, which was one cause for her excitement. The other was Lincoln slipping in next to her, flipping switches and checking gages and generally being competent and manly.

"I knew you could captain a boat, but flying, too?"

He nodded. "Yep. And I'm a mean golf cart driver."

Grace laughed again, pure joy and adrenaline pumping through her veins.

"Don't ask me to operate a train, though. We don't have many trains on the island," he said as he kicked the engines on and the propellor whirled. The noise startled her and though she was still laughing, she gripped the edge of her seat. Lincoln glanced down at her hand clutching the cushion. "You okay? We don't have to go up if you don't want to."

"No, no, I'm fine. I want to go. Let's do it."

The words rushed out. Grace didn't want to think. All she wanted to do was fly with Lincoln by her side.

Ever since he greeted her at the house with a bouquet of flowers and the promise of a surprise if she was up for it, Grace had been giddy with excitement. Not sure what to expect after her abrupt departure the previous weekend, seeing his excitement was reassuring.

"Do you like surprises?" he had asked from behind the giant bouquet.

If it hadn't been for the flowers Grace may have thrown her arms around his neck and given him a big kiss. Filming had been grueling that week. A lot of scenes to get through, a lot of ground to cover, and a lot of Syd's direction, which wasn't always wrapped in the kindest words.

"Grace, lift your chin up when you say your line. Your skin is puckering on your neck."

"Zac, move your hand up so it blocks Grace's stomach."

"Grace, can you keep your eyes open a little wider? You look like you're asleep."

"Great shot, but we need to do it again from a more flattering angle."

And so the week had gone on and on with Syd and the whole crew working their tails off trying to overcome her physical imperfections. Normally that would be enough to send her into a funk, but Grace had kept Lincoln in her mind all week as a distraction.

When she had arrived at the Hill House on Friday afternoon, frazzled and tired from her long week, she was wondering what they might do. Maybe he needed help landscaping. She had never planted anything, but thought she might enjoy it. Though, she would have to wear gloves to avoid being scolded by her makeup people again.

When she opened the door to Lincoln, proud and pleased

with the oversized bouquet of flowers, Grace forgot all about her rough week.

"I love surprises," she responded, and he had whisked her away to the airport.

Sitting next to him in the small cockpit she was more than surprised. Thrilled was a better word.

She glanced behind them at the empty seats. "It's just us?"

"Just us, sweetheart," he said, guiding the plane out towards the runway.

Though they had not left the ground yet, her heart soared.

In the minutes that followed, Lincoln's concentrated piloting, the rush of being in the front seat of a plane racing down a runway, the lift off, the buoyancy of flight, the bright blue waters stretching out beneath them, her mind couldn't keep up with her spirit. They were flying high above the island, but she felt as if they were miles above the earth, so high they may never have to return.

"Is this your plane?" she raised her voice so he could hear her over the sound of the engine.

"No, it's my mate, Arny's. He's got a touring business here, runs people on holiday out and about, sets up romantic dinners, the works."

There was a twinkle in his eye when he mentioned romantic dinners and Grace felt a blush on her cheek. Silly, she knew, how she responded to him, but she couldn't control it.

"It's nice," she said, partly to carry on the conversation and pretend she wasn't blushing, and partly because she meant it. Her private jet was much different than this smaller plane meant to carry tourists around. Built for quiet, luxurious travel, her jet flew more smoothly. On the other hand, this plane made Grace feel like she was on a grand adventure.

With Lincoln as her guide, it was just that. As he flew he

showed her landmarks and places of interest. He guided the plane over Hamilton Island and pointed out his house, and she sensed his pride. He took her over the white and blue swirling inlet she had seen before landing in Faye's jet, then turned the plane and flew fast and low over the unimaginable blue waters surrounding the island.

"It's so blue…so absolutely perfect," she commented.

"Do you know why these waters are such an amazing color?" he asked.

"No, why?"

"The water isn't actually pristine, perfect as you say. There's fine sediment that stays suspended in the water and when sunlight enters the water from above, the sediment scatters the light. That's what makes it this fantastic blue. In a way, it's more beautiful because it's not perfect at all."

Grace's throat tightened with emotion unexpectedly. She looked back out the window at the water rushing underneath. The gorgeous, unique, imperfect water that was easily the most beautiful she had ever seen.

The sun was dipping lower in the sky and Lincoln turned the plane back towards the airport.

"We've seen just about everything possible from up here," he announced.

Grace was a little disappointed the experience was over. She leaned forward and peered through every window, she wanted to soak in every moment.

"You won't see him up here," Lincoln said.

"See who?"

He grinned, "Our humpback, Big Fella!"

Grace laughed again as that thrilling memory came rushing back. "Gosh, wasn't he amazing?"

"He was," Lincoln answered as he turned the plane, circling the airport below.

He announced their arrival to someone on the other end

of the radio and received an all clear to land. They dipped lower in the sky and Grace could see the runway straight ahead, coming closer and closer. She frowned.

"Are you all right?" he asked, noticing her expression.

"Oh, I'm fine. I'm just a little sorry that it's over."

He chuckled, that deep, sexy chuckle she loved so much. "It's not over. We've got dinner waiting for us, the full treatment. Are you hungry?"

"I'm sta-arving," she answered, the word stretched out dramatically as they dropped suddenly, the plane readying for its approach. Grace watched Lincoln as he concentrated on the controls, his piercing blue eyes focusing on the runway below. "I'm so glad you planned dinner…I could kiss you!" Surprised at her outburst and filling with adrenaline as Lincoln pointed the nose of the plane downward, Grace laughed out loud.

Lincoln, his eyes still trained on the runway, his hands gripping the controls carefully, let out a laugh as well and said, "If I wasn't landing a plane, I'd let you."

Minutes later they were rolling to a stop, safely on the ground. Before Grace could figure out how to extricate herself from the plane, Lincoln was there at the open door, holding her hand, helping her down.

With her feet back on earth and her hand in his, Grace was still floating in the clouds. Not quite sunset, the light had turned to magic hour when everyone and everything takes on a magical glow. Lincoln faced her and took her other hand in his, pulling her closer to him. Grace tilted her face up, her hands tingling at his touch.

"Grace…" he said, his voice gruff, but tender. He gazed into her eyes and a shiver moved up her spine. "You're perfect."

The rush of her day came back to her. She hadn't had time to fix her hair or makeup before going to the Hill House like she would have liked. The buggy ride to the airport had mussed her even more, and Grace could only imagine how the excitement of the plane trip had made her sweaty and wrinkled her clothes.

She shook her head slightly, deflecting his words, and glanced at the sun nearing its resting place for the night. "It's the light. Magic hour. Everything looks better at magic hour."

Lincoln dropped his gaze to the ground, bringing it back up slowly, allowing it to touch every inch of her body, neck, and face. "No, it's not the light. It's you. You're perfect." He squeezed her hands tenderly and leaned closer.

"Grace!" A familiar voice rang out behind her and Lincoln stopped, his body poised to kiss her, but put on pause. The voice came again, much closer, "Grace! Grace, what are you doing here?"

CHAPTER 50

At first, Zac didn't know what to think when Phoenix stopped in her tracks and waved her arms frantically back and forth in the air. They were on their way to the helicopter tour, which they were going to go on in secret…again.

Zac had met her and some of the other crew at one of the local watering holes they frequented. He hadn't been able to find Grace for a Friday night date and if truth be told he had grown a little tired of pursuing her with no results.

Phoenix, on the other hand, had been more than happy to give him a ride in her buggy to the bar. There they had drank a little too much and fell into hilarity sharing secret memories of their original helicopter ride.

"We should go again," Phoenix had blurted out before slurping a chunk of ice out of her margarita on the rocks and sucking the margarita off of it.

"Up there?" Zac pointed his finger straight into the air, trying to be discreet.

Phoenix put her thin hand over his finger, blocking it

from the view of everyone else. "Shhhhhhhh," she slurred. "Don't tell!"

It was so unusual for Phoenix to stray far from the rules–twice–that Zac couldn't resist, plus they were more than a little bit drunk.

Making their way through the airport had given them such giggling fits they had both cried.

Zac wondered briefly if anyone around recognized him. He grabbed Phoenix by the shoulder and stopped her. With a deeply concerned look on his face, he scanned the strangers at the airport and asked, "What if someone films us being drunk and puts it online?

Phoenix didn't pause to think like she usually did, she just threw her arms up in the air and almost shouted, "Who cares?" Zac cracked up laughing again. She continued, speaking in a booming, know-it-all, mock producer voice, "Zac, any publicity is good publicity. Don't you know that?"

He couldn't form words through his breathless laughter. She had nailed a perfect imitation of Rigby.

Phoenix turned slowly in a tipsy circle, surveying all of the people around them, pretending to look for any suspicious cell phone that might be capturing their silliness for the world to see. It was when her back was completely towards him that she stopped short. A few seconds later she was jumping up and down, waving her arms.

Zac didn't know what to think. He searched in the distance for what had captured her attention. That's when he heard her shout, "Grace!"

"Grace?" Zac straightened up immediately, squinting his eyes in an attempt to overcome double vision.

Phoenix took off in a determined jog towards a small prop plane parked about 30 yards away. Two people stood next to the plane, a man and a woman. Once his eyes focused in on the couple he could see that the woman was Grace. But who was the man?

"Grace! Grace, what are you doing here?" Phoenix was already halfway to them. Zac took off after her, but had to adjust his speed so he wouldn't swerve too much or trip over his own feet. Too many margaritas.

Grace whirled around at the sound of her name. "Phoenix?" She looked past her slender young producer to Zac veering and bumbling as he tried to catch up. "Zac?" She looked surprised–really surprised–and a little embarrassed.

Phoenix gasped loudly, her normal filters wiped out by liquor, "Were you FLYING?! In THIS PLANE?!"

Grace didn't answer right away, though her tall companion stepped up next to her protectively. Zac slowed down as he approached. There was no reason to get punched in the nose by whoever this guy was.

Grace jutted her chin out slightly in defiance. "Yes, I was flying."

Phoenix gasped again and clapped her hands over the top of her head. "Grace! You're not covered for flying. Not in a plane like *this*!" She waved her hand around dramatically at the less than luxurious airplane behind them.

Zac didn't remind her that they were about to go up in a helicopter for the second time in a month, an activity that was definitely not covered by the production insurance. That was one little fact he figured he could keep to himself.

While Phoenix and Grace discussed the situation Zac took stock of Grace's companion and the way he kept one hand on the small of her back, a silent steady sign of attachment. He was tall, taller than Zac, and fit, but not in weight lifting way, more like the way Zac's uncles who ran their own construction company.

Zac had never seen this guy before…and he didn't like the way they had been standing together before Grace saw

Phoenix...staring into each other's eyes...looking like they were getting ready to kiss.

"What's up?" Zac said to the guy, wanting to seem coolly detached yet tough enough to take him. After the words came out he realized they made him sound more like an impish teenager.

Grace's companion paused, taking in Zac's juvenile greeting. Zac dropped a little under his weighted stare and had to remind himself to stand straighter, look taller. Finally, without saying a word, the guy gave Zac a quick nod in response.

"I cannot believe you would put yourself in this kind of danger!" Phoenix was still ranting in a very un-Phoenix type way.

Grace, it seemed, had had enough.

"I do not need to explain myself to you," she said. Her green eyes, hot with irritation, flicked to Zac. "Either of you."

Phoenix clamped her lips together. Zac was surprised at the reprimand. Heat crawled up his neck as he felt like a teenager once again.

He raised his palms up in front of his chest, surrendering before there was a fight. "No, of course not. No explanation needed. Right, Phoenix?" He caught Phoenix's eye and nodded encouragingly.

Before Phoenix could respond, Grace's eyes narrowed as she looked from Zac to Phoenix then back again. "What are you two doing here anyway?"

Phoenix's face went pale, or paler than normal. Zac raced through all of the possible reasons they could be at an airport together and his mind was blank.

"I wanted to see if I could get some celebratory helicopter rides for the crew when we wrap filming," Phoenix said.

Zac looked at her, a little stunned and a little impressed. The ease with which she lied was unexpected.

Grace zeroed in on him. "And you?"

"Oh, right, well, I was a little bored. Thought I'd tag along."

A queer amusement lifted the corners of Grace's mouth and the tension dissipated. Phoenix seemed calmer, too. The crisis had passed and nobody was the wiser that she had taken Zac up in a helicopter once already, and had been planning another flight just minutes before.

Despite the mood mellowing out between them all, Zac had a hard knot in his stomach. He couldn't shake the feeling that he and Phoenix had just been scolded–and he couldn't let go of the way Grace turned her attention back so completely to the tall, silent stranger at her side.

CHAPTER 51

*G*race shivered at his touch. Her shoulder and back were naked in the balmy night air, but it was the feel of his finger tracing lightly over her skin that made her shiver, she was sure of it.

Keeping her eyes lowered, afraid to look him in the eye and break the spell that she was under as he undressed her, Grace loosened her grip on the flowing blouse she had been clutching to her chest, the last vestige of her clothing, allowing it to slip slowly down her body.

"Are you certain?" he growled, his voice low.

Grace raised her eyes to his, hoping they conveyed all of the love and wonder of a woman about to give everything over to the man of her dreams.

The perfect quiet night around them was suddenly shattered by a loud pop. Instantly the moonlight that softly spilled over her and the man of her dreams shut off.

"Cut!" a voice called out from the darkness. Then, with more frustration, "Cut, cut, cut!"

Grace lifted the falling blouse back up over her chest as she squinted into the darkness. "Syd, what happened?" She could still feel Zac's finger on her shoulder blade where it had paused its caress when the light changed. Without saying anything, Grace shrugged slightly and he pulled it away.

The crew that had been settled in around them, quietly monitoring the equipment as she and Zac pretended to make love, erupted in noise and movement.

"We blew a circuit," Max called out.

Grace sighed, annoyed and tired—and a little cold, "Syd, what is going on?"

"Just hold tight there Grace, we'll get it back in a minute and start from the top."

"Hold tight? I'm cold."

"Yeah, could we get some blankets or something over here," Zac piped up from behind her.

She turned and looked over her shoulder. Zac was positioned behind her, angled so when they kissed he could easily pull her back and get into his position over the top of her and it would all look good on camera, their best sides being seen by the audience rather than each other. In reality, they were sitting too awkwardly to look each other in the eye when they spoke, which was all right with Grace. Sex scenes were always a little too intimate. Avoiding eye contact wasn't the worst thing that could happen.

Shirtless, rippling abs, tan, his hair perfectly roughed up, nobody could deny Zac's amazing looks. Yet there she was, getting ready to be wrapped in his arms over and over again as Syd did take after take to get the scene he wanted, and Grace didn't feel a glimmer of attraction.

Her lack of attraction to him may have worried her at another time, wondering if she could play off Scarlet's love for Ethan when she didn't have any romantic feelings for her co-star whatsoever, Grace was not concerned. She was not concerned because she had a secret weapon and his name was Lincoln Reeves.

After their amazing plane ride, brief encounter with the drunken duo Phoenix and Zac, and the candle light dinner served on a secluded section of beach by Lincoln's friend, Arny, she and Lincoln had gone home together. By the time they arrived at the Hill House Grace could hardly think straight, her brain had been overcome by passion.

Lincoln's touch, the twinkle in his eye, the feeling of his body next to hers at dinner and on the drive home, the way she could sink into his voice as he talked, he filled her every sense completely. She had nothing left to pay attention to anything or anyone else.

He led her into the Hill House leaving off the main light and taking her to the sofa that faced the giant picture windows looking out over the deck and beyond.

"Have a seat." He beckoned to the comfortable pillows and Grace sat. He sat down next to her and put his arm around her shoulders so she could nestle into him. "Do you want a drink?" he asked.

"No, thank you. This is perfect," she said, and she meant it.

Lincoln pulled her into him and she put her hand on his chest, breathing in the delicious scent of him. When she felt his lips brush her hair she lifted her eyes to his, consumed with the desire to kiss him.

Lincoln searched her eyes, his heartbeat increased under the palm of her hand. Grace knew he wanted to kiss her just as badly as she wanted it. Yet, he did not move.

After a long moment, she pulled back, a question on her lips. Lincoln started to explain before she had a chance to ask it.

"I want to propose something to you," he started.

"Propose something?"

He cleared his throat, not sure how to proceed, but

pushing forward anyway. "I am unbelievably attracted to you. Know that, please."

She pulled further back so she was no longer under his arm, but sitting sideways on the couch to listen. This was not turning into the conversation she expected.

"Okay…what's going on?" she asked cautiously.

"I want to be sure you know how I feel before I…propose what I'm going to propose."

Grace didn't know what to think. "I'm getting confused. You keep saying propose. What are you proposing?" Her heart skipped a beat. Was he actually going to *propose* propose?

"It's nothing crazy," he reassured her. He shifted on the couch so he, too, was sitting sideways facing her. "I think we should wait, that's all."

"Wait?"

"I know, I know, it's probably not what you're used to hearing." He ran his hand through his hair roughly. "Honestly, it's not what I'm used to saying."

"Wait for…?"

Lincoln lifted his eyebrows and used one finger to point between the two of them. "Wait…for this."

"Oh!" Understanding set in, quickly followed by more confusion. "So…you don't want to…?"

"No, no, no, that's not it. I absolutely want to…" he hesitated, looking deeply into her eyes until goosebumps rippled up her back and shoulders. Lincoln let his gaze drop to her hands and he reached out, covering them with his. "I don't want to rush into something and somehow ruin it."

"You think making love would ruin things?" Grace still couldn't quite wrap her mind around this conversation. She tried to think of the last time a man refused to go to bed with her.

Nothing came to mind. Never. It had never happened.

"No, not ruin things." He sighed and looked down, frustrated with trying to explain and, hopefully, with having to control his passion.

When he looked back up the blue in his eyes matched the deep turquoise of the waters that surrounded the island he loved so much. The sensation of him looking into her soul with those eyes was so intense she could not tear her gaze away even if she wanted to.

"I think what we have is real, Grace. It's more real than anything I've ever had with anyone else. And I–I want to make sure we don't miss any important steps along the way. I want to make sure we do it right."

Grace couldn't speak. Her heart was caught in her throat, her breath came in shallow gasps.

Lincoln's brow furrowed. "Are you all right?"

"I'm all right," she managed to squeak out. "I'm more than all right."

Lincoln smiled, knowing what she meant without her having to spell it out. "You are more than all right," he said as he lifted her hand to his lips and kissed her fingers tenderly. "You're absolutely perfect."

That was the precise moment Grace Woods fell in love. Completely, unequivocally, unabashedly in love.

That was also the moment she returned to all week when she was away from him, filming. She tapped into her intense desire for Lincoln and the promise that they were involved in something bigger and deeper than a simple island fling and used that energy in her work.

She acted out her scenes as Scarlet holding Lincoln's words in her heart. As she and Zac played out a love affair for the camera, Grace pretended she was looking at Lincoln, that Lincoln was touching her, that it was Lincoln kissing her, laying her back, brushing her hair away from her face, making love to her.

She had to admit the gimmick was working well. Grace could sense the scenes were good and Syd couldn't stop raving about them.

"That was fantastic. Really great you two," he called out after each take. After one particularly emotional scene he was brought to tears. "Wonderful, just wonderful," he said as he wiped his eyes and told Max that was a wrap for the day.

The sex scene was the last scene scheduled before their break and Grace would be glad when it was over. Filming was going well, and that was great, but Grace's heart and soul had shifted to a real man in the real world…with real love flowing between them.

The moonlight turned back on and two assistants rushed to gather the blankets they had thrown over Grace and Zac while they waited.

"All right, ladies and gentlemen, we are back in business. Back to one," Max called out.

"Are you two ready?" Syd asked from his director's chair.

"Are you ready, Grace?" Zac asked from behind her.

She nodded happily. She felt ready to take on the world. "Absolutely."

Zac nodded at Syd and waved his hand. "We're good. Ready to go."

To say filming the rest of the sex scene with Zac was grueling would probably be an overstatement, Grace realized, but it took longer than she had expected and she began to get antsy. She wanted finish up and gather her things to go see Lincoln. Every minute that they worked late was a minute she wasn't going to spend with him.

Finally, Syd called it and she was free to change and go up to the Hill House. She wished she could have someone deliver her bag instead of having to go back to the beach house for it, but she didn't want Faye to find out all of the details of her weekends. She loved her friend, but Grace wanted to keep Lincoln to herself for as long as possible. Do things the right way, like he said.

"Hello, darling, we were wondering if you would ever be finished," Faye greeted her when she walked through the door.

"Yes, it was a long day. I'm ready to–" Grace stopped short when she saw who was in the room.

There was Faye sipping a glass of wine, Ronnie grinning from ear to ear, and Presley. A very pregnant Presley with Hobie by her side.

"Oh my goodness!" Grace covered her mouth with her hands then hurried to them for a big hug.

"Hi! We've come to surprise you for your birthday," Presley explained.

"My birthday? That's not until next week."

"We had to get here and get settled in," Hobie said, giving Presley a protective look.

Grace, still surprised, nodded in agreement and stepped back to see Presley's swollen belly. "Look at you! You're gorgeous," she gushed.

Presley shook her head, smiling, "You don't have to say that. I'm quite lumpy, but I'm fine with it."

"Well, it's great to see you both…all of you I mean," Grace said, circling her hand around Presley's belly to include the baby.

"We're glad to be here…and we're starving," Presley said.

"We waited for you so we could all go to dinner together," Ronnie said.

"Do you want to change first?" Faye said, noticing Grace's wrinkled shorts and T-shirt. She never dressed up to go to the set. No reason to, they were going to put her into her costume anyway.

Grace's mind flew to Lincoln and the Hill House.

"You don't have to change," Ronnie said. "We could order in?"

"Nonsense, this is a celebration dinner," Faye disagreed. "We're all together again…except Ruby. But don't worry, she's coming in a few days," she reassured Grace.

Grace realized that Faye thought she was disappointed about Ruby, but it wasn't that at all.

She looked around at her friends who were waiting expectantly. She couldn't very well get out of this dinner after Presley and Hobie had flown all that way to see her.

She threw on a smile. Everything would be all right. She would go to dinner and make her way up to the Hill House afterward. She had postponed her desire to see Lincoln all week, a few more hours wouldn't be the end of the world. She would just text him and let him know what was going on.

It wasn't until Grace was in her bedroom changing clothes that she realized she had never gotten Lincoln's cell phone number.

CHAPTER 52

*L*incoln sat on the couch where he and Grace had spent most of the previous weekend. He took a sip of the whiskey he had been nursing since he got home from her film set. Whiskey he had picked up on the way, hoping he wouldn't need it, but thinking he might.

It was past 11:30, long after Grace usually showed up, and she still hadn't arrived.

He took another sip, letting the liquor burn the back of his throat before swallowing. The sun had set hours ago leaving him staring out the window into the dark with his own faint reflection glowering back at him.

"Bloody stupid, that's what you are," he said to himself.

He dropped his head, not wanting to see his pathetic miserable face anymore. Instead, he focused on the whiskey remaining in the glass. Not much. He would get up for a refill soon.

"Yes you will," he muttered. "You'll get completely bombed before the night is over. Serves you right."

Lincoln squeezed his eyes shut, blocking the pain in his head. In his heart.

If only he hadn't gone down to surprise her. If only he hadn't gotten too confident. He wouldn't have seen… wouldn't have had to watch her…

Lincoln shook his head sharply and slammed the rest of his drink, the burning almost making him choke. He could not think about what he'd seen again. He stood and went to the kitchen counter to pour another. This time to the rim.

"Why not?" he muttered. Not a soul around to watch him drink himself into oblivion. Why the hell not?

His cell phone rang loudly and buzzed in his pocket. He had set the volume on high after she didn't arrive when expected. Lincoln put his drink down and hurriedly fished out his phone only to be disappointed when he saw Luke's name on the screen. He punched the button to answer.

"Yeah?" he said gruffly.

"Hey, Link. You busy?"

"Why?" Lincoln picked up his drink again and took a healthy swig.

"I was gonna swing over for a bit in the morning."

"Were you?" Lincoln coughed out a laugh.

"Yeah, what's so funny?"

"Nothing. Never mind."

"Anyway, I want to talk to you," Luke continued. So businesslike.

"Isn't it Friday night?" Lincoln asked.

"Yeah."

"I would think you'd be out."

There was a pause before Luke answered, "We're on the boat."

"Who's we?"

"Oh, you know, the usual. Why, you gonna join us?" Luke laughed at the idea.

Lincoln glanced around the empty room and his eye caught his reflection in the darkened windows once again.

He thought about Grace, half nude, wrapped in the arms of that moron actor. He closed his eyes, a wave of nausea moving through his stomach.

"Why not?" Lincoln answered.

Luke laughed, then paused, then asked, "Are you serious?"

Lincoln took another sip of the whiskey. All he knew was that he was going to need a lot more than the small bottle he had bought just in case to forget about watching Grace tonight…to blast out of his memory the fact that he had purposely told her he wanted to move slow and probably blew his chance…and to get over the fact that she wasn't coming to the Hill House tonight. Maybe never again.

CHAPTER 53

"The chef truly outdid herself," Faye told the waiter. "We were all astounded, really." The head waiter tucked his head and gave Faye and the rest of them a tight bow. "Send our compliments to her if you would. Or, better yet, ask her to come out so we can give them ourselves," Faye suggested.

Grace raised her glass to signal her agreement with Faye's suggestion, but inside she was in agony.

When was this dinner going to end? It felt like they had been sitting around talking and eating forever.

"I don't think we can wait around for the chef," Hobie said. "My wife is tired from our trip."

Presley did look tired. No wonder, poor thing, flying halfway around the world while pregnant had to be exhausting.

"You know, I'm a little tired, too, Faye," Grace added. She took the opportunity to look at her phone. "It's almost midnight. We should probably get going."

Faye considered their opinions for a few moments before deeming them valid and waved the head waiter away. "On the other hand, we need to be going now. Send our compliments if you will."

"Of course, Madame," the waiter answered as he stepped away.

Faye frowned. "Madame. Why do they always go straight to Madame these days."

Presley laughed as she took Hobie's hand and let him help her stand. "I think we have to accept it. We're closer to Madame's than Misses."

"Hmph," Faye sniffed.

"How about Ms.? Would that be better?" Ronnie asked.

"I don't know. Would you rather be a Ms. than a Madame?" Faye asked Grace.

Grace wasn't listening. All she wanted to do was get back to the beach house, gather her things, and be gone. She had enjoyed dinner with her friends, but it paled in comparison to the weekend with Lincoln.

Hobie escorted Presley away to their suite to get some rest. The rest of them returned to the beach house.

Faye swept into the room, tossing her purse and scarf on a side table and sinking into the large sectional couch.

"Doesn't Presley look beautiful? Pregnancy agrees with her. Who knew?" Faye chuckled at the idea.

"It really does. They're going to be wonderful parents," Ronnie chimed in.

Grace mumbled something in agreement and turned to go to her bedroom.

"Are you too tired to sit up with us a little?" Faye asked. "I feel like we haven't gotten a chance to visit for weeks, even though we're roommates."

"Well, I'm leaving. I can't visit."

"You're leaving?" Faye sat up in surprise. "Wherever are you going?"

Grace fumbled her answer, still wanting Lincoln to herself as much as possible, but desperate to get to him.

"I'm…I'm going up to my getaway."

Faye's eyes widened. "At this hour?"

"Mm-hmm," Grace responded, a little too meekly.

"You can't wander off into the jungle in the middle of the night. It's after midnight. You'll be dragged off by a jaguar or something."

Ronnie giggled uncomfortably. "I don't think there are jaguars here."

Faye waved her hand around in the air above her head, fending off Ronnie's comment. "If not jaguars there's got to be night snakes or some kind of rabid bats flying around at night."

Grace tried to argue, though fatigue was getting the better of her. It had been a very long day of filming then dinner and several glasses of wine. She was spent.

"I can have a driver take me," she said.

Faye scoffed at that idea, "What if they've been drinking? You could end up all smashed against a palm tree or run off one of these cliffs."

"Faye, I'm sure I can find a responsible driver."

"Why don't you stay here with us. A few hours of sleep and it will be morning. Then you can go up in the daylight. All you're going to do is sleep there tonight anyway."

Grace looked to Ronnie for help, but she wasn't much of an arguer. She gave Grace a weak smile.

The problem was, Grace was tired, so tired that Faye's points seemed to have some merit. She would only be getting there in time to go to sleep. It would be nice to just get some sleep at the beach house then get up early, take a shower, and get freshened up to see Lincoln. She had been filming all day then had a long dinner, she probably looked pretty run down.

"I guess…" she said.

"You guess. I'm right, of course," Faye smiled. She loved it when things went her way. "You just run off to bed and get some rest, darling."

Grace swayed a little as she made her way down the hallway to her bedroom. More proof that she did need some sleep.

As she kicked off her shoes and flopped onto her bed she thought surely Lincoln would understand. He was probably asleep by now anyway. She would be up and on her way first thing in the morning. He might even still be asleep when she arrived.

The last concern that flitted across her mind as she drifted off to sleep was that she wished she had his cell phone number so she could call and let him know. That concern sank into darkness and Grace fell asleep.

The next morning she was true to her plans. Up before dawn, she took a quick shower, making sure to call for a driver before she did so she wouldn't waste any time waiting on anyone.

Her hair still wet, she swept it up into a bun, dabbed on some light moisturizer and enough makeup to make her eyes stand out without looking too over the top. Then she put on a pair of wide legged lightweight slacks and a teal tank top. She packed her getaway bag with more necessities, grabbed her sunglasses and purse, and left the beach house before Ronnie or Faye had even stirred for the day.

By the time she reached the Hill House the sun was up. Birds sang in the surrounding trees as she used her key to unlock the front door.

"Lincoln?" she called out as she entered.

No answer.

Grace rolled her bag into the empty living room and scanned the deck outside through the windows. No Lincoln.

She abandoned her suitcase and strolled to her bedroom…his bedroom…smiling at her confusion, she said quietly, "The master bedroom." Turning the knob and pushing the door open slightly she sang a quiet, "Good morning." The curtains were drawn and the room was dark, but not too dark to see that Lincoln wasn't there.

It only took a few more minutes to look through the whole house and determine he was not home. Not only wasn't he home, but none of the beds looked like they had been slept in. Worry wrung at her heart.

Grace went to the kitchen to make some coffee. Maybe he was running an errand and would be back any minute. She would have coffee ready for him.

A small bottle of whiskey and a used glass sat on the kitchen counter, both empty. Grace chewed her bottom lip, thinking about the possibilities. A growing sense of doom filled her stomach. Before she made coffee she decided to duck back out the front door to see if his buggy was parked outside. She had been in such a hurry to get into the house, she had not thought to look.

She checked the long driveway, her heart sinking. The buggy was gone and Lincoln was gone with it.

CHAPTER 54

*L*incoln couldn't move his right arm–and he was hot.

He opened one eye, but closed it immediately and groaned. The light pierced his eyeball and went straight to his brain, sending splinters of pain through his entire head. He groaned.

"Mmmm…" a woman's voice groaned in response close by. Very close by. "What's the matter, baby?"

Lincoln recognized the voice, like an echo of his past, but not one he wanted for his future. He put his left hand over his eyes and tried opening them again. The dark helped dull the pain a bit so he opened his fingers just enough to peek through them and see who was talking.

Short blonde hair, big blue eyes looking at him blearily. It was Renee, his old girlfriend from high school. No doubt about it. And she wasn't just talking to him, she was laying on him, or at least on his right arm. The rest of her was kind of cuddled up alongside him, her leg over his, her hand on his chest.

"Renee?"

"Live and in the flesh," she said with a giggle.

Lincoln moved his arm out from under her and sat up, which sent more stabbing pain through his head, but he wanted to know where he was. Before he could uncover his eyes to look, a wave of nausea rolled through his stomach and he had to hold himself still to keep from throwing up.

Only he wasn't holding still. He was moving up and down…with the water…he was on the boat.

"Where are you going?" Renee cooed, wiggling her fingers back up onto his chest.

Lincoln pulled her hand gently off of him and stood up. It would be better to throw up than lay there any longer with her, especially since he couldn't remember how she had gotten there or what, if anything, they had done last night.

Lincoln braved removing his hand from his eyes and squinting into the light to find his shirt. The light made his head pound but he would get over it. He needed to get dressed and get out of here.

"Morning," Luke said as he lowered himself into the galley, blocking Lincoln's exit. He had on a pair of shorts and nothing else and looked rough, like he had been up all night. Lincoln figured Luke looked like he felt.

"Hi, Lukey," Renee called out from the bunk bed fit into the far corner of the space, the bed Lincoln had just left.

Luke grinned and gave Lincoln a knowing look. "Hey, Renee. Want some coffee?"

Lincoln stared at the floor, not wanting to give Luke any more ideas than he already had. While Renee was distracted, however, he stole a look at her. She wore a pair of short shorts and a bikini top, but she was still wearing both items of clothing, which was some relief.

"Yeah, coffee'd be good," Renee agreed.

Luke raised the empty pot up to show Lincoln. "Coffee?"

All Lincoln wanted to do was get out of here. "I'll get some at home, thanks."

Luke put the pot in the small sink to fill it up and made a tsk-tsk sound.

Lincoln didn't like the sound of it. "What?"

"It's gonna be a while before you can get home."

"Why?"

"Why do you want to go home so soon, Link?" Renee asked, giving him her version of a sexy look.

Lincoln gave her a weak smile and turned back to Luke, keeping his voice calm, but firm. "Why can't I go home now, Luke?"

Luke cringed a little at the question, then answered, "We're drifting."

"What?"

Luke shrugged and yawned as a thin stream of water poured into the coffee pot. "Yeah, the engine died last night after we took her out. I can't get it going."

Lincoln had to see for himself. He pushed past Luke and onto the deck. As far as he could see, in every direction, there was only water.

Luke popped his head up out of the galley. "No worries, now that you're up we'll have it going in a few hours."

Lincoln wanted to talk to Grace. He'd run off in a hurry the night before, angry and hurt, he could admit that, but he needed to talk to her. He needed to know she was okay and tell her that he would be back at the Hill House in a few hours. He pulled his phone out of his pocket. Maybe he could get her number from Luke.

Luke saw him and shook his head back and forth. "No service out here, mate. Wherever we are."

"What about the radio?" Lincoln asked.

"We've got a little juice for it. Saving that in case of a real emergency," Luke said, then disappeared back into the galley.

Lincoln's shoulders slumped. It wasn't an emergency for him to talk to Grace. Besides, what was he going to do, radio someone at the marina to call Grace Woods and tell her he'd be late?

Lincoln gripped his fists and half-growled half-shouted out at the open ocean in frustration.

"You all right, Link?" another woman's voice asked from the helm.

Lincoln turned in surprise to find Melanie, one of Luke's on again off again girls, sitting in the Captain's chair.

He gave her a sheepish smile. "Sorry, Mel."

"I'll forgive you if you brought me some coffee," she said with a wink.

He held up his empty hands and she giggled.

Lincoln turned around with a sigh. If he was ever going to get them back to shore and get himself back home he had better start working on the engine.

It was early evening before Lincoln made it back to the Hill House. Sunburned, covered in grease and dirt from working in tight quarters to get the engine running, dehydrated, hot, and hungry, Lincoln opened the front door with only a tiny nugget of hope Grace might be there waiting for him.

That nugget quickly disappeared when he was met with silence. No surprise the house was empty. Why would she wait around without hearing a word from him?

He cursed under his breath as he tossed his keys and dead cell phone down on the kitchen counter. That's when he saw the note.

Folded neatly and placed near the empty bottle of whiskey, his name unmistakable on the front. He picked it up, smudging the edges with grease. The handwriting was elegant and neat. Looking at it made his heart sink.

Sorry I missed you. I don't have your cell number! Silly, right?

I hope everything is all right.

Some friends of mine have flown in to visit. I left to spend some time with them. I would like to introduce you to them when you have time.

If you don't have time this weekend, come to the set this week. Or to the Beach House at the hotel.

Grace

LINCOLN READ it over a few times, wondering if she had been angry when she wrote it. Or sad. Or indifferent.

He didn't know.

He didn't know what to do, either.

He put the note down and his eyes flicked to the empty whiskey bottle. Disgusted, he grabbed it and threw it away.

"Bloody idiot," he said under his breath. Leaving the note behind, he went to take a shower and wash away the disappointment of the last two days.

CHAPTER 55

Grace was awake, but numb.

Numb to the brilliant island sun, numb to the conversation around her, numb to everything. Anything she ate turned to dust in her mouth and nothing but water could wash the dust away. If anyone offered her anything else she didn't want it. The taste of any kind of flavored drink made her gag.

"Are you sure you're not sick?" Ronnie asked, worry washing out her normally happy expression.

Grace waved her concerns away weakly. "I'm just a little tired."

She wasn't lying. Grace hadn't slept all night. Torn between worrying that something horrible had happened to Lincoln to being furious that he had ignored her to being riddled with guilt for not arriving when he expected and, perhaps, making him think she wasn't coming at all.

"You need to get your rest," Faye chimed in from her lounge chair. They were relaxing around the infinity pool at the Beach House, waiting for Presley and Hobie to arrive for lunch.

Grace didn't answer. Her numbness extended to her ability to make conversation. She couldn't seem to hold two thoughts together in her head or remember what someone said to her moments after they said it.

She closed her eyes to the sunny day. Covered by a wide brimmed hat, Grace sat underneath an umbrella. She couldn't get sunburned. She was filming tomorrow.

Her thoughts turned briefly to the movie.

Syd assured her they had gotten great footage. The biggest scenes, including the sex scene, had been shot. They only had a few weeks left before they were done at this location and everyone went back to America.

Her throat clenched, hot tears burned at the back of her eyes.

"Grace?" Ronnie stood over her, still worried, Grace could tell by the tone of her voice.

"Mm-hmm," she answered, pretending to be enjoying a moment of zen instead of fighting back tears.

"You should try this. It's a green tea infusion. It's got tons of vitamins and antioxidants. Maybe that will help."

Grace managed a smile. "Okay, just put it down here if you would." She patted the small table next to her chair and Ronnie obliged.

"Sorry we're late," Presley said as she and Hobie joined them at the pool.

"You're like three minutes late. That's not late," Ronnie teased.

"It's perfect timing. Lunch is arriving any moment," Faye informed them.

As if on cue, several wait staff were ushered into the shady side of the pool. They quickly set up a table laden with chilled seafood, warm crusty rolls, fruit trays, and several vegetable salads.

Thankful they were eating outside where she could keep

on her sunglasses, Grace collected a few items on a plate and nibbled on them as her friends engaged in boisterous conversation.

Presley was especially animated. Sitting by her ever adoring husband, eating for two, she was a glowing example of marital and maternal bliss. Watching them talk about what names they were thinking of for their child, Grace's numbness was temporarily stabbed through by a pang of loneliness. She was struck with the realization that, perhaps, she had spent too long chasing movie making and ill suited men instead of finding true happiness like her friend.

Without realizing it, she let out a heavy sigh. All eyes turned to her.

"Come now," Ronnie said. "We know something is bothering you. What's wrong?"

Grace didn't have an answer. She hadn't confided in any of them about her relationship with Lincoln and that relationship seemed to be dissipating, blowing away with the ocean breeze. Where could she begin? How she felt about him? How he had told her they had something real, but just a week later it all seemed to be nothing but fluff?

A thought struck her. Had Lincoln avoided a physical relationship with her because he wasn't actually attracted to her? She clamped her teeth together so she could keep a gentle smile steady on her face, an Acting 101 trick.

"Is it the movie?" Presley ventured a guess.

Grace latched onto the idea. Better to let them think that than try to explain her secret and very short love affair with Lincoln. She nodded.

"Oh, sweetie, I thought it was going well," Ronnie said.

"It is, it's just..." Grace managed to say before getting choked up.

"Is it because it's almost over? You always get pretty attached to the process, don't you?" Presley said.

"We're here for you," Faye said, standing and coming around behind Grace to give her shoulders a quick hug. "And it's about to be your birthday and we'll all have such fun together!"

Grace patted Faye's hand. She didn't feel any better, but it was nice to know they cared.

"Ms. Woods has a visitor," an assistant announced from the patio entrance.

Grace's heart skipped a beat. She dropped the bit of roll she had been pretending to eat on her plate and stood up so fast she upset the table next to her, spilling the glass of infused green tea.

Faye stepped back, giving her room and laughing in delight at Grace's recovery from her gloomy mood. "See, darling! You have a visitor. There's nothing to be grim about."

Grace turned with expectant joy towards the patio entrance, walking to the shadowy figure moving towards the patio entrance, ready to forgive everything and take Lincoln in her arms again.

The figure stepped into the light and Grace stopped short.

"Ruby!" Faye called out.

"Hi!" Ruby said, coming to Grace with open arms. "Happy Birthday!"

CHAPTER 56

*I*f there was one thing Faye adored it was life changing makeovers, the kind they used to have on television before it was taken over by those fake reality shows. The kind of makeover that took someone from blasé to out of this world beautiful.

That was the kind of makeover happening right in front of her. That kind of life changing happiness was why she had decided to stay at the beach house while every single one of her friends was out exploring the islands. She couldn't help it, Faye was dedicated to helping those less fortunate than her.

"Do you really think darker is the way to go?" Phoenix asked, holding up a section of her barely blonde, barely anything, hair.

"Contrast, darling. That's the key, isn't it?" Faye looked to Antoinette for confirmation.

"Contrast is very good place to start," Antoinette, who had a rather thick French accent, looked up from where she was huddled with the hotel's hairstylist mixing color in a small white bowl. "The dark with the fair skin with the big eyes–magnifique!" Antoinette clapped her hands together, applauding the very idea of it.

"And you have to try this," Faye instructed Phoenix from her chair next to the salon chair that had been brought to the beach house for the day's activities.

"What is that?" Phoenix asked suspiciously, eyeing the jar of dark grey lumpy goop in Faye's hand.

"It's everything your skin has ever needed and didn't know how to ask," Faye said with a laugh. She handed it to one of several assistants milling around them. "It literally peels away years of stress," she said.

"Oh," Phoenix answered, leaning her head back in the chair so the assistant could smear it all over her face. "I guess I could use some of that."

Faye was delighted that Phoenix had finally agreed to the makeover. She had been essential in planning Grace's surprise party and since everything was practically ready to go for that on the coming Friday night, there wasn't a lot left to do except play with makeup and hair.

"I'll take some, too," Faye told the assistant. "When you're done with her."

"Excuse me," a man said from the doorway.

People had been coming and going, in and out, all day long, carrying hair and makeup supplies, food and drinks, and clothes for the fashion portion of the makeover, so it wasn't unusual that they were interrupted.

What was unusual was how handsome this man was. Tall- quite tall–blonde, tan, and with the most magnetic blue eyes. She momentarily forgot about Phoenix and turned her attention to the fine example of Australian masculinity waiting at the door.

"Yes?" she asked sweetly. "How can we help you?"

"I'm looking for Grace," he said, almost bashfully. Charming.

"She's not here," Faye responded. He must be a movie person, which made sense. He was a bit dressed down, something the movie types tended to do. "Do you have something to leave for her? I can take it."

"Or me," Phoenix chimed in from her chair where her face was almost completely covered with dark goop.

"You're not working today, don't forget. I'll take care of it." Faye stood and went to the delivery man. She stood quite close to him and drank in his deliciousness for a moment before holding out her hand palm up and saying, "You can give me whatever you're delivering."

He cleared his throat. "I don't have anything for her. I need to talk to her." As he spoke he lifted his shockingly blue eyes to Faye's. The meaning behind his words wasn't entirely clear, but she knew he wasn't just a delivery man.

Faye looked at him more closely. "Do you know Grace?"

She wondered if somehow one of Grace's lunatic fans had snuck past the security during their makeover chaos. Though, as lunatic fans went, he was terribly good looking.

"Yes," he said, looking more and more uncomfortable.

Faye narrowed her eyes. "Where did you meet her?"

"Where did I meet her?"

"Yes, you say you know her, so where did you meet?"

"Uh, on my boat. The boat she chartered when she first came to the island."

Faye thought back to what she knew about that boat trip and thought of the perfect question to find out if this ridiculously gorgeous man was actually a stalker. "And what unusual event happened on that boat trip?"

The man thought for a moment, then cracked a smile. "We saw a humpback whale."

Faye reached out and squeezed his forearm warmly. "Yes! Yes you did, darling. You're the Whale Captain? Marvelous."

With one sweep of her arm she indicated he should come in. "Please, Captain, join us."

He glanced awkwardly at Phoenix with her face covered in goop. Someone had put a slice of cucumber over each of her eyes.

"I don't want to intrude. Do you know when she'll be back?"

"Well, she's making a movie you know. It could be any minute now and it could be midnight. You never know with these movie people." Faye laughed lightly and looked at Phoenix, who didn't respond due to the cucumbers blocking her from any eye contact.

"Right," he said, though he looked quite moody about it. "Do you know if she's planning to go away for the weekend again?"

Faye frowned, that seemed like a personal question. The Whale Captain was handsome, certainly, but she didn't want him to get any ideas about Grace's availability.

"She's having a birthday celebration. It's going to be quite the party." She watched him for a reaction, there was none. So she added for good measure, "She's going with Zac Foster. Her co-star. They're dating, you know."

Phoenix stirred, making the cucumbers slide off of her eyes. She mumbled something unintelligible.

"Don't speak, darling, you'll crack your face," Faye told her. She smiled politely at the Captain. He wasn't reacting, not exactly. It was more that he was purposefully not *over-reacting*.

"I didn't know that. I thought they were just working together," he said.

Faye laughed dismissively. "Well, there's working together and there's *working* together, you know." She looked at Phoenix to back her up, but the girl was being tended to by a team of hovering estheticians. She looked back to the

Captain, gave him a wide eyed smile and said, "Anyhow, I will let her know that you came by."

The Captain nodded and turned to leave. He paused and turned halfway back, looking at her calmly, but with a sadness in his eyes. "No, don't tell her I came by. If that's all right. It's not important."

"Whatever you wish," Faye agreed. As she watched him leave she continued under her breath, "Poor soul. He never had a chance."

CHAPTER 57

"Who, exactly, do I need to talk to so I can get a decent sandwich around here?" Zac spouted off. For the third day in a row craft services had messed up his sandwich order and nobody was around to fix it.

By messed up he meant too much mayonnaise and squished up like someone had sat on it before bringing it to him. And by nobody he meant Phoenix. He hadn't seen Phoenix all week and there was literally nobody else around who could take care of these annoying little problems.

"Hey, hey, what's the problem?" Rigby sauntered to Zac's side.

The older producer had probably been sent over by the production assistants who were too afraid to talk to Zac on their own lest he blow up at them. Zac wasn't proud of that fact, but seriously, how hard was it to get a sandwich that hadn't been sat on to the star of the movie...or one of the stars.

The other star of the movie, the one and only Grace Woods, had also been avoiding him all week, which didn't help his mood.

"I don't want to be a jerk, Rigby, but look at this." Zac held up the flattened BLT and dropped it back onto the paper plate they had delivered it on. "I mean, I honestly think someone might be doing that on purpose."

Rigby chuckled, "Ah, now, Zac, don't be silly."

Zac shot an accusing look at a few nearby crew members, all of them were avoiding eye contact with him.

"Nobody else's sandwiches are flattened before they get them," he complained.

Rigby just chuckled again. Not much help.

"Where's Phoenix? She can usually fix this kind of stuff."

Rigby nodded and gave Zac a placating smile. "Phoenix has been pulled away for a few days. You know that. Didn't I tell you that?"

"Yes," Zac sighed heavily. "I don't get why she didn't tell me. That's all."

"I see."

Zac didn't know what that meant, but it irritated him regardless.

"And what about Grace? Has she been pulled away? I mean, she's still in the movie, isn't she?" Rigby frowned and Zac thought maybe he had gone too far. "Sorry, no disrespect intended. I guess I just feel like I'm out of the loop or something...and I'm hungry."

Rigby patted him on the back again, though a little less chummy this time around.

"There's no loop, Zac. Everyone's busy getting ready to wrap everything next week." He looked at Zac's flat sandwich. "I'll get you another sandwich."

"It's not the sandwich I guess. I think I'm just not feeling up to par. You know, wondering how I'm doing, how it's all going to turn out, and there's nobody to, you know, talk to about it."

Rigby smiled his toothy smile. "I'm here to talk to. The

footage is great, really great. I think we've got a real winner here." Rigby lowered his voice and added, "And all the media attention on you and Grace is gonna keep everything real exciting for a while."

Zac gave Rigby a blank look. Feeling stupid he said, "But there isn't anything going on with me and Grace. That whole thing was a flop, too. I couldn't get in with her no matter what I tried."

Rigby leaned even closer to Zac with knowing eyes, whispering, "There doesn't have to be anything real, my boy. It's all a show. You just make sure you show up at her birthday party and smile a lot and we'll get the PR we need."

Out of nowhere, Rigby produced a new BLT sandwich, perfect in every way, on a crisp new paper plate. Zac looked around, uncertain who had given it to him–and how–when he had been right there next to him the whole time. He took the sandwich, because he was hungry, but his sense of uneasiness had only risen.

Zac wasn't altogether sure about anything anymore.

CHAPTER 58

*L*incoln slept in the spare room of the Hill House for days. He couldn't bring himself to sleep in the master room–her room. Nor could he sleep on the couch where they had spent so much time talking and laughing last weekend, or the hammock that had unceremoniously tossed them out when she woke him up, or anywhere really. Virtually every inch of the Hill House reminded him of Grace. If there was anyplace else he could go to escape her memory, he would have gone.

But there wasn't any place. He was stuck.

He sat on the steps of the deck, not even wanting to be at the table where they had shared so many meals together. He had thought about going to the boat, but even the boat had been touched by her presence. Ruined by it.

Fred and Ginger bobbed around on the floor of the deck behind him making occasional squawking sounds, popping their heads around him to check out what he was doing. They weren't used to him being eye level with them on the floor and they didn't know quite how to react.

Fred waddled back and forth, gently tapping the back of Lincoln's arm with his black beak. "Have a go, mate," he said.

Lincoln snapped a cracker he was holding in half and gave a piece to each bird. "*You* have a go, mate," he said. They took their half crackers and flew up to sit on the railing and eat.

Lincoln looked out at the trees, the light was shifting to the bright light of midday. It was late in the day. A new day.

He had spent all week in a dark pit, not wanting to move or think, but the dark spell was over. It had to be over some time and today was as good a day as any. Today was Friday, the day he would normally expect Grace to be here, but she wasn't coming.

Not today. Not ever.

It was time he faced that fact and tried to get back to a routine of some kind. She was off to some fancy party with her Hollywood boyfriend and everything he had ever thought about her was a lie.

He cringed at that word. He couldn't bring himself to think of her as a liar. Maybe she was more like a mirage. And there was no sense moping around forever over a mirage after it disappeared. They were never real to begin with after all.

Lincoln stood up and brushed the cracker crumbs from his hands. Since the renovations on the interior of the house were mostly complete and being inside reminded him too much of Grace, he had decided to work on the front lawn. It could use a good weeding. He needed to get some exercise to get out of his funk, plus they had spent almost no time in the front yard together.

He gathered a rake and shovel from the shed in the back and went to the front of the house. As he rounded the corner the buzzing of an approaching buggy drew his attention. Luke, freshly shaved and abnormally cleaned up for this time of the day, pulled up, honking the little horn in greeting.

Lincoln nodded his greeting and leaned the shovel up against the house, taking the rake to the edge of the landscaped area in front to start working.

"Good, good, I'm glad you're cleaning up the front," Luke said.

Lincoln grunted his response and started raking.

"Do you mind?" Luke pulled a box out of the back of his buggy. "I'm gonna put this inside."

Lincoln kept raking. "What is it?"

"Kind of a welcome package," Luke answered as he walked past Lincoln and into the front door.

Lincoln paused his raking. "Welcome package?" But it was too late, Luke was already in the house.

Lincoln considered ignoring him, but he couldn't. It was usually better to know what Luke was up to before things got out of hand. Leaning his rake against the house next to the shovel, he followed Luke inside.

He found his little brother with his head inside the refrigerator, positioning the box on the top shelf.

"Welcome package for what?" he asked.

Luke's answer was muffled, "Guests."

A stab of pain hit Lincoln's heart. He hadn't planned on having to explain the disappearance of Grace so soon. "About that–"

"Don't worry about anything," Luke closed the refrigerator door and turned to him. "Everything's taken care of. I know you're not a people person, so you don't have to do anything. I got people coming."

Not sure what he was talking about, but suspicious Luke had some wild plan in place, Lincoln looked him up and down. He was more than cleaned up, he was dressed up, slacks, dress shirt, the works.

"What are you dressed up for?"

"The party, what else?"

"The party? Whose party?"

Luke looked at him like he was simple minded. "Grace Woods' party."

Dumbfounded, Lincoln stood and stared at his brother. As his mind tried to wrap around what Luke had said, Lincoln's heart slipped down, down, down, back towards the black pit it had been in all week.

Finally, he managed to fumble a question, "Wh-what are you talking about?"

Luke explained slowly, as if Lincoln had trouble understanding, "You remember, they wanted to keep the booking here for the weekend, but also throw Grace's birthday party here tonight."

He heard the words, but they couldn't make it past the dark cloud enveloping his mind. Grace's birthday party? The one with her Hollywood boyfriend?

"Here?"

"Yes, here. I told you about it."

"No...no you didn't."

Luke had a thought and looked past Lincoln down the hallway. He lowered his voice, "Is she here now?"

The dark clouds blackened and began swirling. "No, she's not here." Luke looked relieved, but only for a moment. "And you're not having her party here."

"Hold on a minute," Luke's voice raised. "It's all set. It's all paid for. Everyone is on their way."

"I don't care what's paid for and I don't care who's on their way," Lincoln raised his voice to match his brother's. "This is my house."

Luke glared at him. "You already agreed to rent it for this weekend." Seeing Lincoln falter, Luke continued, "What difference does it make if they have a party here for one night? It's big money, Link. Huge money."

The difference was that if he had to serve drinks and make small talk with total strangers while he watched some idiotic American show Grace off as his girlfriend, Lincoln thought he might split in two. He knew his heart would be destroyed, but it might crack his mind and soul in half as well.

"I can't..." Lincoln said, though he couldn't finish. He couldn't explain.

Luke sensed his brother's emotions, even if he didn't understand them. He stepped forward and put his hand on Lincoln's shoulder. "I know you don't like big parties. You don't have to be here. I'll take care of everything if you want to take off for the night."

Take off. Right. That's what he had to do. He didn't know how he would react to seeing Grace again, but the black cloud that had descended on him was not a good sign.

"I'm gonna go now," he said.

Luke didn't seem too surprised. He nodded then smiled broadly, "I promise I won't let them mess the place up."

Lincoln barely heard him as he pulled open his front door.

The drive was full of buggies, like some kind of golf cart convention had arrived. Some of them were pulling little trailers, most of them were packed with various party supplies, and all of them were blocking his buggy. He couldn't drive out of this place and get away from Grace's birthday party.

CHAPTER 59

Grace could barely swallow. The small bite of brie and mango mini-tart sat in her mouth and made her want to gag. She had barely eaten all week and today was no different, even though it was her birthday. She put the mini-tart back onto the tiny plate it had been served on and leaned back into the chair. The massage setting was set to vibrate and it made her whole body jiggle.

"Not hungry?" Ruby asked, her eyebrows arched.

"Not really," Grace answered.

Ruby didn't even try to hide the look she gave Ronnie who occupied the pedicure chair on the other side of Grace. They were all at the hotel spa, which was all mirrors and windows, except for Presley who was taking a nap in a cool room instead.

"Saving room for dinner?" Ronnie asked.

Grace nodded.

"I don't believe it, Grace. I have barely seen you eat one bite of food since I got here. Are you on one of those crazy diets? Again?" Ruby asked.

"I'm not," Grace answered. Ruby's eyebrows arched higher. "I swear." Grace held two fingers up. "Scout's honor."

"You need to eat something substantial by tonight," Faye interjected from her pedicure chair on the other side of Ronnie. "You need energy for your birthday surprise."

"Right…my surprise," Grace gave them the sincerest smile she could muster and hoped her friends couldn't see the pain in it. She had successfully kept her true feelings under wraps all week. All she had to do was get through her birthday surprise and everyone would carry on with their lives, leaving her with her life…which was over as far as she was concerned.

"So what does it matter?" Grace said under her breath.

Again, Ruby gave her a curious look. Grace took a sip of her bottled water and changed the subject.

"Don't you think it's about time you told me what the surprise is? How will I know what to wear?"

Faye let out a sound that could only be called a squeal of delight. She clapped her hands together like a little girl and said, "Just wait! We have it all planned out for you!"

A few hours later, after they were able to coerce Grace into eating a few lemon prawns and a piece of crispy flatbread, she found out the first detail of their birthday plan.

"Oh my goodness, Ronnie, this is really gorgeous," Grace said.

She stood in front of a full length mirror wearing a glimmering green and gold gown. Cut low in the front and even lower, much lower, in the back, the gown hugged the curve of her hips before slipping down over her legs like glimmering streams of water and that pooled around her feet.

Ronnie's eyes shone with admiration and pride as she reached out and adjusted the extremely low cut back that ended right at the bottom of Grace's beautifully shaped spine.

"Thank you, Grace. The dress can only do so much, though. You're the one that takes it over the top."

"Our glamour girl," Faye added.

Presley smiled warmly, her baby bump making her seem wiser than the rest of them. "Grace, you are simply lovely, both on the inside and outside…and I do believe you are getting more and more beautiful every year."

Grace flushed at the kind words and looked back at her reflection. With her hair down and the gown showing off her shape, Grace did feel beautiful.

She looked at the reflection of her friends standing behind her. Ronnie wore a vibrant blue gown, Faye was in all white, Ruby wore a pink and green floral print, and Presley was in a flowing tangerine number. All of them were gorgeous. Generous, funny, intelligent, strong, and gorgeous friends. That's who she had in her life and she needed to remember that blessing.

So her romance with Lincoln didn't pan out. So her heart had been battered and bruised. She had been given so much and she had a lot to be thankful about.

Grace smiled at all of them in the mirror, more sincerely than she had managed all week. She would try, for their sakes, to enjoy whatever celebration they had put together for her.

"Thank you all so much for making my birthday so special," she said.

"Oh, darling, it hasn't even started yet. Let's get the blindfold and get to the buggy," Faye said.

Grace agreed to be blindfolded and they got into two separate buggies. Faye, Ruby, and Grace rode in the first one. Presley, Hobie, and Ronnie in the second. As they whizzed down the road away from the beach house and towards her birthday party, the sadness rushed back into her heart.

She would give anything if Lincoln could be with her on

this little adventure. Her friends would like him, she knew they would. If only…

"No peeking," Faye told her.

"I'm not peeking," Grace said with a laugh. It felt good to laugh.

She wondered if this would be a beach party. That was a reasonable assumption since they were a stone's throw away from some of the most beautiful beaches in the world. She hoped not, just because it would make her think of Lincoln more. The memory of their plane ride that ended with the romantic dinner on a beach was still fresh in her mind. She didn't know if she could enjoy herself if she was being reminded of that evening constantly

The cart carrying them felt like it was going uphill. Grace was relieved. Probably not on the beach if they were headed up. They had left just before sunset and the air was cooling around them. Her exposed back felt a little chilled as they went higher and higher into the hills. The sounds and scents of evening in the jungle were also familiar to Grace. They also reminded her of Lincoln.

Nonsense. She had to stop carrying on this way. Determined to have at least a tolerable birthday, Grace made a decision. She refused to think about Lincoln or let anything or anyone she came into contact tonight remind her of Lincoln.

"Here we are," Faye declared.

The buggy slowed down and turned, making its way down a winding drive.

"Oh, this is nice," Ruby said. "You're gonna love this, Grace. It's just your style," she continued, squeezing Grace's hand.

The buggy stopped and they all got out, Grace waiting for them to guide her. Carefully and with a lot of giggling, Faye,

Ruby, Presley and Ronnie led Grace to her big surprise. Hobie came behind them carrying their wraps.

"Okay, this is good," Faye announced. "Are you ready, Grace?"

Grace giggled, allowing the fun of the moment to overcome her former gloominess. "I'm ready!"

Someone reached behind her and undid the bow of the blindfold, slipping it gently up and off of her head.

Swept away in the moment and excited to see what was going to happen next, Grace opened her eyes.

CHAPTER 60

Zac crouched down behind the couch in the dark. Rigby on one side of him, Indigo Lee on the other. Massively confused at Indigo's presence at Grace's surprise party, Zac hadn't had any time to find out why before the order had come for everyone to hide in the dark.

Grace had arrived and they all knew the assignment. Wait until she had walked in and the lights came on, then jump up and yell surprise.

Seemed pretty juvenile, but the anticipation was real. Nearly 80 people as far as he could tell, all adults, all relatively sane, hiding in the dark together, stifling laughter, holding their breath until the big moment. He was having more fun than he would have expected.

Zac glanced around at the other crouching bodies nearby. He had yet to see Phoenix, wasn't even sure if she was in the room. He knew she would have appreciated the amusement factor of the situation.

"How long do we have to stay like this?" Indi whispered.

"Shhh," someone nearby shushed her, thankfully.

Zac didn't know why she was here, but the least she could

do was go along with the rules of the game. Though he was glad not to have to be the one to shush her. Indi always was kind of a stick in the mud. He was surprised she had stepped foot in Australia after holding such a grudge about that spider bite situation.

"Here they come," Phoenix said from somewhere at the side of the room. Zac knew her voice instantly. That certain blend of sweet authority. He craned his neck to try and look around Rigby towards the sound of her voice. No luck. It was too dark and his eye line was severely limited behind the couch.

The door opened. Everyone hiding in the dark took a collective breath. A few long moments passed before the lights switched on and then, right on cue, they all jumped up from their hiding spots and shouted, "Surprise!"

Grace, looking like some kind of goddess who happened into a house party, was definitely shocked at the outburst. More than shocked, actually. She looked stricken. Zac wondered if she was about to faint and immediately thought maybe surprising someone who had just recently suffered a fainting spell on set wasn't the best idea.

Immediately, his thoughts went to Phoenix. Would she agree? Did she notice the look on Grace's face?

He looked in the direction where he had heard her voice, but didn't see her pale blonde ponytail anywhere in the crowded room. What felt like a sea of people surged around him and the couch, all wanting to go to Grace and tell her happy birthday, but Zac's mind was stuck on finding Phoenix.

"Zac, take me to meet her," Indi said as she grabbed his elbow.

He looked behind him, mildly surprised. He had forgotten she was there. She looked up at him with her pouty eyes and Zac was unmoved. In fact, he suddenly couldn't remember how he had ever pursued her, dated her, kissed her, anything. He turned his attention away from her and back through the crowd to Grace.

She still looked pale and seemed to be leaning on a few of her friends for support. Zac was concerned for her, of course, but once again he couldn't believe he had ever wanted to be with her romantically. Zac stood, stunned in an epiphany as every woman he had ever dated or wanted to date shifted suddenly into a new category: women who were not Phoenix.

Zac's heart started pounding and he forgot about Grace and Indi and everyone else at the party. All he wanted was to see Phoenix. To talk to her, to hear her thoughts on everything that was going on, to hold her thin little hand.

A fervent desire to find her instantly took over.

"Excuse me a minute," he remembered to say to Indi as he stepped away and pressed through the crowd. He knew that Phoenix would be near Grace since she didn't look well. When he got to the group that had formed a tight circle around Grace he still didn't see Phoenix's signature ponytail.

"Zac," her voice came from his side.

He turned quickly at the sound, so excited to see her, but stopped short when he finally did.

Phoenix, thin and pale little Phoenix, no longer had a ponytail. She no longer had her washed out blonde hair or her overly thick glasses. She no longer blended into the background.

Standing beside him was a stunning brunette.

Slight in build, but with gorgeous hazel eyes accented by lavender eyeshadow and deep black eyeliner, wearing a sleeveless floor length lavender lace dress, Phoenix was a changed woman–a beautiful woman.

"Phoenix," he said, her name felt strong and steadfast on his tongue.

Zac dropped his gaze from her eyes down her slim neck and shoulders, let it slip along the lace that trimmed the low cut neckline, then back up to her eyes. He couldn't think of anything to say, nor could he think of how to act. No previously determined facial expression came to mind. All he could do was stare at the vision in front of him and hope that vision never went away again.

CHAPTER 61

When Lincoln escaped from his own house he left so fast he forgot his keys, phone, and wallet. With tunnel like vision all he could think was he had to get out before Grace arrived. Since he couldn't get his buggy out of the drive he took off on foot, traversing a shortcut he knew down the hill to a quiet beach that wasn't normally packed with tourists.

He sank back into the sand and stared up at the midday sun, wishing a giant wave would crash over the top of him and draw him out to sea. Sinking into the blue ocean until he was so deep under the water he could never return, where everything was silent and peaceful, where nobody could ever find him, sounded pretty good at that moment.

The wave never came and eventually the heat of the sun roused him out of his despair. He pulled off his T-shirt, kicked off his shoes, and waded into the water to cool down. When he was waist deep he dove in, plunging under the surface with relief. He knew he could never actually drown himself, his sense of self-preservation was too strong, but being in the other worldly space under the surface of the ocean was comforting for a few minutes.

When he emerged refreshed from his swim, Lincoln ignored the admiring looks of a group of women tourists nearby, gathered his shirt and shoes, and found a shady spot under a few palm trees to dry off. From there he could still see the ocean, but stay away from most prying eyes and possible flirtatious encounters.

He wasn't in the mood to flirt. He wasn't in the mood for anything. The pain remained sharp in his heart, but his mind and his muscles were tired. Lincoln closed his eyes and listened to the rhythmic sound of waves lapping the shore.

When he woke, he wasn't sure how long he had been asleep, though the sun had dropped so far in the sky that he was no longer shaded by the palm trees. He was thirsty and hungry and wished he had remembered his wallet.

"I guess it's Fitz's for me," he said as he stood, brushing sand off his clothes and shaking it out of his shoes.

Henry's bar and restaurant was a twenty minute walk from the beach, but Lincoln wouldn't need his wallet to order anything at Fitz's. There were probably a half dozen other places that would let him pay his tab later, but he was most comfortable at Fitz's.

"Crikey, Link, what happened to you?" Henry asked as Lincoln bellied up to the bar.

"I left my wallet at home, can I get a sandwich on tab?"

"Whatever you want, mate," Henry chuckled. "Did you get tossed out of somewhere? You look a little rough around the edges."

Lincoln tried to smile, but it turned into more of a grimace. "Luke's got a shindig going on at the house so I'm steering clear."

"Right," Henry said as he placed an ice cold beer and a

glass of water on the bar in front of Lincoln. "What'll you be eating?"

A few minutes later Lincoln was devouring a crispy fish and chips plate like he hadn't eaten in weeks. Come to think of it, he hadn't eaten much over the past week. Henry's fish and chips were the first thing in a while that tasted good, that was for sure.

"Delicious," he said through a full mouth as he took a swig of beer to wash it down.

Henry chuckled again. "Even a pig snout tastes good to a starving man." He watched Lincoln curiously. "How long are you banished then?"

Lincoln swallowed, "Oh, I'm not banished exactly. I could go back…I just don't want to."

"Who's at the party?"

Lincoln took another drink of beer and swallowed hard. "It's all those Hollywood types. You know, from the movie."

Henry's eyebrows raised in surprise. "Really? Up at your Grandad's? That's a turn of events, isn't it?"

Lincoln nodded then tried to shrug it off. "They'll be gone soon enough I suppose. I think I'll crash on the boat though."

Henry nodded then thought of something. "I heard Luke's got Melanie staying on the boat with him now."

"Does he?" Lincoln hadn't known that.

"And you know wherever you find Melanie, you find Renee," the waitress, Amelia, added with an exaggerated wink at Lincoln as she leaned in to pick up a tray of drinks from Henry.

Lincoln cringed at the idea of spending the night with Renee and Melanie on the boat. "I guess that idea's out," he said gloomily.

"No worries, Link, you can stay here as long as you like," Henry reassured him.

Grateful for the offer, Lincoln did stay. All afternoon and

into the evening, past sunset and through several more beers, so many that he lost count, Lincoln stayed stuck on that barstool, afraid to go home.

The whole time he avoided thinking about Grace. He talked with Henry, with other patrons he knew, and with some he didn't. He managed to avoid talking about anything movie related, swiftly changing the subject to something else if it came up. It took some effort, but he did it for hours…and hours.

Finally, nudged on by plenty of beer or the fatigue of manipulating too many conversations, or both, Lincoln decided to go home. He knew the party was unlikely to be over, but he was tired.

"I'll sleep in the shed if I have to," he told himself as he made his way up the winding road that led to the Hill House.

He heard the party before he saw it. The unmistakable thumping of a loud bass then, as he got closer, the guitars and vocals of a live band.

He slowed, trying to decide the best way to approach.

First option was to go in the front door, straight into the party, past everyone, including Grace, and back into the bedroom.

Or should he sneak in the back? He could climb up the deck stairs and mingle with people as if he belonged there, avoiding Grace at all costs, until he could make his way to the hallway and back into his bedroom.

He scoffed. As if he belonged there? It was his bloody house after all.

Lincoln started towards the front door. Halfway there he slowed, then stopped, losing his nerve to storm in and face Luke and Grace and whoever else was in there. He was in no condition for a confrontation.

He changed his mind and went around the house to the back. As he rounded the corner he grabbed the shovel and rake from the corner where he had left them earlier in the day. Nobody had put them back.

"If I'm gonna sleep in the shed I may as well put these away," he muttered.

Every window in the house glowed gold. From the back yard Lincoln could see hundreds of strings of shining lights decorating the deck and more on the inside of the house. The thumping of the music was even louder from the back yard and he could hear people talking and laughing. One of those people, though he couldn't pick her out from where he stood, was Grace.

Curious, he moved closer. Then closer.

He climbed slowly up the steps to the deck and was surprised to find it empty. Almost immediately his eyes were drawn to the picture windows revealing a scene he never could have imagined he would see in his Grandad's house.

CHAPTER 62

Grace felt like she was cheating. Being in the Hill House with all of her friends and colleagues but without Lincoln was a betrayal. She knew it was, but she could do little about it. The party was happening whether she liked it or not. A live band, tons of food, over a hundred people, and even roaming photographers that Rigby had hired to capture moments for the press, all of it was past the point of no return.

She didn't have the strength to try and stop it anyway. It was taking everything in her to move through the party without collapsing onto the floor as a blubbering mess.

Thank goodness for Zac and Phoenix.

While Faye and the rest of her friends seemed to be under the mistaken impression that she and Zac were dating, Zac and Phoenix knew that wasn't true.

In the first few minutes after she arrived she had to get over the shock of being at the Hill House, the moment when everyone yelled surprise and scared her to death, and the gut wrenching disappointment when she realized Lincoln was nowhere to be found. She couldn't turn to Faye and Ronnie and the others, they had been the ones who planned the whole thing. How could she disappoint them like that?

Somehow Zac and Phoenix had picked up on her distress, even if they didn't understand the details, and were helping her through it. As her co-star and producer they seemed to be tuned in to her emotions more than others and had a knack for charming and disarming almost anyone. The two them sort of teamed up for the night, one on either side of her, and were acting as conversation buddies, walking her through the socially awkward moments, which were coming fast and furious.

One of the strangest was the appearance of Indigo Lee, invited by Faye of all people. Grace couldn't imagine why Faye would think she wanted Indigo there on her birthday, but Faye kept insisting on including the young actress in conversations.

"I'm sure actresses are always competing for the best roles, aren't they?" Faye asked Indigo, Grace, Phoenix, and Zac as they stood in a small circle sipping their drinks.

Grace knew she was referring to the fact that she had booted Indigo out of the running so she could have the lead role in Heart of Mine. Again, she had no idea why Faye would bring up this old wound right in front of Indigo…and on her birthday. Sometimes the inner workings of Faye's mind were a complete mystery.

"There are always difficult choices made during filming," Phoenix chimed in. "They seem to work out for the best. Every time."

Grace smiled. Phoenix was really coming into her own as a producer and her new dark hair seemed to have made her even bolder.

"Yes, they do," Zac agreed.

He placed his hand on Grace's back as a gesture of support and gave her a light kiss on the cheek. It was the kind of kiss actors shared in a friendly way, mostly air. Grace knew he meant nothing else by it, because she could see the way he was looking at Phoenix. The producer's makeover had done more than make her bolder, it had definitely caught the young heartthrob's eye as well.

Just then something moved outside on the deck. Grace saw a flash of white against the railing just outside where the light faded into dark.

"Fred and Ginger," she said to herself. They must be hungry. To the others she announced, "If you'll excuse me for a moment. I'll be right back." She could step outside and feed them a few crackers so they didn't accost some unaware guest who happened to wander onto the deck.

Grace stepped out into the cool, damp air and took a deep breath. It was a relief to get away from the crowd.

She stepped in the direction where she had seen the movement, "Are you out there?"

There was a shuffle, then a clank out in the dark and she had a split second to second guess her decision to go looking for crazy cockatoos in the darkness when suddenly, unexpectedly, Lincoln stepped into the edge of the light.

She gasped, her hands flew to her mouth in surprise, "Lincoln!"

His clothes were rumpled, his blonde hair had that beach look, windblown and casually ruffled, he was slightly sunburned and looked tired. Bone tired.

He stood cautiously, his shoulders slumping slightly so that his normally tall frame appeared smaller, more vulnerable. To Grace, however, he was still the most handsome man she had ever laid eyes on.

"Lincoln…" she took a step toward him and he took a step back so he was partially hidden in the dark again.

Grace's stomach dropped and her heart quickly followed. He looked away from her, his eyes drawn to the bright windows. Grace followed his gaze and saw what he saw, what he had been watching from outside for who knows how long.

His home packed with people he didn't know, all of them glamorous and posing for photographers or taking selfies, a live band set up in his dining room blasting music through his Granddad's peaceful house. The scene was garish and didn't suit the spirit of the home his Grandad had built by hand. Grace felt sick.

"I'm sorry, Lincoln. I didn't know...I didn't know they were planning all of this."

He turned his attention back to her and it pained her to see doubt in those piercing blue eyes.

She tried to change the subject. "I thought I would see you."

He laughed a little, but there was no humor in it. "No, not me. I don't like big parties."

"No, no, I meant I thought I would see you this past week."

"Oh," Lincoln looked down at his feet and shifted uncomfortably. All of his fidgeting moved him back into the light and for the first time Grace noticed he was holding a shovel and rake in one hand.

He lifted his eyes to hers and she forgot all about the lawn tools. The pain in his eyes pierced her heart and lungs, she couldn't seem to take a full breath.

Neither could he. When he spoke his voice was ragged. "I didn't know how your boyfriend would feel about that."

His words hung between them as she tried to understand. "My boyfriend?"

Lincoln's eyes shot to the nearest window where Zac and Phoenix were still talking to Indigo.

"What are you talking about?" Grace asked as she watched him glare at Zac's back then return that glare to her.

He lifted his empty hand and swished it back and forth, shooing away her question. That move combined with the slight slur in his words made her realize something else. He had been drinking. "I understand, I understand…he's more your type. I don't blame you."

Grace closed her eyes and took a deep breath before answering calmly. "I'm not dating Zac."

Lincoln gave her a 'you can't kid a kidder' face and said, "Come on, Grace. I saw you."

Grace remembered Zac's air kiss a few minutes before. "That wasn't a real kiss. Actors do that all the time. We're a touchy feely bunch. You can ask him yourself."

"No, Grace," his voice grew louder. Not shouting loud, but definitely arguing loud. "I *saw* you."

"You saw me where?"

"Having *sex* with him," Lincoln pointed accusingly at Zac's back.

Grace gasped and whispered hotly, "I've never had sex with Zac."

"You did…on set…I saw it."

She paused. "You were on set?" He nodded sharply, as if this proved his accusation. "That wasn't real sex, Lincoln. We were pretending!" She couldn't keep her voice from raising at his ridiculous jealousy. She saw a few heads turn their way inside the house.

"Well, it looked real enough," he said glumly.

"It wasn't real. Not at all. That's part of my job, you know. Sometimes I have to do sex scenes. It doesn't mean I'm dating the other actor."

He looked into her eyes and Grace could see anger and pain and confusion reeling inside of his soul.

"You're leaving soon," he said softly, defeated.

A fine crack snapped through her heart. The kind of

crack that could go unnoticed for years, but never heal completely.

She nodded and answered quietly, "I am." A single tear dropped down her cheek.

He sighed and let his eyes wander across the deck windows at the party inside then up into the sky where the moon hung low and bright. When they wandered back to her all of the anger and confusion was gone. Only the pain remained.

"We're not the same, you and I. I stay places. I fix things. This house, this island, this is where I belong. But you, you go places and do things. Big, amazing things, Grace. I can't go with you. Not the way you would want me to."

Grace had no answer. Overcome with grief, she was empty of words.

"Captain, you're here," Faye's voice came to them from the doorway. Lincoln stiffened.

"Faye," Grace started, but it was too late, Faye was joining them.

"Are you a Captain and a gardener?" Faye asked, eyeing the shovel and rake in Lincoln's hand.

Lincoln ignored her sarcasm, answering politely, "Just a Captain I'm afraid."

Grace wiped another tear from her cheek, trying to hide the action from Faye. But Faye was not easily put off and she must have noticed their rather intense conversation.

"Won't you come in and join the party?" Faye asked most insincerely.

"Faye!" Grace wanted to scold her, tell her that this was his house, his Grandad's house, that they were practically trespassing in it, and to stop being such a haughty little snob.

Lincoln answered before she had a chance. "No, I won't, thank you. I've got work to do." He raised the shovel and rake in his hand as proof. "You all have fun."

He turned and started down the steps that led to the dark back yard. Grace didn't know what to do. She wanted to cry out, run after him, wrap her arms around him and tell him she was sorry, sorry that they weren't real enough to survive. But she didn't. She couldn't. He didn't want her to, that was obvious.

He paused after the first few steps and turned back, smiling his beautiful smile, the smile that had first melted her heart, "Hey, Grace."

"Yes?"

"Happy birthday."

And then he was gone.

CHAPTER 63

Lincoln walked through the remnants of Grace's birthday party with a plastic garbage bag in one hand. Luke, true to form, had done a dismal job of picking up.

In a way, Lincoln was glad.

Crumpled wads of used napkins, cocktail plates with globs of uneaten food, empty glasses sticky with drying liquor and lipstick marks, every piece of trash he threw away or dirty dish he put on the kitchen counter made him more certain that he had made the right decision to stay away.

The front door pushed open and Luke came in. He carried a garbage bag of his own.

"Link," he said, surprised to see him. He noticed what Lincoln was doing and held up his hand for him to stop. "No, no, no, let me do the clean up. I told you I would."

Lincoln looked at his little brother. Luke was untidy and had bags under his eyes. He had probably stayed up all night.

"It's all right. I'll help. It'll go faster," Lincoln said as he scraped a huge piece of half eaten birthday cake off of a plate and into the trash bag.

They worked in silence and Lincoln found comfort in his younger brother being there. He may have lost in love, but he had this house and he had Luke and that wasn't the worst life in the world.

Before long they were done and Luke dug around in the fridge for something to eat.

"Well, would you look at this," he said as he produced a large section of birthday cake with only a few pieces cut out of it. He held it up to Lincoln, who held his hand up. He didn't want a piece.

It looked like a tier from a stacked cake, an elaborately decorated stacked cake. The frosting was all the colors of the ocean with shining gold veins. Gold sea shells of all shapes were stuck along one side of it. From the cut sections, Lincoln could see it was chocolate.

"Do you think I can eat these?" Luke picked one of the gold seashells off of the side of the cake. Lincoln shrugged, he didn't know. Luke popped it in his mouth and bit down. A look of ecstasy came over him. "Wow. That's so good." He rummaged through the utensil drawer and pulled out two forks, holding one up to Lincoln.

"No, thanks," Lincoln waved him off. "I'm not hungry."

The truth was he was starving, but he couldn't stomach eating Grace's birthday cake.

Luke stuck his fork right into the cake and took a huge bite of it. While he was chewing he dug through his pocket and pulled out a wad of cash holding it up for Lincoln to see.

"What's that?"

Luke swallowed then smiled, chocolate cake all over his teeth. "A tip!"

Lincoln watched as Luke tossed the cash on the kitchen counter, hundreds and fifties unfolding and spilling out into a pile.

"I figured we could split it?" Luke suggested before taking another bite of cake.

Lincoln felt sick. He didn't want her leftover cake and he sure as heck didn't want a tip.

"Who gave that to you?" Lincoln asked.

His mouth still full, Luke answered, "Faye something."

Lincoln scowled. "You keep it."

Luke's eyes widened. He swallowed. "Are you kidding? There's over thirty thousand dollars there!"

"Let's call it even. You keep it and I don't have to rent out the house again."

Luke grinned and gathered up the money. "Deal. We won't rent it out again...until the thirty thousand runs out."

Lincoln rolled his eyes.

Luke laughed, "Come on, mate. That'll give you plenty of time to get back to normal."

Normal. The word hit him hard.

Was that what he wanted? Normal?

He shook off the question. Whether or not that's what he wanted, that's what he had.

Normal was what he focused on all that week. He worked in the yard, ordered some more supplies for some roof repairs that he wanted to get done, and generally avoided going out in public or anywhere he might run into Grace.

She was still on the island. The movie was wrapping up filming and they would all be gone by the coming Sunday, which would be a relief. Lincoln figured if his new normal did not include Grace then he should do his best to get started on it right away.

He did fine, for the most part. He couldn't stomach the sight of any kind of booze. That was one good outcome of the whole wasted affair. He ate and he slept and he stuck to his own company.

Most importantly, he ignored how his heart ached whenever he thought of her and he closed off the desperate part of himself that wanted to seek her out and talk to her again. Normal.

On the day he knew the flights would start leaving the small island airport, taking Grace and everyone associated with her away forever, Lincoln was drawn down the hill.

He had resigned himself to his life without her and there was no changing that, but something in the center of his soul wanted to see her off...to watch her go.

Maybe so he would know the coast was clear and he could wander freely around his island without running into her anywhere. Maybe he wanted one more glimpse of her to hold onto during his new normal life. Or maybe he needed to say goodbye, if only from afar.

Whatever the reason, that Sunday Lincoln found himself leaving the Hill House long before sunrise and hiking down the back roads that would take him to a quiet spot near the runway where he used to watch planes come and go when he was a kid.

He stayed there as the sky turned from deep blue to bright pink and watched the private jets and larger commercial jets prepping for flight. He stayed there and watched passengers and luggage being dropped off by workers in zipping buggies and loaded onto the planes. He stayed there because he had to see with his own eyes that she was leaving.

The bright pink sky was softening into morning and two private jets had already taken off when Lincoln finally saw her.

White shorts and a billowing white shirt, her black hair floating in the breeze, dark sunglasses over her eyes, every movement she made was so familiar to him, so imprinted on his mind, that even from a distance he knew it was her the instant he saw her.

His gut clenched tight. His heart pounded in his chest.

Every muscle in his body wound up and urged him to run to her, take her in his arms, tell her he was sorry, tell her he loved her, tell her he wanted to be with her for the rest of his life.

Yet he stood frozen. Unmoving. Ignoring the screams of his soul. He knew that everything he wanted to tell her was true, but she wasn't part of normal. He knew that, too.

There was one heart stopping moment when he swore she had seen him. As she started up the steps to the plane she stopped and turned in his direction. The ocean breeze that brushed by him made its way to her as she stood there and he imagined it kissing her cheek for him and whispering "goodbye".

She turned and boarded the plane. Lincoln stood completely still as he watched the plane taxi out to the runway then pick up speed then lift into the air.

Then, and only then, did Lincoln move.

He turned away from the airport and the woman he loved and he ran. He ran over the low hill behind him that led to the beach. He ran onto the beach and down the shore. He ran until he couldn't run anymore.

CHAPTER 64

Grace sat limply in the leather seat on Faye's jet, wishing she was already home. Leaving this island was taking its toll on her and she was exhausted.

"I'm going to change," Faye announced as she headed back to the bedroom.

"You just got dressed," Ruby teased.

"I want something more comfortable," Faye pulled on the waistband of her slacks as if to prove her point and sauntered through the bedroom door.

"Now," Ruby settled in next to Grace and patted her hand. "You can tell me what in the world is going on with you."

"With me?" Grace tried to look innocent and happy.

Ruby pursed her lips together and said, "Grace I have been patient with you. I let you have your birthday party. I let you finish filming. I let you enjoy your last day on the island. But now we are alone and we have nothing else to distract us so you are going to tell me what has been bothering you…because I'm your friend and I want to help."

Grace started to protest, but stopped short, choking on her denial.

Her heart had frozen in place when Lincoln told her 'Happy birthday' and walked away. That's how she had managed to get through the rest of the party and the rest of the movie, with a dead cold frozen heart. She had been on autopilot, falling back on her acting training in order to appear to have any emotions at all.

Safely on her way home, away from the turmoil of everything she had just gone through, Grace's heart was beginning to thaw. And as it thawed it cried out in pain.

She stared at Ruby in shock as giant hot tears welled up in her eyes. Ruby took hold of her hand and nodded encouragingly. If she was surprised by Grace's sudden emotions she did not show it.

"Let it out, just let it out," Ruby said.

Grace stuttered through her tears, "I-it's a m-m-ma-man."

"Mm-hmm," Ruby nodded and patted her hand, unperturbed by this news. "Which man, sweetie?"

Grace covered her mouth to try and ebb the flow of sobs. It didn't work.

"Now, now, it's all right," Ruby said soothingly. "Is it Zac? Is that what's got you all upset? Him running off with your little producer girl?"

Grace shook her head violently and managed to say, "N-n-not Zac."

Ruby thought for a moment then tried again, "Is it Syd?"

Grace managed a scoff through her sobs, which created the need for a tissue. Ruby handed her some from the nearby table. Grace wiped her face and blew her nose, which curbed her blubbering for a few moments.

"His name is Lincoln," she managed to get out.

"Okay, Lincoln is his name. Where did you meet him?" Ruby was calm and determined, like a reporter taking someone's confession for a story.

"On his b-b-boat–!" Grace fell back into a weeping fit.

"What's going on?" Faye swept into the room wearing one of her flowing robes and comfy slippers. She sat down across from Grace, concern creasing her normally un-creasable expression.

When Grace couldn't answer Ruby said, "There's some man trouble."

Faye leaned forward and narrowed her eyes. "It's Zac, isn't it? What a beast he turned out to be."

Grace shook her head and tried to explain, but it all came out an incoherent mess.

Faye finally sat back in her seat, frustrated. "I can't understand anything you're saying, darling." She looked to Ruby. "Can you?"

"Apparently his name is Lincoln and she met him on his boat?"

Faye was impressed. "You understood what she said?

"No, she told me before you came out here," Ruby clarified.

"Oh," Faye thought for a minute, letting her mind click through the information. Then she let out a small gasp and looked at Grace. "Do you mean the Whale Captain?"

Grace's sobs grew louder as she nodded. Ruby handed her more tissue.

"Who or what is a Whale Captain?" Ruby asked.

Grace calmed her crying and blew her nose again before answering, "His name is Lincoln Reeves and I think-I think-I think I'm in l-lo-love with h-him!"

Faye's eyebrows lifted in surprise. "In love with him? You barely know him, darling."

"Let the woman speak, Faye. If she says she's in love with somebody then she's in love with somebody," Ruby scolded.

Faye sank back in her chair, pouting.

"Now tell me about this wonderful man who has stolen

your heart," Ruby gently pushed back a stray hair that had fallen into Grace's face.

Her crying fit finally under control, Grace told them everything. The way she and Lincoln had met, how he owned the private weekend getaway she had rented and had been there the first time she went, then every time after, until her birthday party. How kind and funny and charming he was. How he'd wanted to take things slow and she hadn't been able to think about anyone or anything else practically since she met him.

"He never came to see me or called after I was late getting there and then he was so weird when he showed up at the party..." Grace's voice trailed off as her heart sank deeper and deeper in her chest. It was over. She was never going to see Lincoln again.

"He sounds charming, Grace. It sounds like you two had something pretty special," Ruby said kindly.

Grace blinked back tears. They did have something special, something like she had never had before in her life. She wanted to explain it better, to make Ruby and Faye understand how deep her feelings went.

"I p-p-painted his kitchen–" Grace said, but the memory was too much and it came out as more of a wail. She broke into sobs again.

Ruby looked mildly confused at that little detail, but continued to speak in her soothing voice. "That sounds very...intimate, sweetie. I'm sure there's a logical explanation for him not coming to see you and clearing things up. Don't you think there's probably a logical explanation?" She looked to Faye for support and noticed Faye's expression.

No longer pouting, Faye was staring at Grace with ever widening, slightly panicky eyes.

"Faye...what is it?" Ruby asked.

Grace looked up at the tone in Ruby's voice and saw the strange look on Faye's face.

"Grace, I'm sorry. I didn't know," Faye began.

"Didn't know what?" Grace asked with a sniffle.

Faye smiled sheepishly and pinched the air in front of her. "I think I may have made a teensy weensy mistake."

CHAPTER 65

Lincoln got home long after noon, but before sunset. He'd spent most of the morning on the beach, recuperating from watching Grace fly away. Then he took a quick swim and went to Fitz' for a sandwich, a tall glass of water, and some friendly conversation with Henry.

This time he hadn't drank any beer or stayed too late. He had decided he was going to clean up his act a little more. Focus on his health. That sort of thing. He had to try and do something positive to get past losing Grace. He had to make it mean something more than just heartbreak.

The lock clicked as he turned the key in the front door. The sound echoed through his chest. It sounded empty, just like his chest. Empty of joy.

When he stepped into the house it was the same house he had entered nearly every day for decades. All through his childhood, teenage years, and ever since he had become an adult he had been stepping into the same room through the same front door. When his parents were alive, after they passed, through his Grandad's drinking, then after he passed, too, laughing with Luke and fighting with Luke, and living there on his own when Luke went to live on the boat, Lincoln had never felt so alone as he did at this moment.

He put his keys and phone on the kitchen counter, wondering what he was going to do with the rest of his day—with the rest of his life.

A noise interrupted the dreary silence of the room. It came from the picture windows along the deck.

"Fred and Ginger," he muttered as he trudged towards the back door to grab the obnoxious cockatoos a cracker and hush them up. "Have a go, yourself, mate," he called out irritably.

"What is that, exactly, 'Have a go, mate'? I've never understood what it means." A woman's voice came from the couch.

Lincoln jumped at the sound. When he turned and saw who it was, he thought he may have lost his mind and was hallucinating.

Grace.

She uncurled from where she had been napping in the corner of the couch and stood up, facing him.

"Grace," he almost whispered her name, afraid if she was a vision his voice might scare her off.

"Lincoln," she answered, and smiled a smile that could knock a man over.

CHAPTER 66

Grace had fallen asleep on the couch waiting for Lincoln to arrive. The Hill House was so comfortable to her, like home, she didn't have any trouble sleeping there.

She didn't hear him come in until he put his keys on the kitchen counter and woke her up. Every inch of her body tingled with excitement as she listened to him curse Fred and Ginger under his breath and walk across the room. She was overwhelmed with the prospect of seeing him again–of starting over.

When she asked him about Fred's favorite saying and he whirled around to face her, Grace thought her heart might explode it was pounding so hard.

Her throat went dry, uncertain if arriving unannounced and letting herself in had been the right move. She managed to keep her cool and stand up to face him, though the sight of him made her knees weak like always.

Then he said her name. Whispered it, like a wish spoken out loud, and she found hope in that.

"I thought...I thought you flew out this morning," he said.

Confused, but not angry that she was there, which was a relief.

"That's the great thing about private jets, you can turn around whenever you want," she answered, laughing a little, still filled with butterflies.

He paused, uncertain, and Grace found hated seeing him so torn. The shock of her return had him off centered and she wanted to help.

"Did you forget something?" he asked.

"Yes, I did. I forgot something." Grace took a deep breath and gathered all of her courage. She had said a lot of lines in her lifetime, but nothing as important as this one. "I came back because I have something to say to you."

He watched her cautiously, but his body leaned in her direction. "What do you want to say?"

"I think we're real, Lincoln. I think we're the most real thing I've ever experienced."

The careful look in his eyes softened. "You do?"

"I do. I think you were right, I think we're real, and I want us to try again."

A spark of humor flickered across his face and one side of his mouth raised in an almost grin.

She decided to lay everything out on the table and let him sort it out. This back and forth was too much to bear.

"I am not dating Zac, I have never dated Zac. I want you to know that for certain. That was a stupid rumor Rigby put out for PR purposes and it got everybody confused."

"Oh…"

"And I didn't know you came to the set to see me, or to the beach house. I thought you had decided not to come back here when I was here waiting for you and when you didn't come that week, well I thought that you didn't want to see me anymore at all."

"I see…"

"And I had no idea they were going to throw that surprise party here in your house. I would have never allowed that to happen if anybody would have told me what was going on."

"Of course…"

She paused to take a few breaths and realized Lincoln had moved closer and closer to her with each response. They were within arms reach of one another, so close she could see the muscles flexing on his forearms and the twinkle in his eyes.

He paused again, a question coming to his mind. "What about your career, Grace? What about all the movies you're going to make and all the places you're going to go? Will you be happy here with me?"

She stepped forward so she could reach up and touch his cheek, the sensation of his warm skin under her fingertips sending shivers down her spine.

"I've made movies, Lincoln. I've lived all around the world. I've had a wonderful career. Do you want to know what I've never had?"

"What?" he asked, his voice deep, quiet.

"Someone like you," she whispered.

"Grace…"

His hands slipped around her waist and pulled her to him. She ran her hand to the back of his neck, pushing her fingers into his hair.

"I was a fool. Jealous and stupid. I should have trusted you, Grace. I shouldn't have ever let you leave," he said, his voice cracking with emotion.

She gazed into his eyes, those brilliant blue eyes and, just so he would never question it, said, "I'm in love with you, Lincoln Reeves and there's nothing you can do about it."

His arms tightened around her, holding her so close she knew he would never let her go again. He grinned, his eyes dancing with joy and at that moment her heart and soul got lost in those eyes, never to return.

"Oh, I think there's something I can do about it," he said as he brought his mouth to hers and they kissed.

The End

ALSO BY DARCI BALOGH

<u>Lady Billionaires Series</u>

1. Ms. Money Bags

2. Ms. Perfect

3. Ms. Know-it-All

<u>Dream Come True Series</u>

Five childhood friends vow to live the life of their dreams...without men to mess it all up.

1. Her Scottish Keep

2. Her British Bard

3. Her Sheltered Cove

4. Her Secret Heart

5. Her One and Only

<u>Sweet Holiday Romance Series (Box Set - great value!)</u>

Want a quick escape over the holidays? These feel-good romances will get you in the spirit for Halloween, Thanksgiving, Christmas and a brand New Year!

1. Enchanting Eve

2. Love is at the Table

3. Mistletoe Madness

4. New Year in Paradise

<u>Sugar Plum Romance Series</u>

Christmas, cooking, and chefs falling in love!

1. Charlotte's Christmas Charade

2. Bella's Christmas Blunder

<u>Love & Marriage Series</u>

Spicy and sexy with relatable characters, these older woman, younger man women's divorce fiction are both racy and romantic.

1. The Quiet of Spring

2. For Love & For Money

3. Stars in the Sand

ABOUT THE AUTHOR

Darci Balogh is a writer and indie filmmaker from Denver. She grew up in the beautiful mountains of Colorado and has lived in several areas of the state over her lifetime. She currently resides in Denver where she raised her two glorious, intelligent daughters to functioning adulthood. This is, by far, one of her highest achievements.

She has a love-hate relationship with gardening, probably should dust more, adores dogs and is allergic to cats. She has been a writer since she was a child and enjoys crafting stories into novels and screenplays.

Big surprise, some of her favorite pastimes are reading and watching movies. Classic British TV is high on her 'Like' list, along with quietly depressing detective series and coffee with heavy cream.